"

Standing bare-chested in her bedroom, inches from her bed, Steve looked slightly embarrassed as he pulled his T-shirt from his back pocket and wiped his forehead.

"No, that's all right." Gwen stumbled over her words. She'd seen men shirtless before, but never had she seen a man who looked as fantastic as Steve Chambliss did. It wasn't the ideal time to ask her question, but what the heck.

"Steve, I need your help. My producer wants to put together a show on the five sexiest occupations for men. Are you interested in being our representative of a sexy carpenter?" She sounded ridiculous! Where was the sophisticated talk-show host who wowed audiences and hobnobbed with the rich and famous?

"Is that what you think, Gwen?" He inched a little closer. "Do you think I'm sexy?"

ABOUT THE AUTHOR

With fifty novels to her credit, Judith Arnold is one of Harlequin's premier authors. Her versatility and uncanny ability to make her readers laugh and cry have become her hallmarks. Judith, her husband and two sons, make their home in Massachusetts.

Books by Judith Arnold

Judith Arnold

THE MARRYING TYPE

Harlequin Books

TORONTO • NEW YORK • LONDON
AMSTERDAM • PARIS • SYDNEY • HAMBURG
STOCKHOLM • ATHENS • TOKYO • MILAN
MADRID • WARSAW • BUDAPEST • AUCKLAND

To Carolyn,
for teaching me how to write

ISBN 0-373-16553-6

THE MARRYING TYPE

Copyright © 1994 by Barbara Keiler

Prologue

"Her name wasn't Lucy," said Steve, kicking his feet up on the railing and swigging from his open bottle of beer. "It was Lisa. And she wasn't a 40D."

"She was a 39C-plus," Tripp declared.

"She was nothing of the sort," Steve retorted, trying to maintain a straight face. "And her physical endowments didn't matter to me, anyway. What I liked about her was her mind."

This brought hoots of disbelief from Tripp, Ki and Deke. "What you liked about her," Deke needled him in his sultry Georgia drawl, "was that whatever you wanted to do, she said, 'I don't mind.'"

"Hey, give me a break!" Steve's protest was betrayed by the laughter he couldn't stifle. "Lisa Schmidt was a terrific girl. If I were stupid enough to want to get married, she might have made the short list. She liked Clint Eastwood movies, she understood the subtleties of a flea-flicker, and she had her own car."

"And *excellent* posture," Ki pointed out.

Steve laughed again. True enough, one of Lisa Schmidt's most enticing features—or perhaps *two* of her most enticing features—had dwelled between her collarbone and her waist. But that certainly didn't mean he hadn't also appreciated her intelligence. Any female who understood football well enough to know what a flea-flicker was deserved an A in Steve's book—regardless of the letter printed on the tag inside her bra.

They were seated outside on the deck, Steve, Tripp, Ki and Deke, watching the sun turn from gold to coral as it slid down below the mountains to the west. In a while, once the mosquitoes stirred up in the thickening evening, they would probably head inside the cabin and settle around the card table in the living room for some serious penny-ante poker. But the air was still mild, tangy with the fragrance of Sierra breezes and evergreens. The beer was cold and the memories were warm, and no one was in any rush to go indoors.

When Steve thought back to his days at Beckett College, this was what he missed: not the term papers, not the hustle to earn pocket money, not the exams and the lectures and all the rest. What he missed most was the camaraderie—hanging out with Ki, Tripp and Deke.

"You wanna talk about Lisa Schmidt?" he challenged. "The hell with her. Let's talk about...*Candy Kane.*"

Ki rolled his eyes. "Let's not," he pleaded.

"The girl with the name of a porn-film star—and a personality to match. How anyone with the last name Kane could name their daughter Candace—"

"She should have been stuffed in someone's stocking," Tripp agreed.

"But she was *sweet,*" Ki argued, obviously aware of his pun.

"She was sugary," said Tripp.

"And sticky," Deke added.

"We were all young and foolish once," Ki defended himself. "We all made mistakes."

"Gloria," Steve announced, figuring he'd name his most flagrant mistake before any of the others did.

As if on cue, they all groaned and snorted.

"The thing about Gloria," Steve continued after lubricating his memory with another chug of beer, "was that it didn't matter how pretty she was. You could look at her and see exactly what she'd be like in ten years. She'd have one of those houses where the drapes matched the upholstery, and you'd have to use coasters, and she'd have little mushroom-shaped air fresheners in all the bathrooms, and blue water in the toilets."

"I believe the term is anal-retentive," Tripp said helpfully.

"On the other hand, her underwear always matched," Steve reminisced.

"You used to come home from a date with her looking neater than when you left," Deke recollected. "It always made me feel kinda sorry for you."

"Hey, so he left the dorm with his shirttails hanging out and came home all neatly tucked in. Somewhere along the way he must have had to open his trousers," Ki observed. "I never felt sorry for Steve. At least not when it came to girls."

"You held your own," Tripp reminded him.

"Only when he couldn't find someone else to hold it for him," Steve teased, then raised his nearly empty bottle in a toast to Ki and drained it in a few long swallows.

The sky was growing darker, turning the dense fir forest surrounding the cabin into a horizon of black spires. The broad downstairs deck—which Steve had rebuilt last year, with a little assistance from his buddies—was his favorite part of the cabin. Sure, the fireplace was nice, and the hot tub, and that overly macho bearskin rug one of them—he no longer remembered who—had contributed to the living room decor. He liked his cozy bedroom upstairs, and the sturdy furniture, but most of all he loved the downstairs deck.

That and the fact that he shared this cabin with his three closest friends. They'd all gone their separate ways since college, but the cabin held them together. It was their retreat, their lair, their clubhouse. A few years ago, when Tripp had told them he would have to sell the cabin because he was having cash-flow problems, they hadn't had to think long about chipping in, contributing whatever funds it would take for Tripp to hold on to the place. He had said at the time that he would accept their money only if they would accept joint ownership in the cabin, and they hadn't had to think long about that, either.

In the years since, they'd all gone in different directions, pursuing their own dreams. Deke had parlayed his grandmother's old herbal remedies into a multimillion-dollar tea business down in Atlanta. Ki roamed the country tracking gruesome, sensational crimes and turning them into bestselling books. Tripp had turned his athletic gifts into a career designing and selling sports equipment in the Chicago area. And Steve was doing what he'd always wanted to do, despite his fancy college education and the expectations of his parents. He was a carpenter in San Francisco, fulfilling no one's expectations but his own.

But while the four friends had gone their own ways, coming to the cabin would always be like coming home. And Deke, Ki and Tripp would always be his brothers.

Chapter One

"I'm here for your bedroom," said Steve.

The door had opened as far as the safety chain would allow. All he could see on the other side of the threshold was a four-inch vertical strip of femininity: one bare, shapely leg exposed beneath the hem of a short denim skirt, a swath of white fabric above the denim, a tumble of wavy blond hair, a wary blue eye peering out into the hallway.

"My bedroom?" she asked.

It occurred to him that she could take his words the wrong way. It also occurred to him, as he studied the one sparkling eye visible in the narrow opening, the creamy skin of her cheek, the corner of her mouth and the sleek line of her shin, that maybe the wrong way wasn't all that wrong. If the rest of her looked as good as the sample he could see, her bedroom was exactly what he'd like to be there for.

He indulged that mischievous thought for a few seconds before shoving it aside. "I'm Steve Chambliss," he introduced himself. "The carpenter. I buzzed you from downstairs." He checked the impulse to extend his right hand—she couldn't shake it as long as the safety chain remained in place—and instead pulled his wallet from the hip pocket of his jeans. He removed one of his business cards and extended it through the opening.

The hand that took it was slim, pale, the nails enameled a salmon pink. A telephone rang inside the apartment, and she lifted a cordless phone to her ear as she perused his card.

"Hello?" she said. "Oh, hi, Marjorie. Just a sec—I've got a guy at the door who says he's here for my bedroom." The glance she sent Steve's way told him she was amused.

Deciding that was an improvement over wary, he smiled back.

Again he imagined her in the context of bedrooms. Again he warned himself that this was a professional visit. She had phoned his office yesterday and told Karen there was a problem in her bedroom, something requiring the attention of a carpenter. A fellow she worked with, George Maynard, had told her Stephen Chambliss was the best carpenter in San Francisco, and she wanted the best.

Steve recalled that the Maynard job, which had entailed resuscitating several magnificent but long-neglected rooms in a Pacific Heights mansion, had been a tough gig but ultimately quite rewarding, both artistically and financially. Whatever this woman's project was, he hoped it wasn't anything that complicated. He was half done with the renovation of a Victorian near the Presidio, and he had a couple of other projects already scheduled.

As the woman on the other side of the chained door dealt with her telephone call, Steve checked the slip of paper on which Karen had noted the woman's information: "Gwen Talbot," Karen had written, along with a pricey address in the Marina district, along with the word "bedroom."

The woman sent him an enigmatic look from her side of the door, then closed it. Steve heard a muffled trill of laughter as she continued to chat on the phone, and the rattle of the chain being released. She swung the door wide and beckoned him inside, the cordless phone still pressed to her ear.

He entered the foyer and stumbled over a carton. "Watch your step," she said, and then, into the phone: "Not you, Marjorie—although you should watch your step, too." She laughed again, a light, crystalline sound that reminded him of wind chimes. "Do me a favor, call me back in five minutes, okay?" She pressed the button to disconnect the call and smiled up at Steve. "You're the carpenter," she announced.

"I'm the carpenter." Obviously. Not only was she holding his business card, with the words Stephen Chambliss, Carpenter printed on it, but he had identified himself as the carpenter when he'd talked to her via the intercom in the lobby downstairs. Besides, any guy who showed up for a job wearing work boots, faded dungarees and a leather tool belt wasn't going to be mistaken for a lawyer.

"I'm Gwen Talbot. I guess I spoke to your secretary yesterday." She passed the cordless phone from her right hand to her left so they could shake hands.

Folding his long, thick fingers around her small hand, he gave her a quick appraisal. The preview he'd gotten through the barely open door hadn't misled him. She was blond-haired and blue-eyed, with a porcelain complexion and glorious legs displayed to great advantage below the high hem of her skirt. Her build was slim, her height about average for a barefoot woman, and the white T-shirt she wore was intriguingly wrinkled, as if she'd just gotten out of bed.

He really had to stop thinking that way. She was a client, and even if she was the sort of woman who made a man curious about her bedroom—even if he had come to her apartment specifically to make that bedroom a better place—there was nothing deliberately sexy about her, no come-hither look, no seductive grin. Actually, her smile was rather bashful, her eyes round and bright, conveying the impression of youth and innocence. One shimmering gold lock of her hair had gotten snagged in her earring, and as she fidgeted with her earlobe to disentangle the strands, her smile grew even more self-conscious.

Maybe that was it: the appealing awkwardness, the rumpled look, the tousled hair combined with her natural attributes to fill the mind of a guy like Steve with wicked notions.

Her phone rang again. Her eyes remained on him as she lifted the receiver to her ear, and he wondered if she had any idea what he was thinking. Without breaking her gaze, she spoke into the phone: "Hello? Oh—no, the electricity came on just fine. Thanks." She disconnected the caller and shrugged. "I'm sorry, Mr. Chambliss. Things are kind of crazy. I just moved in yesterday, and everything is—"

The phone rang again. She cursed under her breath, and her smile grew even more self-conscious—and even more adorable.

Steve surveyed his surroundings while she answered the call. The carton he'd tripped over was one of three in the foyer. A hallway extended to the right, and straight ahead an arched doorway opened onto a generously proportioned living room with a broad window offering a breathtaking view of San Francisco Bay. The clutter in the room was breathtaking, too—a jumble of boxes, cartons, piles of printer paper, wrapping paper, newspaper, paintings stacked against one wall, a floral-print sofa shoved against another wall, and a long, thick rug rolled and tied, bisecting the parquet floor like a burgundy sewer pipe.

"No, I can't do the window treatments today," she was saying into the phone. "Can I get back to you? Okay, thanks." She disconnected the call and eyed Steve sheepishly. "I'm really sorry, I—"

"No sweat," he assured her, although he didn't want to put her too much at ease. He liked her contrition, her nervous smile, the intelligent blue light in her eyes. He liked her eyes a hell of a lot more than was appropriate under the circumstances.

"I got the phone hooked up yesterday afternoon, and it hasn't stopped ringing," she said.

"It's stopped right now. Why don't you show me the bedroom before—" Too late. The phone rang again.

She groaned and pushed the button. "Hello? Oh, hi, Inez. Can I call you back? Maybe in a half hour." She disconnected the call, sent Steve another apologetic smile, and started down the hall. "It's the master bedroom door," she explained, pausing to turn on a light in the hallway. Along one wall, several cartons occupied the floor. Steve carefully navigated around them as he followed Gwen Talbot to the end of the hall. Her steps were silent, making the clomp of his thick-soled boots sound even louder on the hardwood floor. "It's the door," she repeated, opening and then closing the door in front of her.

The hall wasn't terribly wide. To study the door, he had to stand close to her, close enough that he could see the overhead light threading through the waves of her hair, close enough that he could smell her perfume, a vaguely

musky scent that drew his attention to the smooth skin of
her throat, the contour of her cheek, the edge of her collarbone vanishing into the rounded neckline of her shirt.

"That's a door, all right," he said, willfully forcing his
gaze from her.

"See?" She opened and closed it a second time. "It
doesn't stay shut."

Her shoulders were angular under the loose-fitting
shirt. Her arms were slender, and the thick leather-strap-
ped watch she wore looked bulky circling her graceful
wrist. Her breasts appeared small but firm and delecta-
bly round.

"It doesn't shut," he echoed, pretending to be fasci-
nated by the door she was fanning back and forth on its
hinges.

"It closes, but it won't latch. This thingie here—" she
pointed to the spring-loaded slab of metal protruding
from the door by the knob "—doesn't fit into the hole."

Steve reached around her and tried the door. Sure
enough, the latch wasn't correctly lined up.

He shook his head. "Let me get something straight,
Ms. Talbot—you called me here to rehang a door?"

"If rehanging the door will make it stay shut, then
that's what I want you to do. I want it to close properly.
It's my bedroom, and it's important to me that I can close
my bedroom door when I want to."

She backed up to allow him access to the door. In the
cramped space, she accidentally bumped his hip with
hers, and his gaze darted down to her provocatively bare
legs. If he tilted his head just the tiniest bit to the right,
he could bury his chin in her hair. He tilted his head to the
left as she mumbled an apology and took another step
back.

"Of course it's important that you can close the door," he agreed, refusing to let her nearness get to him. "The thing is, this kind of job is a no-brainer. The super could have taken care of it."

She looked uncertain. "I thought I needed a carpenter, and George Maynard said you were the best...." She tapered off, allowing Steve to devote his full concentration to the problem.

Not that it required much concentration. "See, to do a job like this," he said, swinging the door wide and inspecting the hinges, "all you have to do is pull the door off its hinges and put it back on."

"Well, if that's what you have to do, do it."

He eyed her quizzically, then shook his head again. He wouldn't have pegged her as a helpless female, but apparently that was exactly what she was. "All I'm saying, Ms. Talbot, is that, given what I charge—"

"I know what you charge. George Maynard said you're the best carpenter in the city."

"He's exaggerating. Slightly." The hinges looked good. Steve wondered whether her bedroom was more organized than her living room. For that matter, he wondered whether she had a regular bed, or maybe a heart-shaped one covered in black satin sheets, or a king-size waterbed suitable for orgies—but he couldn't very well peek inside when she was standing inches from his elbow, observing his every move.

"The people who used to own this co-op told me the door hasn't closed properly since 1989," she told him.

That brought him up short. "Why didn't they fix it?"

"I don't know. They said after the earthquake it never worked right. I guess they didn't care. But I do."

"The earthquake, huh."

"I hear it hit this part of the city pretty hard."

"You weren't living here in '89?"

She shook her head. "Yesterday was my first day as an official San Franciscan. And to tell you the truth—" once again she found it necessary to unravel a strand of hair from her earring "—I'm a little anxious about the earthquakes."

"Nothing to be anxious about," he said. "Most of the time, when people in these parts tell you the earth moved, they aren't talking about quakes."

It wasn't the sort of joke he would ordinarily make in front of a client. But Gwen Talbot didn't strike him as an ordinary client. Most clients didn't greet him at the door barefoot, and twist a lock of hair around their index finger while they flashed their big blue eyes at him. Most clients didn't turn him on.

He *wasn't* turned on. Just feeling the way any healthy, red-blooded American man would feel in the presence of a pretty blond lady like Gwen Talbot.

Whatever awkwardness he'd sensed in her before vanished. She raised her chin and narrowed her eyes; her smile grew almost defiant. "Fix the door, Mr. Chambliss."

He chivalrously backed down. "If this was caused by an earthquake, I'm not sure I—"

Her phone rang. This time she looked less apologetic than triumphant. She raised the cordless receiver to her ear, pivoted on one petite pink foot and stalked down the hall, letting the phone continue ringing until she was out of his sight.

Well. Was she put off by his sense of humor? Appalled? Was he going to find the police waiting for him out in the street, ready to charge him with harassment or some such thing?

Somehow, he doubted it. Gwen Talbot might have been disconcerted by his joke, but he'd seen the gleam in her eye, the glitter of suppressed laughter as she attempted to act affronted. She'd handled his line well.

Which made him want to throw her another line and see how she handled it.

Shaking his head, he turned back to the door and studied it thoughtfully. He wasn't looking for a woman—particularly a woman like Gwen Talbot. Anyone who lived in an obviously expensive apartment in one of the fanciest sections of town wasn't his type. What he needed—correction, what he *wanted*—was a woman like himself, someone on his own wavelength, someone who worked hard and partied hard and didn't judge people by the cars they drove or the labels they wore. No upper-crust women for him. Not even if they were cute and disheveled and absurdly sexy.

Fix the door, Mr. Chambliss. Her words echoed in his head, his memory of her voice mingling with the real thing, which floated down the hall from the living room as she chatted on the phone, her words unclear but the melody of her laughter dancing around him.

If his phone rang as often as hers did, he wouldn't be in such a buoyant mood. Obviously Gwen Talbot was a cheerful sort. Even if she was rich enough to have bought herself a co-op with a world-class view of the bay. Even if she couldn't seem to keep her hair free of her jewelry. Even if, for someone who wasn't his type, she sure had a way of holding his imagination hostage.

The door, he reminded himself. *Fix the door, Mr. Chambliss.*

Actually, there seemed to be nothing wrong with the door itself. He closed it, then stepped back and gave it a thorough inspection. He opened it, closed it again, then opened it once more. Succumbing to temptation, he peeked around it into her bedroom.

A big bed, queen-size. A rumpled, summer-weight, white quilt, rose-colored sheets. Two plump feather pillows.

The door, Mr. Chambliss, he muttered under his breath, turning his back on the enticing piece of furniture. Ignoring the cartons and clutter that surrounded her bed, he resumed his inspection of the door from inside the room. He ran his palms along the edge of the molding. Definitely a warp. The strip of wall next to it had a hairline crack. He tapped it lightly, releasing a flurry of powdery plaster. Dusting his hands on his jeans, he scowled.

He ventured back out into the hall. An untrained eye wouldn't have spotted the tiny fissure alongside the molding, but Steve did.

He strode down the hall in the direction of Gwen Talbot's voice. He found her in the living room, standing ankle-deep in wads of packing paper next to an overturned carton, the phone wedged between her ear and her shoulder and a pencil and pad in her hands. In the dining room that opened off the living room stood a long oak table, the top of which was covered with the components of a computer. The monitor swirled with a galaxy of stars, some sort of screen-saver program.

Gwen had her back to him, but she was clearly too busy to contend with him at the moment. He stood quietly in the arched doorway, listening to her babble into the phone. "If we can't get him for Thursday, then let's do it the following Monday. Diane said the others were flexible.... We've got stuff in the can to carry us over the next couple of days, right? I know they're Dallas shows, but at least they aren't reruns. I taped two extra weeks....

Well, I want to do it, too. If we can't do it Thursday—"
she twisted to reach the table and tapped her computer's
mouse, rousing a screen full of data on the monitor
"—according to my schedule we've got the baseball
bachelors lined up for Wednesday. Why don't we run one
of the Dallas shows Wednesday and reschedule the baseball bachelors for Thursday...? What? They have a game
on Thursday? We can tape in the morning and get them
to Gaslight Park by noon...."

"Candlestick Park," Steve murmured.

Spinning around to face him, she accidentally kicked
one of the crumpled pieces of packing paper, which
soared across the room and landed on an arm of the
couch. She sent him a fleeting smile, then said into the
phone, "I have the feeling I'm about to get some bad
news. See what you can do with the baseball players,
okay...? No, don't panic. Everything will work out. It
always does, right? Talk to you later." She disconnected
the call and tossed the telephone onto the oak table.

Steve took a minute to assess the scene: a wide-eyed,
apparently frazzled woman standing amid utter chaos.
The couch was half buried under an avalanche of paper;
knickknacks and file folders lay here and there, curtain
rods stood propped in a corner near the windows, a stack
of framed pictures lay on the floor under a cluttered coffee table, and a ceramic mug rested on the seat of a chair.
In comparison, his generally slovenly bachelor digs
seemed downright immaculate.

And in the eye of the storm, Gwen Talbot glowed.

How could she be smiling in the middle of such a mess?
She obviously had tons of work to do on her apartment,
her phone never stopped ringing, and as she had accu-
rately predicted, she was about to get bad news from the
carpenter who'd come to fix her door. Yet she smiled a

sunshine-bright smile, and nodded to indicate she was ready for him to give it to her straight.

"It's the molding," he said.

"The molding."

"The doorframe. It's warped."

"What do you mean, warped?"

He adopted his gentlest this-is-gonna-cost-you voice. "What I mean is, if having the door close properly is really that important to you, I'm going to have to replace the entire molding around the door. It's out of whack, and it's separating from the adjacent wall."

"Could the earthquake have done that?"

"It probably did. You really ought to see if your super can repair it."

"The building maintenance department told me they already did repair it. If that's the best they can do—" she waved in the general direction of her bedroom "—it's not good enough."

"If you say so." He scanned the living room once more. When his gaze returned to her, he found her smile too contagious not to return. "Have you got an in with the Giants?"

"Who?"

"The San Francisco Giants. I heard you talking about Candlestick Park." Only she'd called it Gaslight Park. Apparently she wasn't up on baseball.

Her grin expanded. "Sure, I have an in with them. Any chance I could pay you for the door repair with a couple of tickets?"

His grin expanded, too. How could he not smile at a woman who seemed to radiate sheer joy despite having just been hit with the news that a portion of her new home was structurally compromised? How could he not appreciate a woman with legs like Gwen's, and those

ballerina-graceful arms, and that slender throat, and her
sapphire eyes and her long, golden hair....

"No chance at all," he told her.

"Box seats right behind home plate?"

She was teasing him. He liked it.

She was a client, though. And he was a businessman.
"The only payment I accept is cash or check. If you want
to throw in the tickets as a bonus, I won't turn them
down."

"How much cash-or-check are we talking about?" she
asked, angling her head in the direction of the hall.

"I'll write up an estimate once I've taken some measurements. It's not going to be cheap, Ms. Talbot. If you
want me to do the job right, I'll have to refit the door
with a new molding, replaster around it and paint the
wall. Maybe paint the entire hallway, if I can't get a good
match on the paint. You could skip the whole thing if you
wanted. The door is perfectly okay the way it is."

"It is *not* perfectly okay," she said, her smile fading.
"Some doors don't matter. But a woman's bedroom is
her sanctuary. It's a private place. How can it be private
if the door doesn't even close?"

He puzzled over her words. A sanctuary? Private?
How private? What did she do in there that had to be
sealed off from the rest of the world? Not that Steve was
an exhibitionist, but he didn't consider it absolutely necessary to shut out the world when he engaged in the sort
of activity he generally associated with bedrooms. He
wondered if Gwen had ever made love in a car, or on the
beach, or someplace like the broad, pine-shaded deck of
the cabin he and his buddies owned up at Lake Tahoe.

And while he was wondering, he wondered why in
God's name he was wasting so much mental energy
wondering about her in the context of making love. She

wasn't the first attractive woman he'd ever done work for. She wasn't the only attractive woman in San Francisco. She was nothing more than a lucrative project—if she decided to hire him. No sense getting sidetracked by her blond hair and her great legs and everything in between, especially when her elite address told her the most significant thing he needed to know about her—which was that she was all wrong for him.

"My truck is parked downstairs," he said. "Let me get some gear and give the job a closer look. Then I'll write you an estimate, and you can decide how you want to proceed."

"Okay." She picked her way adroitly through the rubble and out of the living room. In the foyer, she opened the door and smiled up at him. "I'll leave this unlocked for you," she promised.

Only so she wouldn't have to interrupt her unpacking and her telephone calls to let him in, he reminded himself as he thanked her and left the apartment. She was leaving the door unlocked only for her own convenience.

And he was not going to spend any more time contemplating why it felt so nice to think of Gwen Talbot unlocking her door just for him.

SHE HADN'T REALIZED how completely he filled the apartment until he was gone. The air suddenly grew stagnant. Her phone lay inert on the table; the motor fan in her computer hissed; and for the first time since she'd arisen that morning she felt all alone with her cartons and crates.

She picked up his business card and felt a little less alone. Stephen Chambliss, she thought. Nice name. Nice body.

She smothered a naughty grin and turned to scrutinize the disaster area that eventually would be her living room. The production company had paid all her relocation expenses, so she'd had a small army of moving men pack her things for her back in Dallas three days ago. She couldn't have them unpack for her, however. They didn't know where she wanted anything to go.

Unfortunately, neither did she. Every time her thoughts began to clarify themselves, the phone would ring again, and by the time she was done talking to this or that utility company or Marjorie or the lady from the welcoming committee, Gwen would have forgotten what it was she'd intended to do.

One thing she definitely intended to do was get her bedroom door to close. Last night she'd slept with her windows open, enjoying the balmy September breezes that rose off the bay and climbed the steep slope up from Fisherman's Wharf to her apartment. She didn't enjoy the way her bedroom door kept swinging open with every faint flux of air, though. The first thing she'd done upon arising was to call Marjorie and ask for the name of a carpenter. Marjorie had told her George Maynard, a vice president at the local affiliate that housed her new studio, had had extensive work done on his house last year. Gwen had called George, and he'd recommended Stephen Chambliss.

George Maynard was apparently happily married, with photographs of his wife and children arrayed about his office. He had raved to Gwen about Stephen Chambliss's first-rate work on his house, but he probably hadn't noticed Stephen Chambliss's first-rate body.

Gwen wished she hadn't noticed, either.

So she'd noticed. No big deal. She wasn't in the market for a man, no matter what he looked like. Moving the show—and her life—from Dallas to San Francisco was going to absorb all her energy for quite some time. The last thing she needed was the distraction of a sex life.

Damn. Why did Stephen Chambliss prompt thoughts about her sex life? He was a carpenter who was going to repair her bedroom door, nothing more. Why should Gwen give a rap that he happened to have the sort of lean, limber physique she'd always found irresistibly appealing, and tawny brown hair that was long and floppy without being pretentiously stylish, and spirited hazel eyes, and a slightly cocky, slightly ironic smile, and why did his jeans have to mold to his lower body in such a way that she couldn't stop thinking about his lanky legs and his taut hips and . . .

The phone rang, and for once she was grateful. She followed the chirping sound to her receiver in the dining room. "Hello?"

"It's Marjorie," her producer announced. "You're going to make me gray before my time."

"I'm already making you rich before your time," Gwen shot back. "A little gray won't kill you. Were you able to rework the schedule?"

"We've got the baseball bachelors set for Thursday morning. We'll do the Exploratorium show Monday. You win, Gwen. I concede."

"I told you it would all work out." If it was Marjorie's job to panic, to assume the worst, to fuss and fret over the scheduling of Gwen's guests, then Marjorie was magnificent in her job. Gwen refused to worry about the details. Everything always seemed to fit into place, one way or another.

She heard a sound at the front door, a quiet click as it opened. There was something strangely domestic about the sound, something natural about it. Something disturbingly appealing about the notion of a man entering her home as if it were his.

Not that she'd want a stranger to let himself into her house. But Stephen Chambliss wasn't a stranger. George Maynard trusted him; certainly she could, too.

Marjorie was yakking into her ear about which of the taped Dallas shows they'd broadcast for the rest of the week. Gwen remembered to interject murmurs of assent when necessary, but her mind zoomed off on a tangent: the Stephen Chambliss tangent. She visualized him closing the door behind him, and moving in confident strides down the hall to the bedroom. *Her* bedroom.

Her pulse shifted up a gear, and her cheeks grew warm. Honestly! He was a carpenter, striding down the hall to her broken bedroom door, with its expensively cracked molding.

Just to make sure that was what he was doing, she tiptoed through the dining room into the kitchen and across to the door that opened onto the hallway. Glancing down the hall, she saw him. Armed with a tape measure, he knelt in the bedroom doorway, measuring the door's width. His broad, strong shoulders stretched the fabric of his shirt taut across his back as he worked. His hair covered the collar with a thick fringe of chestnut brown. His hands worked with a crisp efficiency that did weird things to her nervous system.

She'd never been a sucker for laborers, never the sort of woman who swooned over faded dungarees and callused palms. She'd always preferred intellectuals, men who worked in corner offices hatching brilliant schemes for their companies, or in laboratories curing society's ills, or in classrooms inspiring children to use their brains. Yet there was something awfully beguiling about a man who worked with his body. Brains weren't sexy the way muscle and sinew and brawn were.

Her cheeks felt feverish. She ducked back into the kitchen and commanded herself to cool off. Stephen Chambliss had the oddest effect on her. She hoped the door repair wouldn't take more than a day or two. Having him in her home was too distracting.

"Are you still there?" Marjorie bellowed through the phone, jolting Gwen from her ruminations.

"Oh—sorry. Yes. I'm still here."

"Well, which show do you want on Friday? The one with that nut who says pregnant women can make their babies smarter in utero by eating vitamin K? Or the one with the belly dancers?"

"The belly dancers," Gwen answered. "That vitamin-K guy *was* a nut. I'd just as soon put that tape in deep storage."

"Well, it's there if we need it. So, we'll do the baseball bachelors Thursday and the belly dancers Friday. Welcome to San Francisco."

"Right. I've got to go," she said, turning to discover Stephen Chambliss filling the kitchen doorway.

She disconnected the call and peered up at him. He was terribly tall—she'd noticed that when she'd bumped into him in the hall earlier. He had to be more than six feet in height, and most of it seemed to be leg. Yet his taut, powerful physique didn't intimidate her. Something about him made her want to smile: the enigmatic humor that illuminated his eyes, perhaps, or the sly curve of his mouth, or the way he seemed utterly at home in his lean, lanky body. Even as he handed her the piece of paper on which he'd scribbled his estimate—even as she glanced at the number on the bottom and winced—she couldn't quite stop smiling.

"You don't have to decide right now," he suggested. "Sleep on it, get another estimate—"

"No," she cut him off, setting the paper down on the counter and sighing. "I don't have time to go shopping around for other workmen. I want the job done—and why not have it done by the best carpenter in San Francisco?"

He chuckled, although his eyes looked serious. "Let me give you a bit of advice, Ms. Talbot. In the future, if you're dealing with contractors, don't show your hand so fast, okay? Don't let the contractor think you trust him. There are a lot of rip-off artists in this town."

"But you aren't one of them." She wasn't sure what it was about Stephen Chambliss that convinced her he was honest. Maybe his eyes. Maybe his affable smile, his posture, his quiet voice with its undertone of wry amusement.

Or maybe she was a fool, and he was the biggest rip-off artist of all.

He shrugged. "There are some guys in town who'll do this job for less. I can give you their names, if you want. They may not do a double-coat of paint, and they may not get the plaster quite as smooth. They probably won't go with a molding identical to what you've got on your other doors. But you can save yourself some bucks if you go with them."

"Do you not want this job, Mr. Chambliss?"

"If I didn't want this job—" he grinned "—the number on the bottom of that estimate would be three times as big. I'm just telling you your options."

"I'm opting to hire you. When can you get the job done?"

He did a mental calculation. "Assuming my supplier has the molding in stock, I can get started day after tomorrow, give or take. This isn't a one-shot job, though. Once I've got the wall replastered, it's got to dry twenty-four hours before I start painting. Then I've got to let the paint dry and come back another day to do the second coat."

"That's fine."

"I'll need a deposit," he continued. "Also, you might talk to the super and see if you can find out what paint was used on the hall, the brand and color. If we can get a good match I won't have to paint the entire hall."

"I'll check with maintenance." She rummaged through her purse, lying on the counter near the refrigerator, and pulled out her checkbook. "How much of a deposit do you want?"

"Two hundred fifty should do it."

She wrote the check, tore it from the book and handed it to him. "There you go."

He gave her a speculative smile. "You really must want that door fixed."

"I really must." Either that, or she really must want to formalize her relationship with Stephen Chambliss. Handing over a check established in her mind that, whatever his potent male presence did to her nervous system, he was in her world only as a carpenter. As soon as she paid him, there could be no question but that he was working for her. Giving him a check settled things, somehow.

So why, when she gazed up at him as he folded the check and stuffed it into the chest pocket of his shirt, did she feel as if nothing was settled at all? Why did his easy grin make her feel like a giggly schoolgirl rather than a calm, successful television personality taking steps to make her new home livable?

Why couldn't she shake the suspicion that the only reason she'd hired Stephen Chambliss was to give herself an excuse to see him again?

Chapter Two

Marjorie inched open the kitchen door just wide enough to spy on Stephen Chambliss, who was spreading a large canvas drop cloth across the floor in the hallway outside Gwen's bedroom. Marjorie had glimpsed him in the foyer when he'd entered Gwen's apartment, clad in faded jeans, thick-soled boots and a snug-fitting T-shirt, and armed with the drop cloth and a large steel toolbox. From that moment on she'd been twittering and fluttering and refusing to return to the dining room table, where she, Gwen and Diane were supposed to be putting together a schedule for the next two weeks.

"Who *is* he?" Marjorie asked from her lookout perch beside the kitchen door.

"He's here to fix my bedroom door," Gwen told her, refusing to reveal that she found him as much of a knockout as Marjorie did.

"Ohh," Marjorie sighed. "I'll bet he could fix *anything.*"

Gwen grabbed Marjorie's arm and dragged her away from the door. "Behave yourself. If you leer at him, he might charge me more."

"How much is he charging you? I'll chip in. I bet Diane will, too. How about it, Diane?"

"The Gwen Talbot Show's" new administrative assistant crossed the kitchen and glanced down the hall, then let the kitchen door swing shut. "Atheists take note," she whispered. "There is indeed a God, and his gift to women is kneeling outside Gwen Talbot's bedroom door." Winking at Marjorie, she added, "You bet I'll chip in. That man is worth a year's salary, if you ask me."

Gwen glared at the two women, one of whom she'd been working with since the launch of her show in Dallas three years ago, and the other of whom she'd met the day she'd arrived in San Francisco. Marjorie Bunting, the producer of "The Gwen Talbot Show," resided on the young end of middle age and looked like a proper Junior Leaguer. She'd been an assistant producer on the local Dallas news show that had hired Gwen as a researcher eight years ago, and she'd groomed Gwen into a fine talk-show hostess. But after three years in Texas, both she and Gwen agreed that they'd fairly well exhausted the local pool of guests. "The Gwen Talbot Show" had been syndicated nationally for two years, and it was already risking becoming stale. Both Gwen and Marjorie had agreed that broadcasting out of San Francisco would liven things up.

Diane DiMeo, the secretary they'd plucked from the clerical pool at the local San Francisco network affiliate where they rented production facilities, was exactly the opposite of Marjorie: a twenty-five-year-old punk, with close-cropped hair, a nose ring and a wardrobe consisting entirely of two colors: black and black. Yet she was smart and savvy and knew her way around a television studio. Marjorie had been working with Diane for two months before Gwen had arrived in San Francisco, and despite their very different styles, Marjorie and Diane seemed to be on the same wavelength about a lot of things.

Men, for instance. Gorgeous, hazel-eyed carpenters.

Gwen shook her head, half annoyed and half amused by their ga-ga reaction to Stephen Chambliss. "Seriously, ladies, just because I've got a good-looking handyman in my home doesn't mean we should act like sexists. I know I hate being ogled. Don't you?"

"Not since I turned forty." Marjorie inched past Diane to indulge in another peek down the hall. Spinning around, she clasped her hand against her bosom and let out a swooning moan. "He's wonderful. Is he married?"

"*You're* married," Gwen reminded her, although a laugh leaked through her reproach. She knew Marjorie was exaggerating her response to the magnificent hunk of manhood kneeling outside the bedroom door.

Then again, Gwen herself was more curious about his marital status than she would have liked. Three days had passed since his first visit to her apartment, three days during which she really ought to have been too busy to waste a minute thinking about him. Yet she *had* thought about him, about his tall, trim build and his playful eyes and the seductive rumble of his voice, and about whether the absence of a gold band on his left ring finger meant he was single, and about what the hell difference it should make to her if he was. She'd just moved to a new city, a new environment, and she was about to enter a new phase of her life. She shouldn't be fantasizing about a carpenter who was going to tear her doorway apart, put it back together, and charge her a whole lot of money for his efforts.

Yet when he'd telephoned her last night to tell her he'd gotten hold of the moldings he needed and to ask if he could start work the following morning, she'd experienced not satisfaction that the repair was going to get done, but...joy. Absolute, irrational, inexplicable joy at the prospect of seeing Stephen Chambliss again.

She was relieved to have Marjorie acting like an idiot over him. It made her aware of how close she herself could come to acting like an idiot over him if she wasn't careful.

"That's the fellow who worked on George's house?" Marjorie inquired.

"One and the same."

"George never told me he looked like that."

"He wouldn't have noticed," Diane pointed out. "George is the last of a dying breed—straight and monogamous. He only has eyes for his wife." She crossed back to the counter, where she'd left the stack of paper Gwen's computer printer had just spewed forth. "What I'm wondering is what that guy has on under his T-shirt," she remarked as she began collating the pages.

"Nothing, probably," Marjorie said, visibly wrestling with the urge to glimpse the carpenter one last time. Losing the battle, she tiptoed across the kitchen and peered around the door. "Definitely nothing," she reported.

Naturally he would have nothing on under his T-shirt. The day had dawned uncomfortably hot and sticky. Gwen was wearing a loose-fitting dress of Indian cotton, and she'd pinned her hair up off her neck. Marjorie, whose attire always bespoke decorum even when her attitude didn't, had on a sleeveless shell blouse and a skirt of lightweight linen that already looked wilted, even though it was only ten in the morning. Diane's outfit consisted of black culottes, a black tank top and black sandals. All the windows in the apartment were open, but the bay was sending no breezes up the hill to Gwen's apartment today. If such weather was typical for San Francisco at the tail end of summer, she would have to consider buying some air-conditioning units.

In the meantime, she was going to have to cope with the sultry weather—and she was going to have to cope with Stephen Chambliss, whose presence in her apartment seemed to have elevated the temperature a few extra degrees. Much as she wanted to believe she was better behaved than Marjorie and Diane, she couldn't help noticing the traces of perspiration that streaked his forearms and stained the back of his body-hugging T-shirt.

Through the closed kitchen door, she heard the sound of wood squeaking and splintering. "Good Lord, what's he doing?" Marjorie asked, racing eagerly back to the door to check on him. "Tearing the place to shreds?"

"Probably," Gwen said glumly.

"With his bare hands, no less," Marjorie reported, returning to the counter and grinning conspiratorially. "Imagine what those hands would feel like—"

"Enough," Gwen silenced her. She'd spent far too much time during the past several days imagining what his hands would feel like. "We have work to do. The wedding show is coming up at the end of the month and we still haven't filled all the slots in between. Next Friday's show, for instance...."

"Let's do something sexy," Marjorie declared. Gwen shot her a scowl, but Marjorie shrugged it off. "I mean it, Gwen. Thursday we've got the show on computerized houses of the future. Wednesday we've got the show on human-canine communication."

"Tuesday we have the show on sex after a mastectomy. That's sexy."

"That's medical," Diane interjected. "You need something playful, Gwen."

"Talking dogs are playful."

"I'm thinking *sexy*," Marjorie stressed. "I'm thinking..." Her gaze drifted toward the door, toward the hall, toward the carpenter at the other end of it.

Before Gwen could object, Diane piped up. "I read this article in *Women-News* magazine the other day, all about the sexiest occupations for men. Carpenter made the top five."

"No," Gwen said immediately. She had a good idea of where this discussion was leading, and she didn't like it.

Ignoring Gwen's protest, Marjorie clapped her hands gleefully. "Wonderful! The sexiest occupations for men. Let's go for it." She started toward the kitchen door once more.

"Wait a minute!" Gwen snagged Marjorie's arm and hauled her back to the counter. "You want to have a carpenter on the show? Fine. Get a carpenter who isn't fixing my bedroom door."

"But he's perfect," Marjorie said, dismissing Gwen with a breezy wave of her well-manicured hand. "What were the other four occupations in the top five, Di?"

"Let me see if I remember." Diane studied the ceiling as if the information were printed up there. "Cowboy was one."

"Of course," Marjorie said, grabbing a pencil and scribbling notes on the back of one of the collated schedules. "What else?"

"Stuntman. Detective. And...something scientific."

"Now you're talking," Gwen muttered, recalling the doctoral candidate in chemistry she'd dated when she'd been an undergraduate. He'd been damned sexy, and if she had managed to find a position in Boulder instead of having to move to Dallas for her first job out of college, she might still be with him.

"Astronaut," Diane remembered.

Gwen sighed. She knew a good concept for her show when she heard one, and a show featuring representatives of the five sexiest occupations for men was bound to be a hit. The show they'd taped yesterday—featuring the baseball bachelors—had had a similar concept, and it had been a winner. The audience for "The Gwen Talbot Show" primarily comprised women between the ages of twenty-five and fifty, and as much as they enjoyed the shows that dealt with how computers were going to make housekeeping easier in the twenty-first century, or how to deal with demanding bosses, or how to coexist peacefully with adolescent children, or how to talk to dogs, the shows that always spiked the ratings were the ones that dealt with sex. In particular, with young male sex objects.

"He's fixing my bedroom door," she said weakly.

Marjorie's frown brooked no opposition. "Yesterday the baseball players took a couple of hours out of their lives to tape your show, and then they went back to the ballpark to swing their bats and spit. Surely your carpenter can tear himself from your bedroom door for a couple of hours next week to tape the Friday show."

Gwen sighed again. Marjorie was right. But Gwen simply couldn't imagine asking Stephen Chambliss if he would be willing to appear on her show in his capacity as a sexy carpenter. The whole idea made her uncomfortable.

"I'm going downstairs to get my mail," she said. "Marjorie, we're not doing a show on male occupations unless you can get me an astronaut." She handed her producer the cordless phone and stomped out of the kitchen.

She'd intended to march directly out of the apartment, but in the foyer she hesitated. How could a woman just walk past Stephen Chambliss without permitting herself to look at him?

Actually, the first thing she saw, when she turned to gaze down the hall, was plaster. The drop cloth he'd spread across the floor was covered with chunks of it, and a haze of plaster dust hovered in the air. The doorframe stood exposed, a skeleton of vertical beams. The door, removed from its hinges, leaned against a side wall.

Amid the rubble Stephen Chambliss hunched over his toolbox, picking through its contents. Sweat pasted his unruly hair to his cheeks; his shirt was damp and clinging, offering Gwen an unwelcome hint of the sleek torso underneath. The thick leather tool belt girding his hips looked almost unbearably masculine.

Before she could tear her gaze from him, he glanced up and sent a dazzling smile her way. His teeth were too straight and white, his cheeks too dimpled, his hand too masterful as he snapped a tape measure shut.

"That's quite a mess you've made," she observed.

He stood, dug a dark blue bandanna from his hip pocket and mopped his glistening cheeks. "Enough to make you want to run for cover, huh."

"I'm sorry it's so warm in here. I haven't got any air-conditioning."

"Ninety percent of the time, you don't need AC in San Francisco. It's the other ten percent that kills you."

"Well." Why did her mouth feel so dry all of a sudden? Why did his eyes bewitch her? She was a thirty-year-old television personality. She'd interviewed movie stars on her show, politicians, models and athletes and Pulitzer-prize-winning authors. What was it about Stephen Chambliss that reduced grown women like Marjorie and Diane and Gwen herself into tittering ninnies? ''I have to go downstairs for a few minutes,'' she informed him. ''My colleagues are in the kitchen if you need anything.''

''All I need is an arctic breeze.'' He presented her with another heart-stopping smile before turning back to the disaster area that had once been the threshold to her bedroom.

Gwen gazed after him for another wistful moment, then stalked to the front door and out. She couldn't possibly ask him to appear on her show, not without stammering and blushing and acting like a first-class fool.

And she was not going to make a fool of herself. Not for her show. Not for Marjorie. And certainly not for Stephen Chambliss.

DAMN, BUT IT WAS HOT. Hotter than when he'd arisen that morning, hotter than when he'd driven the truck down to Daly City to pick up the molding from his supplier, hotter than when he'd pressed the intercom button next to Gwen Talbot's name and lugged his gear up the stairs to her co-op, hotter than when he'd spread out the drop cloth and set to work. Back in Connecticut this would be called an Indian summer. In California it was called hell.

The open windows in the bedroom didn't help. The air was thick, almost oppressive. The two women who were holed up with Gwen in the kitchen seemed to make the place even hotter with their constant yakking.

And Gwen herself, her sylphlike body set off by swirling gauzy cotton and her hair a whirlwind of blond curls heaped up on her head, and her eyes as blue as the sky and as bright as the merciless sun.... Damn. Thinking about her made him even hotter.

He wondered what all the chatter in her kitchen was about. From the little evidence he'd seen, he suspected that Gwen was an Important Person. She knew professional baseball players, she kept her computer running constantly, and her colleagues came to her rather than making her come to them. He'd seen the two women spying on him through the kitchen door. The younger one looked funky enough to make Steve feel like an old geezer, but the other woman had the prim, impeccably tailored demeanor of a museum curator or a senator or, heaven help him, a bank vice president.

It shouldn't matter to him what Gwen Talbot did, who she was, how she earned enough money to afford this prime piece of real estate in the city's Marina district. Yet he could expend only so much energy on the physical labor of yanking nails out of studs. Part of his mind kept circling back to her, to her gaminlike beauty in her flowing cotton dress, to her long, shapely legs, to the few rebellious golden curls that had unraveled from the hairpins to drizzle around her face, making him all too aware of how alluring the nape of her neck was.

She couldn't be a bank executive. She smiled too much. The only time Janet had ever smiled was when some major deal went through and the bank stood to reap a huge profit.

Janet was past tense, a lesson he'd learned well. Gwen Talbot was no tense at all, neither present nor future. Even if she wasn't a banker, he could figure out everything he needed to know: that she had clout, that she played in the major leagues, that despite her tantalizing hairdo and her flower-child apparel, she had a polish and a poise that marked her as the sort of woman who would give him a hard time if he ever got close to her. He'd had his affair with a high-powered professional, he'd given it his best shot, and he'd found out that high-powered professionals mixed with laborers about as well as toreadors and bulls.

Man, the heat! He was edging toward meltdown. Tug a few nails, and he had to dry his face with his bandanna. Another nail, another once-over with his bandanna. His hair was so wet, the added weight strained his scalp.

He slumped against the dismantled doorjamb and gulped in a lungful of sweltering air. Across the master bedroom the door to the master bath stood open. Maybe a drink of water would cool him off.

He dusted the plaster from his boots before entering Gwen Talbot's bedroom. She'd done a fine job of straightening the place up, and if he'd had a shred of decency he wouldn't have stopped to inspect her private boudoir. But he was too hot to care about propriety. And anyway, she couldn't expect him *not* to look into her bedroom when he was rebuilding her bedroom door.

In the few days since his last visit, she had arranged her furniture and removed all the cartons from the room. A blond oak triple-dresser stood against one wall, with a mirror above it. Its surface was relatively clear, except for an intriguing collection of crystal bottles holding equally intriguing tinted fluids. Perfumes, no doubt. He wondered if she dabbed her perfume or splashed it liberally, if she touched it only behind her earlobes or also behind her knees, between her breasts.

Beige area rugs stretched across the hardwood floor. A carved oak screen decorated one corner. Oak night tables flanked the broad platform bed, and a vase holding an assortment of flowers stood on one of them. Sent by an admirer? Hand-delivered by the admirer, perhaps. Brought to her by the admirer last night. And that lacy scrap of whatever it was that lay draped across one of the two feather pillows—had she been wearing that when her admirer had shown up with the flowers? Had the admirer pulled the delicate garment over her head and tossed it aside, and taken her into his arms, and...

Cripes, but it was hot in her bedroom! He strode to the bathroom, a small cubicle with the required plumbing and a few more crystal bottles cluttering the pearly white counter that surrounded the sink. He cranked on the cold water, splashed his face and then scooped some water from his cupped hands into his mouth.

The refreshment cooled him only until he U-turned and headed back through her bedroom, passing the broad, unmade bed with its rumpled rose-colored sheets and that slinky white negligee on the pillow. And then he was sweating again.

It was silent out in the hall. Maybe Gwen's associates had decamped. Steve hoped so. Their incessant blabbing had given him a headache.

He lifted the claw hammer and wrenched a few more nails from the studs bordering the doorframe. A chunk of plaster separated above the frame and spattered into his face. The droplets of water and sweat glued flakes of it to his neck, making him itch.

He tried to dust off the neckline of his shirt, but that only dissolved the plaster into a pasty grit. What with the heat and the dust and the sweat and his unwelcome consciousness of that filmy, lacy thing on Gwen Talbot's pillow, he was surprised steam wasn't rising from his skin.

He glanced down the hall. Empty. Not a sound, not a sign of life. The ladies must have left while he was in the bathroom, and if Gwen had returned to the apartment he would have known. For the moment, he was all alone.

He peeled off his T-shirt and used it to wipe the sweat and powdered plaster from his neck and upper chest. The air was still suffocatingly hot and humid, but drying his skin brought him relief. He breathed deeply, scrubbed the back of his neck with the shirt and rolled his shoulders to loosen them.

Just a few minutes, he promised himself, and then he'd put the shirt back on. Just a few minutes, so Gwen wouldn't have to nurse him through heatstroke. He'd be appropriately covered before she got back.

GWEN COULDN'T BELIEVE how hot it was. The apartment had been muggy when she'd left, but in the twenty minutes she was gone—first to empty her mailbox and then to argue with the super about when he was going to deliver the cans of paint he'd assured her he had stored in the basement—her home had transformed from merely tropical to downright equatorial. Potatoes could bake in here, she thought, closing the door behind her and thumbing through the stack of mail that had crammed her box.

"Marjorie?" she hollered, wondering whether her producer and Diane had abandoned the place for a cooler setting. They'd offered to come to her house that morning because she had wanted to be home when Stephen Chambliss was working. But the studio building was air-conditioned, and Marjorie and Diane might have been driven from Gwen's apartment by the sauna atmosphere. Just because she had a carpenter in her house didn't mean they had to suffer in this mind-numbing heat.

The carpenter. She cast a quick glance down the hall—and gasped when she saw him standing bare-chested, staring at her and looking incredibly sheepish.

"I'm sorry," he mumbled, shaking out his wadded shirt as if he wanted to dive headfirst into the gray fabric. "I just got so hot, I—"

"No, that's all right." She'd seen men shirtless before. Perfect strangers at the beach, and overly muscular fellows in advertisements for boxer shorts, and even, on occasion, carpenters doing outdoor construction on particularly hot days like today. But never had she seen a man who looked as fantastic out of a shirt as Stephen Chambliss did. If the air in her apartment was fiery, her cheeks were blazing even hotter.

"I thought your visitors were gone, and—"

"It's okay, Mr. Chambliss. It's so uncomfortable in here, I don't blame you. I mean, really, if it's safe to do the kind of work you're doing without protective—I mean—" *I mean I'm babbling like a lame-brained fool, because you've got the most spectacular chest I've ever seen.* It was sleeker than she'd imagined, a glorious stretch of lean muscle tapering from broad, bony shoulders to a tight, hard abdomen. No hair obscured her view of his sun-bronzed skin, his small brown nipples, his narrow navel. His arms were sculptures of bone and tendon, curved biceps and sinewy wrists. His neck was strong without being thick. And then her gaze skipped back to his chest, his flat stomach, the alluring shadows where his hips began and the emphatic underline of that erotic tool belt of his.

"You can call me Steve," he said, giving his wadded shirt another shake.

Good God. He was standing half naked in her bedroom doorway, asking her to call him Steve. "I don't know how it got so hot in here," she mumbled, sounding even more foolish. Without a doubt, his having stripped off his shirt certainly contributed to how hot it was—for her, at least.

"I don't make it a habit to parade around clients' houses half dressed. It's just, between the heat and the plaster dust, I was getting pretty uncomfortable."

"Well," she murmured, doing her best not to gawk at him. She'd hosted shows in which her guests tried to throw her off-balance, or sometimes didn't even try but simply became tongue-tied or said stupid things. She'd always managed to cover her uneasiness, smoothly gliding into a new question or a commercial break. One of her greatest skills was that she could remain poised in the face of all sorts of disasters.

Steve's physique was not a disaster. It was more on the order of a miracle. The only thing that resembled a disaster was her reaction to him. "I wish I had a fan for the window."

"That's all right." He shook his shirt out one final time, and she knew that if she didn't say something he'd put it back on. She considered telling him she didn't mind his leaving it off if it would make his work any easier, but the words died on her tongue as her vision snagged on a drop of sweat skittering from the thick ridge of his collarbone down, meandering toward his sternum and then skimming below his ribcage, detouring past his belly button and vanishing into his pants just above the belt buckle.

She swallowed.

He pulled his shirt on.

"How's the door?" she rasped.

He glanced over his shoulder, as if to refresh his memory of what door she was referring to. "It's coming along."

"Do you need anything? Any help, or a cold drink?"

"No help. I may take you up on the drink in a while, though." A strip of molding slid free of a nail beside him. He deftly caught it, pulled it loose and tossed it onto the canvas at his feet as if it were no heavier than a toothpick. Even in his shirt she could see the flexing of his arm muscles. She could sense the easy strength in his hands. She wondered what his hands would feel like...

She resolutely spun away and hurried into the kitchen, nearly knocking over Marjorie and Diane, who were huddled behind the door, eavesdropping. They scattered, giggling. "What do you think?" Marjorie mouthed.

Gwen scowled. "Will you grow up?" she whispered, her gaze following Diane over to the wall near the dining room door, where the thermostat was located.

Diane wiggled the dial, then murmured, "I'll go open the living room windows."

Before Gwen could question her, she'd skipped out of the room. Gwen raced to the thermostat. The dial Diane had been twisting was currently set at sixty-five, but the thermometer read eight-one.

Tossing her mail onto the counter, she confronted Marjorie. "What have you two been up to?"

"We've been very busy," Marjorie reported, sweeping her thick, dark hair back from her face and smiling unapologetically. "We've got a cowboy from Yuba City lined up for the Friday show. Nancy Howard over at the station is getting us a stuntman, and NASA said they'd be thrilled to send us an astronaut. I'm sure San Francisco's full of detectives. And—'' she gestured toward the hall ''—you're in charge of our sexy carpenter.''

Gwen took a minute to digest this. ''NASA's sending an astronaut?''

''Public relations is part of their job. Astronauts are frequently asked to make appearances. It helps keep interest high in the space program, so we won't complain about how much of our tax money goes to NASA.''

Marjorie's explanation gave Gwen the time she needed to recover from her encounter with Steve—and to assess the evidence in the kitchen. ''Why is Diane opening the windows in the living room? They've been open all morning.''

''Except for the last twenty minutes.''

''And you tampered with the thermostat.''

''It worked, didn't it? He took off his shirt.''

''I can't believe you two!'' Gwen tried hard to look outraged, but she couldn't hold back her laughter. ''You actually cranked up the heat to get him to strip?''

''It worked, didn't it?''

''You're insane!''

''I'm your producer, and I think we've got a top-notch show all set for next Friday. It's going to be bigger than the baseball bachelors. Even bigger than the wedding show, if we can pull it off. Go ask that stud-muffin if he'll strut his stuff on 'The Gwen Talbot Show.' ''

''I can't believe you cranked up the thermostat! Have you no shame?''

Marjorie shrugged and gathered her leather briefcase from the counter. ''None whatsoever,'' she confessed blithely. ''People who have shame don't become talk-show producers.'' Diane swept back into the kitchen, and Marjorie handed her the stack of schedules. ''Diane and

I have to go line up a detective. You talk to that darling man out there.''

''Marjorie—''

''It'll start cooling off soon,'' Diane promised, hoisting the schedules into her arms and grinning. The tiny gold ring adorning her nostril glinted in the overhead light. ''And listen, Gwen, if you don't want him, give him my number, all right?''

''Now wait just a minute—''

Ignoring Gwen, the two women waltzed out of the kitchen, sending appreciatively hungry looks down the hall in Steve's direction on their way out of the apartment.

Gwen remained in the kitchen doorway, listening to the front door close behind them. Then she let out a long breath. She knew as well as Marjorie did that having a carpenter on her show—along with an astronaut, a cowboy, a stuntman and a detective—would make for a great hour of stimulating entertainment. Her audience would love it. The sponsors would love it. Even Gwen would love it, except...

Except that she'd seen Steve's body. She'd seen the flicker of awareness in his eyes as she'd gaped at him, and the twitch of a smile, and that tantalizing trickle of sweat skittering down his chest. And for the life of her, she didn't know where she was going to find the nerve to ask him to be a guest on her show.

She heard a snapping sound down the hall, followed by a muted thud. Steeling her spine, she entered the hall and watched as he laid the last piece of warped molding on the drop cloth. ''Steve?'' she asked, appalled by how timid she sounded.

He turned and straightened up, a strip of new molding in one hand. Even fully clothed he was too handsome. The way he gripped the molded board, the way he flung a damp lock of hair off his face with a sharp toss of his head, the way his eyes flashed green and gray in the uneven light of the hallway, the way his enigmatic smile latched onto something inside her—maybe Marjorie and Diane hadn't been so very insane when they'd contrived a way to get him to remove his shirt....

"Let me get you a drink," she said, ordering herself to think of him only as the person she'd hired to fix her door.

His gaze narrowed slightly, and she realized she'd chosen her words poorly. A man like him probably got propositioned all the time by women he was working for, being offered drinks and more. Clichés filled her mind: the bored housewife in the silk lounging pajamas, the frustrated spinster who paid him to shift the books on her shelves, the madcap heiress with too much time and money on her hands. All he'd have to do was make a joke about the earth moving, and they'd hook their fingers around his tool belt and drag him off to bed.

Gwen was neither a housewife, a spinster, nor a madcap heiress. She was a television talk-show hostess whose producer had maneuvered her into a tight spot.

Shoring up her courage, she presented Steve with a stiff smile as he lowered the board back to the floor and wiped his hands on his bandanna. "I guess I could use something cold and wet," he said.

"I have iced tea or lemonade." *Nothing stronger,* she wanted to add. *Nothing that by any stretch of the imagination you can take to mean anything other than normal hospitality on an abnormally hot day.*

He followed her into the kitchen. The room suddenly seemed much smaller than it had when the real estate agent had shown it to her two months ago. Something about Steve's large boots, his large hands, his large, lean body...

"Iced tea?" she said brightly.

"Sounds good."

Grateful for the chance to do something, she got busy collecting two tumblers, ice cubes and a canister of iced-tea mix. "Do you take lemon?" she asked. "Sugar?" She wondered if she sounded as stilted as she felt.

"That mix already has lemon and sugar in it," he observed.

"Oh. Right. Of course." She spooned the powder into the glasses and filled them with water, causing the ice cubes in the glasses to crackle.

Frantically, she recalled awkward moments from her past: the time the guest on her show, a seemingly typical minister, had without warning released a snake onto the set; the time a show on circuses erupted into a fistfight between two rival clowns; the time a cabaret performer abruptly stopped singing, climbed on top of the piano and yanked off her blouse before the startled eyes of a national television audience.

Gwen had sailed through those bizarre incidents. Why did sharing her kitchen with Steve Chambliss make her feel she was in way over her head?

She stirred the contents of one glass and handed it to him, her lips curved in what she hoped was a brave smile. He nodded his thanks and took such a large swig that when he lowered the glass it was half empty. "I needed that," he murmured, then lifted the glass to his forehead and touched the cool surface to his skin.

"There's something I have to talk to you about," Gwen said before taking a dainty sip of her own drink.

He studied her face and misread it. "Don't worry about the mess out there. I'll clean up when I leave. Even though the job won't be done, you'll be able to use the room and the hallway."

"No, it's not about the repair. It's about...well..." She sighed, then revived her smile. "Do you know who I am?"

He frowned slightly. She'd never thought of herself as particularly short, but he seemed to tower above her, his gaze slanting steeply toward her upturned face. "Gwen Talbot," he said.

"I'm the host of 'The Gwen Talbot Show.'"

"Uh-huh." Obviously that meant nothing to him.

"It's a TV show. A daytime talk show."

"Oh." He smiled tentatively. "I don't watch much daytime TV. I'm afraid I haven't caught you on the air."

"That's all right. No apology necessary." Rugged young workmen were not her target audience.

His expression altered slightly, and he stood straighter. "So—that means you're famous, huh. Gee, I didn't realize—"

She chuckled, feeling somewhat more at ease. "Apparently I'm not so very famous. You've never heard of me."

"I've never heard of most people." He shrugged, then grinned and shook his head. "I'm working for a TV star. I should have quoted you a higher price."

"Oh, please!" Gwen scolded, then burst into laughter. Steve's teasing relaxed her even more. "You're already charging me a fortune."

"So, any chance you can get me a couple of Giants tickets? Actually, I'd prefer the 49ers, if you've got access."

"I've got something better," Gwen told him. "A chance to be on my show."

That brought him up short. He stared at her for a minute, then tossed back his head and guffawed. "Me? On your show? Hey, *I'm* not famous. What would you want me on there for?"

Here came the tough part. "Well, see, Marjorie—one of the women who was here earlier—she's my producer, and she wants to put together a show about the five sexiest occupations for men. There was this survey in a magazine, and..." Dear Lord, did this sound as inane to him as it sounded to her? "Anyway, one of the five sexiest occupations listed in the magazine was carpenter, and Marjorie thought maybe you'd be willing to come on the show and represent carpenters."

He took a slow sip of iced tea. He tapped his teeth on the glass. He rested his hips against the counter and crossed his legs at the ankle. Throughout, his gaze never left Gwen. She felt pinned down, held in place by the steady green-and-silver glow of his eyes as he considered the idea—and the woman who'd verbalized it.

"You want me to come on your show."

"As a representative of a sexy carpenter," she said. "We don't pay our guests, but it could be a lot of fun. We're also having a sexy stuntman, a sexy cowboy and a sexy astronaut."

"Oh, so I wouldn't be the only sexy male." He sounded miffed. "I'd have to share the show with all those other sexy men."

She realized he was teasing again. A spark of laughter illuminated his eyes, and he fought a losing battle against a smile.

She didn't bother to fight her own smile. "Also a sexy detective, if Marjorie can line one up. This would be your chance to prove that carpenters are sexier than astronauts."

"Are they?"

The teasing remained, but in an altered form. He was challenging her, and making her remember the way he'd looked without his shirt, the way his body moved when he worked, the way sweat streaked his chestnut brown hair with shadows. Of course, she wanted to shout, of course they're sexier than astronauts!

What she said was, "Please do it. I think you'd have a good time. And I'm very nice to everyone who appears on the show. I never embarrass them."

"Sure," he said.

"I mean it. My show is about having fun, not humiliating my guests."

"No. I mean, sure, I'll do it. What the hell. It sounds like a trip."

A warm surge of pleasure seized her. More pleasure than when she'd lined up three players from the San Francisco Giants, more pleasure than when she'd arranged for a guest appearance by the conductor of the San Francisco Opera, more pleasure than when she'd seen the lovely new set being built for her friend Inez's wedding, which was going to take place on Gwen's show at the end of the month.

Steve Chambliss was going to appear on "The Gwen Talbot Show." He'd be natural, he'd be perfect, he'd have the audience gushing over him.

Gwen only hoped she wouldn't embarrass herself by gushing over him on camera in front of eighteen million viewers nationwide. Because the truth was, she'd never had a guest on the show who could affect her equilibrium as wildly as Steve Chambliss did.

Chapter Three

"You're kidding," Tripp said once he'd gotten his snickering under control. "You, on TV? As a sexy carpenter?"

Steve sank deeper into the overstuffed cushions of the sofa, used his foot to nudge the newspaper out of his way, and propped his legs comfortably on the coffee table. On the other side of the living room, the doors of his custom-built entertainment cabinet stood open, and through the speakers Bruce Springsteen crooned softly about the darkness at the edge of town. Usually Steve cranked up the volume, but tonight he was on the phone, and The Boss had to settle for being background music.

Steve had already called Ki and Deke to alert them about his upcoming appearance on "The Gwen Talbot Show." They'd both reacted predictably. Deke had let out a rebel yell and then implored Steve to make sure he mentioned, on the air, that he owed everything he was and ever would be to the ingestion of great quantities of Deke's million-dollar product, Dr. Feelgood's Herbal Tea. Ki had asked Steve to plug his latest true-crime book on the air. Now it was Tripp's turn to have a chuckle at Steve's expense.

"Yeah," Steve confessed, laughing along with his friend. "I'm going big time. Flashing my stud smile on the small screen and giving a cheap thrill to the seven people who have nothing better to do at three o'clock Friday afternoon than watch a stupid TV talk show."

"Seven people, plus those of us with VCRs. Seriously, Steve—a sexy carpenter?"

"Typecasting, obviously." He took a swig of beer from the bottle at his elbow and caught the newspaper with his toe before it tumbled off the edge of the coffee table.

"How on earth did you get roped into doing it?"

Good question. Ever since Steve had told Gwen Talbot he would appear on her show, he'd been asking himself the same thing.

He didn't want to think he could be so easily suckered by a pair of big blue eyes and a dazzling smile. He didn't want to believe his ego was in need of nationally syndicated stroking. Yet there he was, less than fifteen hours from taping time, less than twenty from airtime, with no idea of how Gwen had managed to push his buttons and pull his strings.

"I don't know. Gwen insisted it would be fun."

"*Gwen?* You're on a first-name basis with the lady, huh."

Steven grinned. How could he call her Ms. Talbot after she'd seen him topless and sweating? How could he maintain that kind of formality when he was going to appear on her show?

It wasn't as if he were still working for her, anyway. He'd applied the last coat of paint to her wall yesterday—and she hadn't been home. The building manager had let Steve in, he'd finished up the job, the manager had given him the check Gwen had already written as final payment, and he'd left.

In fact, he hadn't seen her since the day last week when she'd talked him into doing the show. He'd been back to her place three times, and she'd been out all three times. Without her in it, her apartment had looked like what it was: a rich woman's residence. The rug had been laid in the living room, paintings had been hung on the walls, fresh flowers had been placed not just in her bedroom but also on the mail table in the foyer and on the dining room table, alongside the perpetually purring computer. Her bed had been made, her lingerie carefully put away.

A rich woman's residence, all right. And Steve knew better than to get hung up on a rich woman.

Yet the strangest thing of it was, he'd wanted to talk to her. Last night, he'd been sorely tempted to dial her number and ask her if she was satisfied with his work. He knew she was—he'd done a damned good job, and if she hadn't found it acceptable she would have called him to complain and ask for her money back. But she hadn't called. And he'd spent the evening pretending to watch a baseball game on the tube while his mind toyed with the notion of phoning her, and asking her...

Asking her for a date? Nah. He already knew she wasn't his type. Too upwardly mobile. Too famous. Too capable of manipulating him into doing things that were totally out of character for him—like appearing on her TV show.

"She convinced me that the reputation of all carpenters everywhere rested on my shoulders," he explained to Tripp. "She's going to have an astronaut on the show, for God's sake. An astronaut and a cowboy. I *have* to go on the show, if only to prove that carpenters can hold their own with astronauts and cowboys."

"Yeah, sure." Tripp snorted in disbelief. "Carpenters the world over will be forever in your debt for carrying the banner. Come on, Steve. Why are you doing this?"

Because... Because of Gwen's big blue eyes, and her dazzling smile, and that intriguing lace thing he'd seen on her pillow. Because of her slender shoulders and her long, lithe legs. Because of the energy she radiated, and the certainty, and the fact that doing the show would give him an excuse to see her again.

He swallowed some beer, then sighed. "I don't know why I'm doing it, Tripp. Maybe some latent yearning for the spotlight."

"Of course. That's you in a nutshell, Chambliss. Latent yearning. Well, look—if you're going to do it, I'm going to tape it. Then, when you make an ass of yourself, I'll have the moment preserved on tape for black-mailing purposes."

Steve laughed. "I knew I could count on you."

"Have you notified Ma and Pa Chambliss about your impending stardom?"

Steve let out another sigh, this one less baffled than just plain weary. "I guess I'll call them when I'm done with you."

"You'd better be done with me, then. It's 8:30, Chicago time, and it's an hour later where they are."

Steve glanced at his watch. Back in Connecticut it would be nine-thirty. Not terribly late, but his parents weren't exactly night owls. If their telephone rang after ten, they would assume someone had died.

He ended his conversation with Tripp and drained the bottle of beer. He knew he should call his folks and get it over with, but he procrastinated, rising and crossing to the kitchen to inspect the fridge for edibles. None of the frozen microwave dinners jamming his freezer tickled his taste buds. He pulled a couple of slices of leftover pizza from their foil wrapping and stuck them in the oven.

He had to call his parents; there was no way around it. If he didn't call them, one of his mother's friends would see "The Gwen Talbot Show" and inform her that Steve had been on it, and then his folks would be furious with him not only because he'd gone on national television and flaunted his lowly occupation but also because he hadn't given them advance warning.

He wished they could laugh about it the way his buddies had. But a decade had passed since he'd quit his fast-track marketing job and taken up a hammer and nails. More than a decade since he'd become the first member of his family to graduate from college. His father drove a truck for a local supermarket chain, his mother worked part-time as a warehouse clerk, his older brother was a mechanic and his sister a beautician. Steve, the family academic, had gone to college with the help of a scholarship, a few loans and a great deal of sacrifice from his parents.

And what had he done with his hard-earned diploma? Left it in a box in his parents' attic and embarked on a life of rewarding physical labor.

As if that wasn't bad enough, now he was going to appear before television cameras, before a studio audience and a national audience, and gloat that not only was he a laborer, but his labor made him sexier than a cowboy. Talk about an accomplishment to fill a guy's parents with pride.

The kitchen warmed with the aroma of hot cheese and tomato sauce. He pulled the reheated pizza from the oven and took a bite. What the hell. He was thirty-three years old, and he was under no obligation to live his life to please his parents, or his friends, or his lovers, or anyone but himself. His family couldn't turn him into a button-down executive. Neither could his last girlfriend, Janet, the bank vice president. If they were disappointed in him, that was their problem, not his. He was used to being disapproved of by people who believed the only careers worthy of respect were those that didn't leave calluses on a man's hands.

Maybe they were right. Maybe Steve had blown his future by abandoning paper-pushing for carpentry. But Gwen hadn't invited any marketing executives to appear on her show, had she?

Steve could have been one of those marketing executives if he'd listened to people who claimed to know what was best for him. Who knew? He could have had a closet full of Brooks Brothers suits and tasseled loafers. He could have been pulling down six figures a year, and managing a fast-growing portfolio in his spare time. He could have been driving an Infiniti instead of a heavy-duty van with Chambliss Carpentry painted on the sides. He could have been living in an apartment with a view of San Francisco Bay, like Gwen Talbot's.

But he hadn't listened to anybody but himself, and he had no regrets. Evidently, listening to oneself added to one's sex appeal. And if Steve's parents didn't like the idea of his going on TV to talk about it, well, it wouldn't be the first thing he'd done that they didn't like. And it probably wouldn't be the last.

THE THEME MUSIC CUED UP. Gwen held still as an assistant dusted a cosmetics brush across her chin and throat one final time, and as another assistant handed her a cordless microphone. Lights glared on the stage where her five guests sat, but she kept her gaze fixed on the studio audience.

The assistant gave her a gentle shove. She shaped a broad smile and strode from the shadowed wing and up the two well-lit steps to the stage. The one hundred women in the audience burst into applause.

"Hi! I'm Gwen Talbot, and I'm surrounded by five of the sexiest men in the working world!" she announced, following the print that scrolled down the TelePrompTer screen. She had reviewed the script several times that morning; she ought to know her opening speech verbatim. Yet for the first time since her rookie year as a talk-show host in Dallas, she depended on the prompter. She was too nervous to trust her memory.

The show was going to go well. When Marjorie had faith in a show's concept she whistled. If she trusted both the show's concept and its guests, she hummed. That morning when she arrived at the studio, she'd been belting out "Ain't No Mountain High Enough" at the top of her lungs.

By nine-thirty, word had reached Gwen's dressing room that the cowboy, the astronaut and a local detective were already waiting in the green room for the ten o'clock taping. Ordinarily, Gwen visited the green room before the show to meet her guests, exchange small talk and give them a preview of some of the questions she would be asking them while the cameras rolled. But that day she'd asked Diane to handle the loosening-up-the-guests chores for her.

Why was she so anxious? Why had she spent a half hour that morning groping through her closet, unable to decide whether she should dress in a demure suit or cut loose with a funky slacks outfit? Why did this one show—which Marjorie's off-key warbling guaranteed would send the ratings through the roof—have Gwen in such a tizzy?

She knew the answer, and she didn't like it.

Every evening when she entered her apartment and smelled the faint, lingering scent of fresh paint, she knew. Every time she closed her bedroom door and heard a clean, solid click as the bolt shot into place, she knew. Every time she closed her eyes and pictured Stephen Chambliss's sleek, sweat-streaked torso, his seductive gaze and his ironic smile...

She knew.

She was a professional. She would treat the carpenter the same way she treated the astronaut and the detective and the other guests. She would tape the show and be done with it, and perhaps, once it was over, she would be able to put Steve out of her mind.

Her audience was revved up; Marjorie had seen to that with a pretaping pep talk. Gwen glanced past the prompter and forced herself to relax. "*Women-News* magazine conducted a recent survey of the sexiest occupations for men," she said, "and the top five vote-getters were astronaut, cowboy, stuntman, detective and carpenter. Today on the show, we've got representatives of each of those occupations. They're going tell us a little about what makes their work so irresistible to women...and what do you say, ladies? Are these guys irresistible, or what?"

She turned and gestured grandly toward the five men seated in easy chairs on the stage. The audience erupted in lusty cheers. She couldn't really blame them. Her guests were all remarkably good-looking.

They'd dressed for their roles, too. The astronaut wore a snappy-looking NASA jumpsuit. The cowboy was clad in full rodeo regalia—Stetson hat, fitted shirt, leather chaps and boots. The detective bore a vague resemblance to Humphrey Bogart in his Sam Spade mode, complete with a slouchy fedora and a trench coat. The stunt man was a sculpture of chiseled muscle encased in spandex, with a glossy crash helmet perched on one knee.

And then there was Steve.

Unlike the others, his getup wasn't the least bit flashy or eye-catching. He looked much as he had the first time he'd come to her apartment: a comfortable T-shirt, faded blue jeans, thick-soled work boots and his low-slung leather tool belt. The corner of a red bandanna peeked out from his hip pocket. Gwen didn't notice it until he shifted in his chair, drawing her attention to his lean, hard hips.

Her gaze remained on him only long enough for him to send a mysterious smile her way. It was the same smile he'd sent her the morning she'd returned to the apartment after Marjorie and Diane had sabotaged the thermostat and Gwen had found him standing in the hallway, half undressed and sweating. His smile then had been a bit bashful, a bit defiant, and much too virile.

His smile was bashful, defiant, and excessively virile now, too.

Refusing to let him rattle her, she turned back to her exuberant audience. "After each of these good-looking fellas tells you a little about what makes his job so sexy, they'll answer your questions. At the end of the show, we'll have our own informal survey and see which of the five professions you think takes the cake when it comes to sex appeal. But first, a few words from our sponsor." The light on the camera aimed at her went off, and she pivoted to greet her guests. "Guys, you look great! What do you think, ladies?" she asked the audience. "Do they look great or what?"

The audience responded with wolf whistles and whoops of pleasure. Someone shouted her phone number. "Hey," Gwen said, still smiling, although her tone grew serious, "no phone numbers when we're taping, okay? This show is seen all over the country. You don't want your phone number going out across the airwaves." She caught a hand signal from one of the cameramen. "Are we ready to roll again?" she asked. At his nod, she pulled a stack of index cards from a blazer pocket of the chic suit she'd finally decided to wear, cleared her throat, waited for her cue and began speaking in her more formal on-air voice. "Let's meet our sexy male professionals now. We'll start with Lyle McKay, a cowboy from Yuba City. Tell me, Lyle, what is it about cowboys that turns a woman's knees to jelly?"

He gave an aw-shucks grin and tipped his Stetson. "Way-ell," he drawled, "I reckon the thing about cowboys is, what we do is dangerous. I mean, yer out there, just you and yer horse and all them cattle, and it's just you against all of 'em. You gotta be able to rope strays and ride broncs and contain stampedes. It takes a tough man to be a good cowboy. A tough man, and a fearless one. And a good horse."

Gwen suspected he was overstating the difficulty of the cowboy's lot in the twentieth century, when most cattlemen controlled their herds from the driver's seat of an off-road vehicle. Lyle's accent sounded more West Texas than northern California, but the audience clearly adored him. When he was done, they applauded rambunctiously.

The astronaut went next. In a deep, stentorian voice he talked about space walks, fighting G-forces, the incredible risks astronauts faced during takeoff and reentry, the immense courage required of a human being to allow himself to be launched into an airless, lifeless universe. He talked about the thrill of discovery, and about the fierce dedication and levelheadedness astronauts needed in order to overcome the many emergencies that cropped up during space flights. He wasn't a cowboy, Gwen concluded, but he held his own. When he was done, the audience cheered.

Gwen introduced the detective, who described his career of sleuthing and stalking and being shot at, staring death in the eye, knowing how to use a firearm and having the guts to use it when he had to. He discussed the perils of dealing with criminals, the bravery necessary to do his job. He was tough and macho, and the women filling the seats of the studio responded enthusiastically to his gritty arrogance. They also shrieked their appreciation of the stuntman with his rippling muscles and his fearlessness. He talked about racing motorcycles through fires, jumping off buildings and other feats of derring-do.

The four men were admirably intrepid, defining their manhood by the amount of danger they had to overcome in their work. Gwen almost felt sorry for Steve. What kind of danger did a carpenter encounter on the job? The possibility of smashing his thumb with a hammer, or falling off a ladder, or nicking himself with a saw? How could Steve compete with the flagrant bravery of the other guests?

She eyed him from the opposite end of the stage. His multicolored eyes glinted with amusement, and she found herself thinking that maybe bravery was overrated as a source of sex appeal. Anyone with eyes like Steve's—slightly sleepy, slightly cocky, much too knowing—had plenty enough going for him.

"Our last guest today," she told the audience, "is Stephen Chambliss, a carpenter here in San Francisco. Steve, why don't you tell us a little about your work?"

He leaned forward in his chair, and she caught another glimpse of the red tip of his bandanna poking out from his hip pocket. Facing the audience, he grinned affably. "I've got to tell you, ladies," he said, "what I do isn't about risking my neck. Carpenters operate in a whole different way. We don't shoot people or rope animals or pay house calls on extraterrestrials. What we do is *make* things. We work with our hands," he said, displaying his hands for the audience. For all their blunt strength, they were surprisingly graceful, his fingers thick but nimble, his palms leather-smooth. "Carpenters are really tuned into the way things *feel*. We like to take our time and do the job right, to make something that'll last.

"One thing we do is use our *tools*. We carpenters always say you've got to have the right *tools* to do the job." His eyes twinkled; his mouth skewed in a wicked smile. The way he pronounced the word "tools" made the word sound X-rated. Gwen felt an uncomfortable warmth stroke the back of her neck. "Now, I brought some of my tools with me—"

"Let's see them!" shouted a rowdy audience member. A few women giggled. They hadn't missed his innuendo.

His grin widened. "There's nothing I'd rather do right now than show them to you," he said, making a big production of rearranging himself in his chair so he could reach into a slot of his tool belt. He pulled out a square of brown paper and held it up for the audience. "This is sandpaper," he said. "It's a little rough—" he ran a finger along its abrasive surface "—but when you use it right, it makes things real smooth. Carpenters like things to be smooth. We'll rub and rub until it feels right, just as smooth as it can be."

A few women in the audience sighed. One woman murmured, "I like it smooth, too," which provoked a spate of laughter.

Steve put away his sandpaper and pulled from his tool belt an old-fashioned hinged ruler. "This is a carpenter's rule. A lot of carpenters use tape measures, but I thought you might want to see this. It's stiff. Long and hard and very stiff." His innocent smile was belied by the mischievous gleam in his eyes. "This tool can be used for all sorts of things. Like measuring studs, for instance." A tide of laughter rolled through the audience. Even the other men on the stage were laughing. So was Gwen, although she could feel her temperature soaring into the fever zone.

Steve continued, his expression spuriously earnest. "One of the features of a carpenter's rule is that if you need it bigger—" he opened a hinge "—it gets bigger. It can be just as big as you want it to be. And it's always straight and hard." He folded the rule and slid it back into his tool belt.

The warmth creeping down Gwen's neck transformed to a heat that pooled at the base of her spine, in the cradle of her hips. She was relieved to be off-camera, where no one outside the studio could see her squirm and shudder in an attempt to fend off her response to his teasingly erotic words. She'd dealt with more embarrassing guests on the air, more suggestive subjects, but she'd never found herself thinking about roughness and smoothness and measurements in quite the way she was thinking about it right now. If she was blushing—and she was certain she was—she'd rather not have her flaming cheeks broadcast into homes all over the country.

He pulled from his belt a three-inch screw. "This is a screw," he said.

Most of the audience erupted in laughter, although the sound had a certain breathlessness about it. The stuntman shook his head in grudging admiration. Gwen glanced into the wing toward Marjorie, unsure of whether she ought to let Steve keep going. Marjorie sent her a thumbs-up. If Steve crossed the line into blatantly bad taste, the tape could always be edited before airtime. But for now, Marjorie clearly wanted him to keep going.

"You'll notice," he said as he held up the screw, "it's a very, very *long* screw. This isn't a screw for someone who wants to rush. But carpenters don't rush things. We like to take our time. And this is the kind of screw that takes a long, *long* time."

He pulled a screwdriver from the belt. "You all know what this is. Notice how the tip fits just perfectly into the slot here—it just nestles right in there." He demonstrated by placing the screwdriver into the head of the screw. "A carpenter turns it and twists it, always with just the right amount of pressure—not too much pressure, not too little. When it's all done you've got two items joined firmly together, and they don't want to come apart. And I'll tell you, we carpenters feel *real* good when we've joined two things together with a good, long screw."

Women in the audience were giggling and sighing. The muscles in Gwen's thighs were clenching. She wondered whether Marjorie had tampered with the thermostat in the studio, or whether Steve's wicked insinuations were enough to put everyone into a sweat. She'd have to make sure her face received a fresh powdering during the next break. Her forehead and upper lip were damp. As for other parts of her body...she didn't even want to think about what Steve's presentation was doing to her.

Pretending to be unaware of his effect on the audience, Steve returned his props to his tool belt and leaned back in his chair. "These other gentlemen—" he indicated his fellow guests "—I admire their courage. I respect it. They face danger head-on. But as far as carpenters go, well, we aren't fighters. We're lovers."

A brief, stunned silence followed his speech, and then an explosion of clapping and stamping feet and whistling. The light flashed red on the camera aimed at Gwen, and she made a joke of how flustered she was, fanning herself frantically with her index cards. "Well," she said in an unexpectedly thick voice. "We're going to take a quick break to cool off, and then you'll have a chance to ask these very sexy guys some questions." The audience responded with more whistles and hoots.

The camera light switched off, and Gwen felt herself go limp. Marjorie bounded onto the stage from the wing, clapping wildly, first at the show's guests and then at the audience. "You're all fabulous!" she roared, sweeping past Gwen and opening her arms toward the men, as if to gather them all in one big, maternal embrace. "Absolutely fabulous."

The astronaut scowled. "Are you sure there won't be any problems with censors?" he asked, shooting a chastening look in Steve's direction.

Steve arched his eyebrows in mock astonishment, as if to say, *Why look at me? What did I do?*

"No problem," Marjorie assured the astronaut. "We're doing great. Are you ready to roll?" she asked Gwen.

Gwen managed a smile. The good news was that in the upcoming segment of the taping she would be out in the audience, far from the one guest who could arouse her mercilessly with a few impish puns. The bad news was that once she was in the audience she'd have little recourse but to look at him.

At all her guests, she reminded herself as, clutching the cordless mike, she ascended the steps up one of the aisles. A camera followed her deep into the audience and the light went on. "Hi, I'm Gwen Talbot, and we're talking with a quintet of gentlemen who represent the five sexiest occupations for men, according to a recent poll in *Women-News* magazine. It's time for some questions from the audience. Yes?" She aimed the mike toward one of the woman seated near her.

The woman stood up and batted her eyes furiously. "Um, I was just wondering..." She grinned sheepishly at Steve. "Are you free tomorrow night?"

Gales of laughter. Gwen had no choice but to join in. Another woman waved toward her, and she edged down the row to take the question. "I was wondering if any of you are married," she asked all five men.

It dawned on Gwen that she had no idea if Steve was married. Or the other four. She really had to make sure she didn't ignore them.

It turned out that the astronaut and the detective had wives. The astronaut, who seemed miffed by Steve's prurient speech, went on at some length about how marriage and sexiness weren't mutually exclusive, and how knowing a wife was waiting for him back on the planet Earth made it easier to face the dangers of outer space. The detective, in his best hard-boiled manner, said he'd met a long-legged broad on a case. "I had to marry her," he explained. "She's the only person who's ever managed to lay me out flat." His joke won him appreciative laughter.

The cowboy said he wasn't married because the cowboy's life was a loner's life. The stuntman mentioned that he wasn't married because he found it impossible to choose among all the cute starlets he worked with in Hollywood. A few women booed good-naturedly.

Then Steve spoke up. "I'm not married," he said. "I have nothing against marriage in theory. But personally, I'm just not the marrying type."

"Why not?" an audience member shouted. Gwen repeated the question into the microphone.

Steve shrugged. "It seems that when a woman decides she wants to marry you, the first thing she does is try to change you. She says she loves you, but could you please be more like this and less like that, and could you stop putting your feet up on the table, and could you drink your beer out of a glass instead of a bottle...and the next thing you know, she's changed you completely, and you're not the same guy you used to be. I like women, you know? I love them. But I'm pretty happy with my life the way it is. I guess that means I'm not good marriage material."

"Marriage is a noble institution," the astronaut retorted.

"It's an institution, all right," the stuntman countered. "Like a booby hatch."

"Now, now, now," Gwen chided with a smile, then grabbed the opportunity to plug an upcoming show. "I agree with our astronaut. Marriage can be one of the sexiest occupations of them all. And don't forget—" she addressed the camera directly "—that on Friday, October 1, right here on this show, we'll be broadcasting a real, live wedding! Inez LaPorta, San Francisco's premier television meteorologist, and celebrity restaurateur Tom Blanchard will be tying the knot on 'The Gwen Talbot Show,' and all you viewers are invited to join the festivities. We're going to take a brief break for our sponsors, and when we come back, our studio audience here is going to hold their own poll to see which of these five fine gentlemen represents the sexiest profession for men.''

The camera light flicked off and Gwen let out a shaky breath. Even from the shadowed heights of the back row, Steve's cryptic smile drew her attention. He leaned back in his chair, looking much too leggy, much too comfortable. It didn't seem fair that he could be so relaxed when, with his sly words and his easy humor, he'd managed to turn on every woman in the room.

At least one woman, she amended, unable to speak for anyone but herself. But it was *her* show. She was the one who was supposed to be a natural at this. Yet there Steve sat, his head tilted at an angle that implied both confidence and bemusement, as if he wasn't quite sure how he'd wound up in this predicament but had every intention of enjoying himself. And she was a tangle of quivering nerves.

She knew that once the taping was over, the show ran and the ratings came in she'd be able to reminisce fondly about this morning. Steve would be gone from her life. She would no longer have to worry about the way his eyes mesmerized her, and the way his smile plucked sensations from deep in her gut, and the way his legs forced her to reevaluate the very concept of faded blue denim.

As she descended the aisle stairs back to the stage, Diane and a few stagehands distributed ballots to the audience members. On the stage the guests chatted among themselves. A woman in the front row informed the cowboy that she'd always had a soft spot in her heart for a man in spurs. The woman next to her declared that she'd always had a soft spot in her heart for a man who took his time, even if he wasn't the marrying type. A third woman muttered that she herself had a soft spot in her brain for men who weren't the marrying type.

"We've got all the ballots," Diane called from the opposite side of the studio. "A couple of minutes, and we'll have the totals."

"Kind of like election night, isn't it," Gwen teased. "I hope four of you have concession speeches ready." Actually, she was more than interested in how Steve would react if he lost the audience's vote. Not that she expected the poll to turn out that way, but she wondered, just wondered...

Did he know how incredibly attractive he was? Had he guessed that his routine with his "tools" would melt not just an audience of ebullient women but the host of "The Gwen Talbot Show"? Gwen prided herself on being reasonably sophisticated. She'd done shows featuring striptease dancers, sex therapists, even a rather mousy, bald businessman from Corpus Christi who had been married to fifteen women simultaneously. Three of his alleged wives had appeared on the show with him and claimed that he'd more than satisfied them in bed.

But in his own Caspar Milquetoast way, he'd been a fighter. Like the astronaut, the cowboy, the stuntman and the detective.

Steve Chambliss wasn't a fighter. He was a lover. Merely thinking about the way his low, laughter-filled voice had wrapped around the word *lover* caused longing to wrap around her soul like a drawstring, pulling tight.

She didn't want to long for Steve. She didn't want to like him. She sure as hell didn't want to be so vulnerable to his smile. He'd just boasted, to a national audience, that he had no interest in changing anything about himself just to make a woman happy. Who needed a selfish, stuck-up man like that?

She focused on the other four guests, who passed the time by exchanging competitive barbs. The cowboy contended that no man could possibly be sexier than one who knew how to straddle a filly, although he allowed that a dude like Steve had probably straddled a few sawhorses in his day. The detective bragged that it was the adrenaline a man felt when he stared down the barrel of a gun that gave his performance in bed an extra edge. The stuntman commented on the importance of resilience, flexibility and endurance. The astronaut pointed out that only a man who had circled the earth in a space shuttle could understand how to send a woman into orbit.

Steve merely shifted his lithe, supple body in his chair and smiled. Gwen ordered herself to ignore him, but she couldn't resist his smile, all teeth and dimples and devilry. She almost hoped he came in last in the poll. Maybe if he did, he'd seem less appealing in her eyes.

Diane sidled up to her with a folded sheet of paper. "Ready in five," she whispered, then vanished as the director counted down the seconds. The light flashed on the camera, and Gwen flashed her smile. "Welcome back! We've got the final tally on our poll of what the sexiest profession for men might be. Is it a cowboy?" She watched as camera two zeroed in on what was visible of Lyle McKay's craggy face beneath the dented brim of his Stetson. "Or is it an astronaut?" The camera panned one seat over, then panned again as she said, "A detective? A stuntman? Or a carpenter? I've got the results in my sweaty little hand here...." Her own camera came back on as she unfolded the paper. She tried hard to look amazed. "Well, our studio audience says the sexiest occupation is...a *carpenter.*"

Thunderous applause. Hoots and hollers. Steve looked abashed. The cowboy shook his head and chuckled. The stuntman gave Steve a friendly sock in the arm. The detective obviously shared the cowboy's shock at having not won, and the astronaut looked indignant but also a bit relieved.

"Kiss the winner, Gwen!" a voice rose from the audience.

"Oh, now, now, now..." She held up her hands in protest.

"Go ahead! Kiss the winner! Kiss the winner!" More audience voices chimed in. Gwen wasn't sure, but one of the voices sounded a lot like Marjorie's.

"Now, really, folks! This is a clean family show!"

"Give him a clean, family kiss!" That was definitely Marjorie's voice, singing out from the wing where she was standing with Diane.

Gwen looked helplessly at the men on the stage. "If you don't do it," Lyle drawled, "you're likely to have a revolt on your hands."

"The hell with him," the stuntman piped up, jabbing a thumb in Steve's direction. "It's us losers that could use a kiss."

"Kiss the winner!" the audience chanted. "Kiss the winner!"

"Oh, Lord." Chuckling to cover her chagrin, Gwen glanced at Steve—and was transfixed once again by that smile of his, all fun, all trouble.

If she didn't kiss him, the cowboy's prediction might come true. If she *did* kiss him, her nervous system might rise up in revolt.

She glared at Marjorie, who remained with Diane in the wing, waving her fists triumphantly in the air and clamoring with the audience: "Kiss the winner! Kiss the winner!"

Gritting her teeth and silently vowing revenge on the despicable producer of her show, Gwen turned back to Steve. He shoved himself to his feet as she crossed the stage. When she was halfway across, he spread his arms in welcome. "I won't bite," he promised as she drew to a halt several inches from him.

"Just keep your tools to yourself," she warned. She would have liked to sound composed, unaffected by any of this. But her voice sounded tremulous, her scalp tingled, her hands went icy and her breasts seemed to burn.

Steve looked disgustingly untouched by the hoopla. "It's just show-biz, right?"

"The things I do for ratings." She took one step closer, rose on tiptoe and offered him her cheek.

Rejecting the offer, he cupped his marvelously strong, graceful, callused, capable hands around her cheeks and steered her face to him. Before she could protest, his mouth claimed hers.

Chapter Four

If the closing theme music cued up, Gwen didn't know. If the studio reverberated with wolf whistles and shrieks and the cameras were panning the studio to capture audience members waving and mouthing greetings to friends and relatives, Gwen wasn't aware of it. If Marjorie was churning up hysteria from the sidelines, and a voice-over was listing the show's sponsors, and four representatives of the sexiest male occupations were standing just a few feet away from her, watching her kiss a carpenter, she didn't care.

For one timeless, mystifying instant, all that mattered, all that existed, was Stephen Chambliss, his hands warm and firm on her skin, his lips brushing hers. He tasted of mint and magic, heat and power, safety and danger—a danger she wanted to experience as surely as the astronaut wanted to fly to the moon or the detective wanted to stare death in the face. She wanted to test the limits of the universe and the limits of her soul with Steve.

But almost as soon as the kiss began it was over. As reality crept back into her consciousness she recognized that what had occurred between Steve and her hardly qualified as a kiss at all. His lips had merely touched hers. His breath had barely whispered across her upper lip, her

body had scarcely felt the shadow of his. No more than
a couple of seconds had elapsed before he withdrew.

Gwen ought to have been grateful for the brevity of the
contact. She wasn't a performer playacting passion for
the entertainment of the masses—and she certainly
couldn't consider the kiss anything more than playacting. Steve's eyes, his hands, his long, rangy body and his
victory in the studio-audience poll meant nothing. As he
himself had said, it was just show biz.

Gwen was a professional. She hadn't relocated herself
and her show fifteen hundred miles to a bigger studio and
a site with better access to major population centers just
to go berserk over the guy who'd fixed the master bedroom door of her apartment.

Yet as her gaze fleetingly met his, she was almost positive she glimpsed a reflection of her own astonishment
in the glittering depths of his eyes. He appeared uncertain, his grin gone, his breathing shallow and unsteady.
He dropped his arms, and when she glanced down she
saw his fingers flexing and unflexing, as if his hands had
gone numb.

Had the peculiar spell that had momentarily transfixed her affected him, too? Had they both been bitten by
the same bug?

She didn't need this. She didn't need to be feeling
whatever the hell it was she was feeling—and if she *was*
going to feel it, she didn't need to be feeling it in the context of a brawny carpenter. Gwen had always been par-
tial to intellectuals, mental heavyweights, refined,
educated gentlemen who used multisyllabic words. She
didn't engage in lighthearted affairs, and she had no interest in the sort of man who went on TV to brag about
how he wasn't the marrying type because marriage meant

nothing more than being nagged by a woman to drink his beer out of a glass.

If her heart was beating just a bit too fast, if her eyes seemed unable to focus on anything but the tall, gorgeous hunk looming before her, it was only because her resistance was weak. She'd been working too hard lately, what with the frenzy of moving to a new home and getting used to a new studio, a new staff, a new city... and a bedroom door that didn't work until the tall, gorgeous hunk had fixed it for her. With his tools. And his hands. Taking his time, making things smooth, joining things together with a good, long—

"Great show!" Marjorie exclaimed, bounding onto the stage and shouting to be heard above the din of the audience members standing, stretching and milling around the studio. "Gentlemen, you were fantastic! Really, a terrific show. Better than those baseball players."

"Of course we're better," Lyle McKay gloated, his Texas drawl in remission now that the camera wasn't on him. "Baseball players are overgrown boys. We're men."

"And wonderful guests. You've all been great sports," Marjorie said, moving among the men and shaking their hands. "If we ever do another show like this, you can bet we'll get you back on the air. Steve..." She'd reached the carpenter and pumped his hand vigorously. "Sorry we couldn't invent an excuse for you to remove your shirt. But you practically made up for it with that lewd speech. Congratulations on your election to the sexy-occupation hall of fame."

"The hall of fame, huh." Steve laughed. "And here I always thought being a television producer was as sexy as it got."

"You're a shameless flirt," Marjorie scolded, then sent Gwen a rapturous look. "Next time we've got any on-the-air necking with a good-looking guest, I want to be on the receiving end."

"You'll be on the receiving end, all right," Gwen muttered.

"Don't blame her," Steve said in Marjorie's defense. "The kiss wasn't her idea. It was those raunchy ladies in the audience. Right?"

Gwen considered explaining to him that Marjorie was a consummate manipulator, nearly always in control of everything that happened on "The Gwen Talbot Show." No doubt she had coached some of the audience members before the show to shout for a kiss once the winner of the election was announced.

Marjorie's talents as an impresario didn't bother Gwen as much as Steve's breezy attitude did. He seemed to have recovered fully from the jolt of their kiss—assuming he'd been as stricken by it as Gwen had been. Maybe it hadn't stirred anything in him at all. Maybe she'd only been reading her own stunned response in his expression.

The lights came up bright in the studio, and technicians began to swarm through the room, coiling wires, stacking chairs. Marjorie ushered the cowboy and the stuntman off the stage; Diane chatted with the detective, who apparently found her nose ring intriguing. The astronaut was signing autographs for a few audience members.

Gwen peered up at Steve. She remembered once again the way he'd looked last week in the hallway of her apartment, without his shirt... the way he looked every night when she got into bed and closed her eyes. She'd be relieved to have him out of her life. Relieved—and curiously bereft.

"You have any plans?" he asked.

His voice startled her out of her ruminations. "I beg your pardon?"

"We could get a cup of coffee or something."

"Oh—uh—" She felt tongue-tied all of a sudden, she who made a career out of talking, putting people at ease, getting them to open up. "I—uh—don't know," she hedged. "I guess I'd have to check my schedule."

"For a cup of coffee?" A low chuckle rumbled up from his chest. "You must be one important lady."

"No, it's just—" *It's just, I haven't decided whether I can spend any more time with you without getting myself into trouble.* "I know I've got a meeting later today. I'm just not sure what time it's scheduled."

"Ah. A meeting. You *are* important."

His sardonic tone puzzled her. Ninety percent of her waking hours were spent in meetings; it didn't mean she was important. It just meant that that was the way television talk shows were put together.

Still, his smile held a challenge. He was baiting her, hinting that he knew she'd been overwhelmed by his kiss. The slight tilt of his head seemed to say, *I don't care how important you are—I've got your number.*

Like hell he did. She would have to have a cup of coffee with him, if only to prove to herself that she was immune to his charms. She would go somewhere with him, drink some coffee with him, and discover that despite his handsomeness and his wicked wit and his flair for kissing, he was nothing but a skilled craftsman, a Mister Fixit, a stud in a tool belt. She and Steve would spend ten minutes talking about her bedroom door, and she would be so bored she'd break whatever hold he had on her fantasies.

"I'm sure I can spare a few minutes," she said coolly. "Let's have that cup of coffee."

STEVE CONTEMPLATED the play of emotions in her eyes. He wondered if she knew how transparent she was, if she had any idea of how eloquent her gaze was, and her smile.

For that matter, he wondered if she had any idea of how soft those smiling lips of hers had felt against his mouth. Like velvet, like rose petals, like the sweet, dewy skin of a peach. Only different. Better. Delicate and tentative, yet holding a whisper of a promise.

The irony of the whole thing simmered inside him. Imagine what the rambunctious members of the audience would think if they knew the guy they'd voted the sexiest of the sexy had turned into a cliché-ridden poet after one brief, chaste kiss from Gwen Talbot, who just happened to be exactly the kind of woman he preferred to steer clear of.

It was nearly eleven-thirty. He himself had little more than a few minutes to spare; the rehab job on the Victorian near the Presidio beckoned. He had two men on it, but they could use an extra pair of hands. The sooner he made his way across town and got to work, the sooner that job would be done and he could move on to renovating a kitchen on Nob Hill, and constructing a cedar deck down in Pacifica.

But he couldn't say goodbye to her. Not yet. Not when his body was still humming with electricity from that one silly kiss.

He followed her out of the studio and into a narrow hall floored in linoleum and walled in cinder-block. Steve had never been in a television studio building before. He would have thought it would be a little more glamorous, with carpeted floors and papered walls. Here the only decorations were bulletin boards and clipboards, posted schedules and No-Smoking signs. The corridors were laid out in a neat grid, some wider and some narrower. The doors lining the hallways were uniformly black steel, with white numbers painted on them and light bulbs affixed to the walls above most of them. "Are these all studios?" he asked.

Gwen nodded. "When the light above the door is on, it means they're taping in there. You're not supposed to open the door unless the building is on fire—and even then, it had better be a three-alarm fire." She glanced at her watch, then gestured toward a door above which the light had just gone on. "They're probably setting up for the noon news broadcast in there."

"Really?" Steve tried to act blasé, but he wished he could peek inside and see the local news reporters. The sports reporter, in particular. He'd spent the whole month of August predicting a miserable season for the 49ers. Steve would like to have a word with him about his negative attitude.

But he kept pace with Gwen, who managed to walk at a sprightly gait despite her high-heeled shoes. He wondered if she was a sports fan. He wondered if she was athletic. Her calf muscles were taut ovals, her ankles appealingly slender. Her insteps were enticing, smooth and sexy in her stylish leather shoes.

He recalled the feel of her cheeks against his hands, soft and inviting. And the feel of her lips beneath his.

When it came to Gwen Talbot, he acknowledged, he wanted a hell of a lot more than a cup of coffee. Even if she was wrong for him. Even if her chic beige suit might have cost as much as the repair he'd done on her door. Even if she hobnobbed with television reporters and NASA astronauts. Steve wanted to find out if her insteps, her calves, her thighs, felt as silky as her cheeks.

That hazardous train of thought was derailed when a heavy black door opened beside him, releasing into the corridor the familiar sound of sawing and hammering. A skinny young man in a ponytail emerged from the room, shouting over his shoulder, "Yeah, I heard you—root beer, not cola!" before colliding with Steve. "Whoops!" he said cheerfully, then turned and loped down the hall in his high-top sneakers.

The noise of carpentry continued to spill out of the room. Curious, Steve poked his head inside.

He felt Gwen brush against him, then past him into the room. For a moment his lungs filled with her scent, part ginger and part vanilla, rousing all sorts of hungers inside him. He pictured the crystal bottles of perfume arranged on her dresser, and then he pictured her platform bed . . . and then he switched off the troubling parade of images and followed her into the room.

It was larger than the studio where they'd taped "The Gwen Talbot Show," with a steeply sloping audience area big enough to hold twice the number of people, and a broad stage cluttered with lumber, electrical cords and workmen. "Hi, guys," Gwen shouted above the buzz of a power saw. "How's it coming along?"

"Ms. Talbot." A stocky man with a beer gut and thinning silver hair approached, smiling deferentially. "Nice to see you. What do you think?" He waved toward the stage.

"It's hard to judge at this point, but I'm sure it's going to be beautiful. Has Inez had a look at it?"

"Yeah. She said she wants us to put flower boxes high up, all around the bridge piece. I dunno how that's going to work out."

"Well, if that's what she wants, try your best to accommodate her, Frank. God willing, this will be the only time she ever gets married. I want the set to be perfect."

"We'll do what we can."

"Is the bridge going to be that steeply sloped? I know she wants it to rise, but that seems awfully steep."

"I'll double-check the drawing. I just sent Jeff out for some lunch, and at two I've gotta get the crew back to the theater up on Geary. Union rules—we can have 'em only for three hours a day."

"I understand. I really appreciate what you're accomplishing here, Frank. I know Inez and Tom are going to appreciate it, too."

The silver-haired man turned and strode back to the stage. Steve absorbed the entire scene—the scaffolding, the two-by-fours, the odd ramp splitting the stage. "What are they building?" he asked.

Gwen surveyed the mess and smiled. "A stage set. When it's all done it's going to have all sorts of San Francisco landmarks—the TransAmerica building on one side, a cable car on the other, and the Golden Gate Bridge running right down the center. You heard me talking about the show we're doing for Inez LaPorta's marriage. This studio is where we're going to tape it."

"Inez LaPorta is the meteorologist on this station's evening news, isn't she?"

Gwen nodded. "She's also an old friend of mine. We went to college together, majored in communications and planned our assault on the television industry. Anyway, she's a public personality here in San Francisco—and so's her fiancé, Tom Blanchard. Maybe you've heard of him—"

"He owns a restaurant down on the Wharf, right?" Steve said.

Gwen nodded again. "Also a movie-industry hangout in L.A. Inez asked me months ago if I'd be in the wedding party, and then when I told her we were moving the show to San Francisco, she and I started joking about what her wedding would do for my ratings, and we decided to have the ceremony right on my show. What do you think?"

Steve shrugged. He couldn't imagine anyone wanting to watch a wedding on TV, but then he wasn't representative of the sort of person who tuned in to "The Gwen Talbot Show" on a regular basis. "I guess it could be fun."

"Inez had the idea of building a set that would reflect all the symbols of the city. We needed more space than my regular studio, so we've arranged to build a special set here."

"You need more than extra space," Steve observed, scowling at the flimsy ramp halving the stage. "If you build that up to look like the Golden Gate Bridge, it's going to be mighty top-heavy."

Gwen eyed him quizzically. "Are you saying it's dangerous?"

"It might be—especially sloped the way it is. Those two-by-fours are awfully heavy. They need proper buttressing if you're going to use them topside. And the other stuff that guy was saying, about flower boxes overhead..." Steve shook his head. "You can't put flower boxes above people. They'll have water and dirt dripping down on them—assuming the weight doesn't pull the whole structure down."

"Oh, I don't think they'll leak on anybody. Not if they're placed properly."

"Yeah, and if the earth doesn't move."

She eyed him again, looking a little less sure of herself. A hesitant smile crossed her lips, and then something lit up in her eyes, so abruptly she might as well have had a cartoon light bulb flash on above her head. The lady had a brainstorm, and it involved Steve.

"Let's go get that coffee, shall we?" she suggested, moving briskly toward the door.

He wasn't sure he wanted to be a part of her brainstorm. For that matter, he wasn't sure he wanted to be a part of her world. As he followed her out of the studio, he once again assessed her elegant outfit, her fancy leather pumps, the porcelain perfection of her makeup, her impeccable manicure.

He was used to working for rich folks. Hell, he loved working for rich folks. Their checks never bounced, and thanks to them he was comfortably well-off himself.

But gorgeous rich women who turned him on were a whole other situation. After having spent two years in a relationship with a representative of that species, he had learned to keep his guard up—especially when one of them was having a brainstorm about him.

They reached an elevator, and Gwen pushed the up button. Steve watched her out of the corner of his eye. She was still smiling, looking perky and smug. The flat light of the hallway layered her hair with platinum highlights.

The elevator door slid open. Four people were already in the car, one holding a pizza and another a bag from a fast-food joint. As Steve and Gwen entered, the smell of hot grease assailed his nostrils. He was as fond of hot greasy food as the next guy, but he would rather have been inhaling Gwen's sweet, spicy fragrance.

Stupid thought. He concentrated on the grease.

They rode up five floors and exited into a hallway that could have been in another building. Here, at last, were the carpeted floors, the tasteful decor, the fancy oak doors. "My office is just down the hall," Gwen told him. "I'll have Diane bring us some coffee."

Coffee in her office hadn't been what he'd had in mind when he'd asked if she was free. He'd been thinking of removing her from her television milieu and bringing her somewhere a bit more down-to-earth—the deli around the corner from the lot where he'd parked his truck, for instance. He'd wanted to talk to her in a place where he wasn't her employee and she wasn't "on," just to see whether the shock that had sizzled through him when his lips had touched hers had been a freak occurrence or an indication that they were plugged into the same powerful current. And he'd wanted to pick up the tab.

Then again, if he saw her in her office, surrounded by the trappings of upwardly mobile success, it would probably short-circuit whatever attraction he might be feeling for her. He'd see her seated behind a huge, intimidating desk with a multibutton phone at her elbow and a view of the city spread below her window, and the effect on his libido would be a complete power outage. Which would be for the best.

Her office was pretty much what he'd expected. A little smaller, and the view was of the building next door. But the furniture was walnut, not steel, and the windows had cloth drapes, not plastic-slat blinds. Besides the desk and a tweedy-looking chair, the room held a love seat of the same tweedy fabric, with a glass-topped coffee table in front of it. A centerpiece of fresh flowers adorned the table.

Steve recollected all the flowers Gwen had in her apartment. Did her boyfriend send her flowers at work, too? Or did she buy the flowers herself?

She indicated with a wave toward the sofa that he should take a seat. He did, but the upholstery was too stiff and short for him to fit comfortably. Gwen moved to her desk, lifted the handset of her predictably elaborate phone and pressed one of the buttons on the console. "Diane, could you bring two cups of coffee? I've got Steve Chambliss in here.... No, we're talking shop. I mean it. Stop!" She burst into laughter and hung up the phone. When she turned back to Steve, she looked as if she was trying hard to squelch her smile.

But the smile remained, even as her lips attempted a semblance of a straight line. The smile was in her eyes, in her cheeks, in the twitching of her nose.

Steve smiled back. "Are we talking shop?" he asked.

She stopped fighting her smile and leaned over to pluck off her shoes. A wavy strand of hair slid forward to brush her throat. Steve's fingers itched to trace its path.

The office, he commanded himself. *Focus on what makes her all wrong for you.* He steered his gaze to the framed lithograph behind her desk, the onyx pen stand, the crystal paperweight, the flowers, her high-style suit, with its fitted jacket and slit skirt, and her long legs, and her stockinged feet and her gently arching insteps....

"Diane asked me to find out if you wrote that speech yourself."

"What speech?"

She stared at his tool belt, and a fresh spate of melodic laughter spilled into the air. "All that nonsense about your *tools.*"

He leaned back on the sofa, trying to fit his large body into its ladylike proportions. "Yeah, I wrote it. Why?"

"It was obscene."

"There wasn't a single dirty word in it."

"I have never heard anyone say the word *tool* as obscenely as you did."

He shrugged again. "It's part of being a carpenter," he conceded, although he was secretly pleased. After calling his friends last night, he'd decided that if he was going to do the show, he was going to have some fun with it. "I didn't really write much of anything. I just made a few mental notes, filled the belt with my *tools,* and ad-libbed."

"Really?"

"Really."

"You're a natural for TV."

Other people might be flattered by such a remark. Steve only laughed. "If I was a natural, I would have done a better job of kissing you," he said.

Her smile vanished, and her cheeks turned a delightful pink, the same shade as the pale carnations in the vase on the glass-topped table. The light rap on the door caused her to start.

Steve politely stood as Gwen's morbidly attired assistant entered with a tray holding two steaming mugs, a plastic bowl of sugar packets and a bowl of powdered creamer. She beamed Steve a blinding smile as she carried the tray to Gwen's desk. "Everyone's buzzing about you," she said. "Everyone wants to know how they can get a big, long screw like yours. Enjoy your coffee." She gave Steve a saucy smile, then left the office, closing the door behind her.

Gwen lifted a mug and passed it to Steve. Her cheeks were still pink. The blush diminished her professional aura—which made it harder for him to think of her as the hotshot she was. "See?" she said. "You *are* a natural."

"I was just having a little fun with that speech."

"Well, that's what my show is all about—having a little fun."

"Good." As he took the mug from her, his fingers brushed hers. She started again.

So did he, although he did a better job than she did of hiding the reaction. There really seemed to be sparks between them, static electricity, tiny eruptions of lightning. If he had any brains, he'd take a giant step backward.

Instead he remained by her desk, by her. "You said we were going to talk shop," he murmured.

She turned her back to him and spent an inordinate amount of time stirring sugar into her coffee. "I've been thinking about your criticisms of the set for Inez LaPorta's wedding. I was wondering if I could hire you—"

"No."

His immediate rejection surprised her. It surprised him, too. But once he'd caught his breath, he realized he didn't want to work for Gwen ever again. He either wanted to kiss her again, a real kiss, a kiss that led straight to that wide platform bed of hers—or, if need be, to the stiff, cramped cushions of the love seat on the other side of the office—or else he wanted to clear out and regain his sanity.

She peered up at him, her complexion still slightly flushed, her eyes glittering with facets of blue light. "I didn't mean you'd build the set. I only thought you might review the design and make sure they aren't making big mistakes with the flower boxes and the bridge...."

"No," he said, more calmly this time. She was too close, too tempting. He decided to worry about regaining his sanity later.

He set his mug back on the tray, then eased hers from her hands and put it down beside his. Then he circled his arms around her and lowered his mouth to hers.

She had less than an instant to whisper his name, whether in protest or pleasure he didn't know. And then his lips covered hers, and his arms tightened around her, and he pulled her slender body closer.

Her hands had gotten trapped between them. She flattened them against his chest, but she didn't push him away. Nor did she resist when he coaxed her lips with his, when he skimmed her lower lip with his tongue, when he slid one hand up into her hair and sighed at how unbelievably soft all those thick blond waves felt. Her fingers inched upward, nearing his shoulders, exploring the ridges of his collarbones through his shirt. When he pressed his tongue against her teeth she opened fully to him.

She tasted better than ginger, better than vanilla, better than the sweetest delicacy a gourmet chef could conjure. Her breath mingled with his, her tongue tangled with his, and one item of personal equipment he wouldn't have dared to mention on the air grew as hard and stiff as a carpenter's rule.

He wanted her. Standing up, if need be. Across her desk. On the floor. In full view of the people in the building across the alley. He didn't care. All he knew was that he wanted Gwen Talbot.

"Steve..."

His tongue surged. His hips surged. She felt so dainty in his arms, so slender, so utterly feminine. If his mind hadn't gone south, he would have reminded himself of her expensive clothes and her hoity-toity job. But he couldn't think when her fingertips were digging into the muscles along his shoulders, and her breasts were pressed so tightly to him that he could feel the tight points of her nipples, and her hips mimicked the rocking motions of his. He couldn't think.

Unfortunately, she could. "Steve," she whispered, then tore her mouth from his and hid her face against his shoulder.

He was panting, his thighs aching, his blood searing his veins. "Wow," he groaned, loosening his hold on her only enough so he wouldn't smother her.

"I know." She let out a shaky breath.

He stroked his hands through her hair, partly to soothe her and partly because her tousled golden tresses felt so good. "That was pretty special."

"I know." She edged back just far enough so she could tilt her face back and view him. "Steve, I—I'm not—I wasn't looking for something to happen here."

He could have taken her words as a brush-off, but he chose not to. "Sometimes, even when you're not looking for something, it finds you, anyway."

"I guess."

"So." He combed his fingers through her hair one last time, then grinned. "Where do we go from here?"

"Steve..." She sighed and averted her eyes, leaving him to understand they were going nowhere. He could have made things easier by saying that before she did, but he decided not to. If she wanted to trip the circuit-breaker, he saw no reason to help her.

She took a step back, fussed with her hair, glanced wistfully at her coffee. Then she lifted her eyes back to him. "I'm new in town. I've only just gotten here. I'm still trying to get my footing, you know? This is all a little too fast."

"Sure." His cheeks cramped from his artificial smile. He should have been grateful to her for recognizing what a lousy match they were, but he didn't feel grateful. He felt hot and horny and anxious to brace himself for the blow his ego was about to take.

"It has nothing to do with you," she insisted.

"I'm just the wrong guy in the wrong place at the wrong time."

"You were in the right place at the right time," she argued.

Then he was the wrong guy. Okay. She was the wrong woman. There was a certain symmetry to the situation.

If only his hips weren't still throbbing. If only his heart didn't beat in double-time whenever he gazed down into her eyes. If only he hadn't felt the firmness of her breasts as she leaned into him, and the eager play of her tongue against his. If only he didn't know she craved him as much as he craved her.

"I don't suppose you'd be interested in helping out with that wedding set, would you?" she asked.

Her words were more effective than a cold shower. So this was the way she did business: kiss a guy, soften him up and harden him up, and then, when he's suffering from terminal lust, try to get him to work for you. "No," he said.

"I shouldn't have kissed you, Steve," she said, the words spilling out in a frantic rush. "You're a terrific carpenter, and really, I think if you just spent a couple of hours going over the design, and—"

"No."

"—and talking to Frank Trivelli, pointing out where he's going wrong on the bridge, and the flower boxes, and I'd pay you, of course..."

The last thing he wanted was Gwen Talbot paying him. "Sorry," he said curtly. "No."

"I wish you didn't look so offended, Steve. You're a fine carpenter. George Maynard was right: you're the best in the city. You should be flattered." There was a pleading quality to her voice, an apology underlying it.

"Okay. I'm flattered. Thanks." He was also acting like an ass. He raked his hair off his forehead and tried for a smile. "Look, Gwen...I can't work for you, okay? Let's just say goodbye, and I'll be on my way." He headed for the door, keeping his spine straight and his breath regular.

"I've hurt your feelings," she murmured contritely.

He yanked the door open, then spun around and put a little more effort into the smile. "No hurt feelings, Gwen," he assured her. "It's just that I don't take money from women I've kissed."

Before she could respond, he stepped outside and closed the door behind him. Like the door to her bedroom, it latched with a cold, decisive click.

Chapter Five

The small group of women clustered on the sidewalk a few paces from the building's main entrance looked vaguely familiar to Steve. As he stepped outside they flocked toward him, pencils and paper clutched in their hands. He remembered them then; they'd been the studio audience members who had asked the astronaut for his autograph.

If they intended to ask Steve for his autograph, he might just lose it. At another time he would find his brush with fame worthy of a good chuckle, but right now, his nerves were stretched nearly to snapping. All he wanted to do was shut himself up in his van and analyze exactly how much he hated Gwen Talbot—and *why* he hated her.

But there he was, surrounded by a band of women wielding pencils, all of them twittering about how cute he'd been on "The Gwen Talbot Show," how they'd voted for him, how it had been a foregone conclusion that he would win the title of sexiest occupation for men, how they'd all take lovers over fighters any day.

Steve sucked in a deep breath and tamped all his rage and frustration into a corner of his mind. "Thank you, ladies," he said as politely as he could. "I'm afraid I'm in kind of a hurry. I've got to get to a job site, so..." He waited for someone to hand him a pencil and paper.

None did. Instead, one of the younger ones said, "All I want is your phone number."

His smile dissolved into a frown of bafflement. "My phone number?"

"Forget about her." An older woman nudged the younger one out of the way. "Here's my daughter's number. She's twenty-five and single, a preschool teacher in San Mateo and just as sweet as can be." Flipping through the transparent sleeves in her wallet, the mother produced a photograph of a pleasant-looking young woman. "Her name is Sara Beth. Isn't she lovely?"

"She's—uh—very pretty," Steve said, embarrassed. "But I'd rather not—"

"Here, just take her number," the mother said, stuffing a slip of paper into the chest pocket of Steve's T-shirt. "You'll call her, you'll ask her out—I'm telling you, you're made for each other."

"He's made for *my* daughter," another woman argued, elbowing her way to the front of the group. "You want to ask that lady's daughter out, go ahead. Then you ask out my Jennifer. You'll see who's made for who."

"The hell with their daughters," one of the younger women overruled them. "I'm a bird in the hand. I'm right here, right now."

"This is all very flattering," Steve mumbled, trying to extricate himself from the persistent women. "But I'm really not looking to hook up with anyone—"

"You don't have to hook up," the second mother told him, shoving another slip of paper into his shirt pocket. "Just give my Jennifer a call. You'll see what I mean."

Steve forced himself to smile again—though it was more of a grimace, his jaws rigid and his teeth bared.

With a nod and a wave, he slipped out of the proud mothers' clutches and sprinted down the street to the lot where he'd parked his van. He didn't dare look over his shoulder. He didn't want to know if the women were chasing him.

Once inside the van, he locked the door and let out his breath. A weak laugh escaped him. They hadn't been so bad. He might have actually enjoyed his run-in with them if he hadn't been so keyed up over his encounter with Gwen.

The air inside the cab of the van was hot. Once he was sure the women hadn't followed him, he rolled down the window. The dashboard clock read nearly noon; he had to get over to the Victorian rehab. But as his amusement over the women on the sidewalk faded, his irritation over Gwen sharpened.

Kisses weren't supposed to be like that. He'd done more than his share of kissing during the past eighteen-odd years, and he'd found that in general, kisses were like matches—they were essential for getting a fire started, but you didn't expect them to give off much heat or light.

With Gwen, though, a kiss was an explosion.

And then, as she and he had emerged from the conflagration, the lady—and "lady" wasn't the first word that came to mind—had tried to *hire* him.

Granted, in the matter of that goofy stage set, she needed his expertise more than she could begin to guess. He wouldn't want to tangle with unionized stagehands, but the set had to have some heavy-duty common sense imposed on it. That ridiculous ramp was just begging for someone to trip and break an ankle—probably the bride, in her white gown and dainty shoes. And elevating the flower boxes so they hung directly above the heads of the wedding party wasn't exactly smart. And the lumber they were using was sure to make the whole thing top-heavy. Steven had noticed inadequate buttressing. The design was a calamity waiting to happen.

He could spend an hour poring over the design and whip it into shape. But he wouldn't. Not for Gwen. Not for a woman who could go from kissing him to offering him money in the blink of an eye.

Particularly not for a woman whose kisses were as dangerous as arson. He ought to count his blessings that he'd escaped with only minor burns.

Shoving his key into the ignition, he tried to list everything he loathed about Gwen. Once he took inventory, perhaps he would find it easier to recover from the blazing arousal he'd felt in her office.

Her office. There was a dandy place to start. As he revved the engine and navigated through the lot to the booth by the gate, he reflected on Gwen's swanky office, a room that bespoke prestige and power. He recalled the plush carpet, the solid walnut desk and that ghastly love seat. Sit too long on it and a guy might need a chiropractor to straighten him out. Make love on it and a guy might wind up crippled for life.

He paid the attendant, then steered out onto the street, heading west. *Her outfit.* Now, there was a big negative. The jacket of Gwen's suit had to have been silk—it had felt almost as smooth and sleek as her hair. And the skirt was way too long. He remembered his first meeting with her, when she'd been wearing that wonderfully abbreviated denim skirt and no stockings. And his second visit to her apartment, when she'd been wrapped in that sleeveless gauzy dress, the fabric so lightweight he could see the outline of her body when the light shone behind her. And her hair had been pinned up then, displaying her swanlike neck and her throat and her delicate chin, and . . .

His jeans felt as snug as when he'd been kissing her. The idea of compiling this list was to cool him off, not keep him overheated. He groped through his thoughts in a desperate search for more of Gwen Talbot's flaws.

Her money. Not that he objected to rich women on principle, but he'd be damned if he was going to let her *pay* for him. Especially when he knew she desired him. What was he supposed to do, take her money, fix her set and service her on the side?

He turned onto Locust Street. The Victorian rehab loomed ahead. Jimmy's truck was parked in the driveway, and Steve pulled up behind him and shut off the engine.

Some good, hard, sweaty labor was exactly what Steve needed. Not memories of how well Gwen had fit in his arms and how poorly she would fit in his life, but a good, solid afternoon of finishing the attic into two cozy bedrooms. And then, when he was done, he would go home, pop open a beer and forget he'd ever met Gwen Talbot.

IT WAS AFTER SIX when he finally let himself into his apartment, his hair sprinkled with sawdust and his arms cradling a bucket of barbecued chicken from the fast-food joint around the corner. Visions of a long, refreshing shower filled his mind.

On his way to the kitchen with the chicken, he pressed the button on the CD player, and the apartment filled with Bob Seger's gravelly wail. Steve set the steaming bucket on the table, thumbed through the mail he'd pulled from his box downstairs and tossed it aside. Returning to the living room, he noticed the light on his answering machine flashing.

And flashing. He stopped counting after seven flashes.

His parents, probably. Even though she knew he would be at work, his mother would likely have been trying him nonstop ever since the tape of "The Gwen Talbot Show" had been broadcast at three o'clock that afternoon. No doubt his mother had a complete critique of his performance. He should have worn a suit and tie. He shouldn't have said all those dirty things about tools. Mrs. Donahue down the street had been so shocked, she'd called all the neighbors and told them that Steve Chambliss had turned out to be a no-good bum just like she'd always said he would.

Flopping onto the couch, he pressed the message button and tugged off his boots while the tape rewound. He heard a beep, and then the voice of Karen, his office manager: "Steve, check in with me when you can. The phone hasn't stopped ringing since the show ended. Twenty people all want you to come to their houses and do estimates. And guess what, Steve? They're all women."

Closing his eyes, he pictured the gaggle of women waiting for him outside the studio after the taping. Surely all the women who'd phoned the office weren't calling just to describe their single daughters to him. Hadn't Karen just said they wanted him to do estimates? They must have legitimate business. It was just a coincidence that they'd all called in one afternoon.

The second message began. Karen's voice again, laced with laughter: "Hi, Steve, it's me. It's five-thirty and I'm closing up shop. We've got a total of twenty-seven calls, all from women. Maybe appearing on that show was good advertising. Can't wait to get home and watch you on my VCR. See you tomorrow."

A beep, and then a sultry alto: "Hi, Steve. This is Bettina Hargrave, your neighbor in apartment 3A. We've met downstairs in the parking area behind the building a few times—I drive the black Supra. Anyway, I saw you on 'Gwen Talbot' this afternoon, and I just wanted to say you're *very* telegenic."

Beep. "Steve, it's Deke. Batten down the hatches, old boy. You're gonna get swamped."

Beep. "Hi. It's Marilyn." His sister. "Listen, I don't care what Mom says, I thought you were great. We set up a TV in the shop and everybody watched, even Lorraine, the manicurist, who swears she hates TV, but let me tell you, she was right up there in the front row. Anyway, we all voted for you. But listen, Steve—*dumb move* announcing to the world that you're not the marrying type. That's like telling a kid he can't have a lollipop. You know he's gonna spend the next year of his life trying to wheedle a lollipop out of you. And you, brother of mine, are going to have women pounding down your door. Be good, or be careful, or whatever. Talk to you later."

Beep. Two voices, apparently on separate extensions of the same line, both quite young and giggly: "Um, this message is for Steve Chambliss—" "No, let me say it!" "No, *me*, it's my phone—anyway, we love you, Steve!" "We love you, Steve!"

Beep. "Steve? Ki. Remember—I've got first dibs on ghosting your autobiography, man."

Beep. Heavy breathing, and then: "My number is 555-2387, and I'm yours, lover."

Beep. "Steve? It's Tripp, and yes, I've got you preserved on tape for posterity—or blackmailing purposes, whichever comes first. Way to go, pal."

Beep. "Steve? It's your mother. You ought to be ashamed of yourself, going on TV looking like a good-for-nothing. You're such a handsome man, and you show up in jeans? On TV? I should be used to you breaking my heart by now, but I'll tell you, that Louise Donahue from down the street called me right after the show ended, and she said, 'What's with that son of yours? Goes to college, gets a job, and then he throws it all away and moves all the way to California and dresses like a bum. On TV!' And all those things you said, about—I can't even say it—*screws*, Steve! I'll never be able to show my face at the Stop-and-Shop again!''

Beep. ''Steve? It's Marjorie Bunting, the producer of 'The Gwen Talbot Show.' Please call me at the studio first thing tomorrow. Or if it's not too late, call me at home. It's important.'' She left her number and hung up. Hers was the last message. The machine rewound.

What could be more important than the news that his mother was woefully predictable, and that if he dialed 555-2387, a panting woman would be his? Sighing, Steve closed his eyes and listened as Bob Seger warbled about Mary Lou taking his diamond ring and his credit cards and running off. *What had he gotten himself into?*

He wondered about Marjorie Bunting's call. She'd seemed okay when he'd met her that morning at the studio, much more composed and sensible than the morning she'd been at Gwen's apartment when Steve had commenced work on the bedroom door. His only memory of her that day had been fleeting glimpses of her and the one with the pierced nose—Diane, was it?—spying on him from behind the kitchen door, and giggling as much as the two silly girls on his answering machine.

But that morning, Marjorie and Diane had been poised and organized. Diane had greeted the guests in the green room, brought them coffee and reviewed the show with them, explaining in what order they'd be seated and how much time they'd have to describe their work. Then Marjorie had come in and energized them with her confidence about what a great show it was going to be. Throughout the actual taping, Steve had caught glimpses of her off to the side, orchestrating things, smiling and signaling Gwen.

Her hunch had been correct. It had been a great show, great enough to have garnered Chambliss Carpentry more than two dozen calls for estimates. So why had she sounded so urgent on his machine? Had the sponsors been outraged by his bawdy humor? Had some antisex cult put out a contract on him?

One way to find out. He fast-forwarded the tape to Marjorie's message, played it and jotted down her phone number in the margin of the previous day's sports section, which was still lying on the coffee table. He went into the kitchen and opened a bottle of beer, then returned to the living room, sprawled out on the couch and dialed Marjorie's number. She answered on the third ring.

"Hi. This is Steve Chambliss," he said, then checked his watch. Six-thirty. "You called me, and I—"

"Yes, thanks for calling back," she said, then paused. When she next spoke, her voice was cloyingly sweet. "Steve. I'm so glad you called."

God help him if she started breathing heavily, too. "I'm probably interrupting your dinner, so—"

"Oh, no, that's all right. We haven't sat down yet." Another pause, and then that icky-sweet voice again. "Steve. I'm so glad you appeared on the show today."

"Well . . . yeah, it was fun." *Cut to the chase, lady.*

"I know Gwen had a ball with it."

Swell. Gwen had a ball. She could have had a ball with him in her office, too, if she'd played her hand a little better. "That's great," he said blandly.

When Marjorie next spoke, her tone was devoid of all the molasses gooeyness. "Look, Steve, we have a bit of a problem."

The censors. The sponsors. Everyone in America who didn't like men joking about their tools. "Yeah?"

"It has to do with a special set we're building for our wedding show on October 1. Gwen told me she showed you that set."

Steve took a long sip of beer straight from the bottle and used the time to sort his thoughts. Yes, Gwen had showed him that set. Yes, he'd told her she had a bit of a problem. But then he'd kissed her and everything had changed.

"She also told me," Marjorie continued when Steve said nothing, "that you pointed out some serious flaws in the design."

"Uh-huh." He didn't like the direction this was heading in, but he couldn't very well hang up on the woman.

"Steve, she really, really respects your qualifications when it comes to carpentry. According to her, you did a magnificent job on her bedroom door—"

"It was a door," he cut her off. "It was no big deal. I'm not a stagehand. I'm not an expert when it comes to building television sets. I'm sure the guys you have working on the set know what they're doing." Right. And the earth never moved in San Francisco.

"Steve." Marjorie was sounding syrupy again. "We borrowed those carpenters from the American Repertory Theater. They're used to an entirely different kind of construction—flats and scrims and scenery that doesn't have to project well on television. They're used to creating impressionistic stage sets. Inez LaPorta drew them up a design, and they're executing it without the proper knowledge. Gwen and I are both convinced that you could revamp the set to make it safer."

"Any carpenter can revamp the set."

"But you're the best in San Francisco. George Maynard said so. And now, so does Gwen."

He drank his beer.

"Steve. What if someone gets hurt on that set, on the ramp or something? Do you want that hanging over your head?"

No, he didn't want it hanging over his head, any more than he would want heavy flower boxes hanging over his head. But it wasn't his responsibility.

"Let's speak frankly, shall we?" Marjorie said, her voice changing yet again. There was an undertone of steel, something firm and tenacious. When she spoke that way, Steve could believe she was a successful producer. "Gwen seems to think she offended you today, although I can't for the life of me imagine how someone with your delicious sense of humor could take offense at anything she could do."

What she'd done hadn't been offensive, exactly. She'd only been herself: a lovely woman who could kiss like a miracle but wanted to employ Steve, who couldn't bear the thought of being employed by a woman who kissed like a miracle.

"What I'm looking for is maybe just an hour or two of your time to review the blueprint and tell the crew where they're going wrong. We'd pay you your going rate. Just an hour or two, Steve, to prevent someone from getting hurt during the taping of the wedding."

Once again he wanted to shout that none of this was his responsibility, and in any case he couldn't abide the thought of having to see Gwen again, wanting her but knowing she'd turn out to be just another high-powered lady who loved Steve just the way he was, except for everything she wanted to change about him. He gazed down at his attire with its light blanket of sawdust—yeah, he looked like a bum—and at the bottle of beer in his hand, no glass, and he remembered all the times Janet had tried to change him. "Couldn't you clean yourself up a little before you pick me up at the bank?" she would say. "Couldn't you change into something a little more respectable? Maybe a nice sport coat and khakis? And Steve, I'd like to introduce you to my colleagues as an engineer. It's not really a falsehood—you *do* engineer things. It's just that as a bank vice president, I have a certain reputation to uphold. I do love you, Steve—you know I do. Let's not fight about these superficial issues."

They hadn't been superficial to him. They'd been the very definition of who he was, what his life was all about.

He sighed. Gwen hadn't made any disparaging remarks about his wardrobe. She hadn't introduced him as an engineer—although, of course, his being a carpenter was the point of her show. But still . . . he couldn't quite explain it, even to himself, but there was a class thing between him and Gwen. And when she talked about paying him, that class thing reared up and punched him in the face.

"Steve?" Marjorie broke into his ruminations.

He pictured that ridiculous ramp. The precarious flower boxes. A woman's wedding resulting in someone's being injured. "What are we talking about? An hour's consultation?"

"Give or take. We'll pay you for your time. If it's two hours, we'll pay you for two hours. Three. Whatever you need to get the design corrected."

"Okay." Gwen had nothing to do with it. It was simply professional pride. Self-respect. The obligation not to stand by while people made disastrous mistakes and put other people at risk. "When do you need this done?"

"The sooner the better. If you're free tomorrow—"

"Tomorrow's Saturday," he said, not that that made any difference. He'd been planning to put in a few hours at the Victorian rehab tomorrow, anyway. Carpenters worked when they worked. Five-day work weeks were irrelevant—particularly when he had twenty-seven potential jobs waiting for him at the office.

"Why don't we meet for breakfast in my office?" Marjorie suggested. "I'll serve coffee and pastries, and you can review the designs and fix what's wrong. How does nine-thirty sound?"

It sounded just about right. He could stop by his office at nine and see what Karen had for him, then put in a couple of hours at the studio with Marjorie, and then cruise over to the Presidio for an afternoon hanging drywall in the attic of the Victorian. The only thing bothering him about the plan was the possibility that Gwen might be in Marjorie's office when he got there.

So what if she was? They'd kissed and she'd stopped him. He was a big boy; he could be cool about it.

"Sure," he said. "Nine-thirty."

"Thank you!" Marjorie sounded as exuberant as she had that morning during the taping, when she'd shouted, "Kiss the winner!" from the sidelines. "You're really saving our lives here, Steve."

He didn't doubt it. "Having me save your life doesn't come cheap."

"But you're worth every penny. I can't tell you how much Gwen is going to appreciate this."

Steve said goodbye and hung up the phone. Then he sank into the lumpy cushions and swore under his breath. He could think of any number of things he wanted from Gwen—her kisses, her incredible golden hair spilling through his fingers, her slimly curved body under him, taking him, absorbing him . . . or simply her ability to relate to him without bringing payment into the picture.

But her *appreciation?* That was one thing he could sure as hell do without.

Chapter Six

The cool, damp fog shrouding the city Saturday morning reflected Gwen's mood perfectly. She knew San Francisco was famous for its fog, but she herself wasn't famous for being glum and overcast. When she'd tried out for her high school's cheerleading squad years ago, the coach had informed her, "Gwen, even if you couldn't do the splits and jumps, you'd make the squad just because of your sunny disposition."

What sunny disposition? she thought morosely as she wandered from room to room in her apartment, drawing open the curtains and gazing through the windows at a mass of gray vapor so dense she couldn't even see the roofs of the houses across the street, let alone the bay. Her first genuine San Francisco fog ought to have excited her. But that morning she viewed it as nothing more than an omen that her day was doomed.

She had promised Marjorie she'd attend the meeting with Steve at nine-thirty. Inez was going to be there, too, since she was the bride-to-be. And it was Gwen's show. She *had* to go.

She didn't have to like it, though. She didn't have to be thrilled by the prospect of seeing Steve once more, seeing his beguilingly crooked smile and his rugged torso and his lean, leggy height.

He was the wrong man for her. In spite of his extraordinary skill at kissing, and the erotic power of his embrace, and the way his body had aligned with hers, and the infuriating fact that even though he was wrong for her she couldn't get him out of her mind... He really wasn't her kind of guy.

She dressed in an outfit that matched her state of mind: an old pair of stone-washed jeans and a sweatshirt bearing the logo of the network affiliate in Dallas where she used to tape her show, back when her life was fogless and she'd never heard of Steve Chambliss. She ran a brush through her hair a few times, then donned her raincoat and left her apartment.

She briefly considered taking the bus rather than her car—she believed that one of the best ways for a newcomer to acquaint herself with an unfamiliar city was to use the public transit system—but that morning she was too grumpy to inflict herself on the innocent riders who would be sharing the bus with her. Instead, she descended the stairs to the garage in the basement of her building, climbed into the Acura she'd rewarded herself with last year, after she'd won her time period for three sweeps in a row, and drove through the slowly stirring streets of the city, careering up and down the hills without her usual gee-whiz joy over their absurd slopes.

She arrived at the studio with a few minutes to spare and parked in the underground garage reserved for employees. She had the elevator to herself; on a Saturday morning, when the station broadcast cartoons from a network feed, the building tended to be sparsely populated.

Marjorie's office was located down the hall from Gwen's. Although twice as large, it didn't seem terribly huge because most of the extra space was consumed by a conference table. It was around that table that the majority of the meetings Gwen attended took place. And while she wasn't a big fan of meetings, she'd never dreaded a meeting as much as she dreaded this one.

Inez was already in the room, along with a gurgling urn of coffee and a heaping platter of doughnuts. The sight of all that sugar and jelly and custard made Gwen's stomach twist into a knot.

As she entered the office, Inez darted over, her large brown eyes glistening with a combination of panic and relief. "You're saving my life, Gwen!" she babbled, her on-the-air meteorologist composure nowhere in evidence. Gwen had watched Inez's televised weather forecasts religiously since she'd moved to San Francisco. On the air, Inez was the epitome of decorum, her dark hair arranged neatly around her face and her wardrobe appropriately demure. Today, however, she wore an exercise suit of shocking pink and her hair was irredeemably frizzy thanks to the clammy morning air.

"I haven't saved your life," Gwen argued, trying not to sound too grouchy. "I can't possibly save your life without some coffee in my bloodstream."

Inez eyed Gwen speculatively. "What's wrong?"

"Nothing." Gwen busied herself filling a cup from the urn. "You want some?"

"You look like you haven't slept in days."

"One day," Gwen let slip, then groaned. "Insomnia last night. I thought I felt an earthquake." Not exactly. Rather, it was that whenever she'd thought about Steve— and she was apparently unable *not* to think about him, so whenever she thought about him was pretty much all the time—she'd remembered his joke about the earth moving...and she'd imagined him making the earth move...and she hadn't slept a wink.

Inez accepted her explanation at its most literal. She settled onto one of the chairs, the fabric of her slacks whispering as she crossed her legs. "Relax. *I'm* the one who's supposed to be a bundle of nerves. It's *my* wedding."

"It's *my* ratings," Gwen quipped, handing Inez a cup of coffee.

"Talbot, the last thing you need to worry about is your ratings. After yesterday's show, I wouldn't be surprised if you'll be hearing from the network brass with a seven-figure offer to host your own prime-time show."

Without adequate caffeine in her system, Gwen couldn't begin to comprehend Inez's statement. "What are you talking about?"

"You know what I'm talking about. Yesterday's show."

"The five sexiest occupations for men?"

"That show was incredible, Gwen. We almost had to cancel the five o'clock news and run it a second time."

Gwen's forehead ached from her frown. She sank into a chair, clutching her cup and staring at her friend. "What are you talking about?" she repeated.

"Yesterday's 'Gwen Talbot Show.'" Inez enunciated each syllable, as if she were addressing a nincompoop. "With the five foxes. Or should I say, four foxes and a guy who can make a lecture on his professional equipment sound pornographic."

Gwen guzzled some coffee, scorching her tongue. She cursed, then groaned, closed her eyes and prayed for Inez's remarks to make sense. "What happened? Did the station get complaints from the bluenoses?"

"Complaints?" Inez tossed back her head and laughed. "Honey, the switchboard lit up—"

"Great. I'm toast." Just what Gwen needed: to have her show canceled thanks to antipornography crusaders, right after she'd finished setting up her apartment—as well as paying a small fortune to have her bedroom door fixed.

"You're the toast of the town," Inez corrected her. "They *loved* your show."

Gwen flicked a suspicious glance across the table. "Who loved it?"

"Everybody. They especially loved the carpenter. He was sensational."

"You didn't see the show, did you?" Gwen knew that when the show was broadcast locally, from three to four in the afternoon, Inez was usually in the weather room preparing her forecast for the six o'clock news.

"They always leave a monitor on in the newsroom," Inez reminded her. "I wandered in, and I couldn't leave. Not after I saw that stud with the long screws." She preened unconsciously, smoothing down the kinky halo of her hair.

"The other guys were cute, too," Gwen argued, wishing she could convince herself. "Didn't you think that cowboy was a knockout?"

"He was all right for a cowboy."

"And the astronaut. You know me, I've always considered brain-power the ultimate turn-on in a man. On that scale, the astronaut had the others beat, hands down."

"The astronaut was married."

"You're going to be married, too, in a couple of weeks."

"That doesn't mean I can't appreciate a display of male pulchritude every now and then. And that carpenter was definitely worth appreciating. I wasn't surprised he won your studio poll. Everyone in the newsroom was rooting for him."

"Even Dave Kaplan?" Gwen asked, naming the male half of the news show's anchor team.

Inez laughed. "He said Steve wasn't his type. In fact, he said you ought to do a show about the five sexiest occupations for women. He said you could have a swimsuit model, a stripper, a go-go dancer, a *Playboy* bunny and a prostitute."

"What a sense of humor," Gwen muttered.

"That's why every woman in America is drooling over Steve Chambliss instead of Dave Kaplan," Inez pointed out. "It was his sense of humor that really won them over."

"You're getting married in two weeks," Gwen reiterated, glaring at Inez. "You'd better behave."

"You know I love Tom—who also, I might add, has a great sense of humor. But just tell me this—what was it like kissing the carpenter?"

Gwen felt her cheeks grow warm. Then she realized Inez was alluding to the quick, chaste kiss she and Steve had exchanged on the air, not the torrid kiss they'd exchanged in the privacy of her office.

Actually, that first kiss, while quick, hadn't been chaste. The instant Steve's lips had touched hers, chaste became an inoperative concept. "No comment," she said testily. "Where is Marjorie, anyway?"

"Downstairs, waiting to let the carpenter in. The receptionist doesn't come in till noon on Saturday, and Marjorie didn't want to leave the poor man to the mercies of the security guards." Inez shook her head. "This guy must really be amazing. Not only does he look like a million bucks, not only does he have that all-important sense of humor, not only does he kiss like a dream—''

"Who says he kisses like a dream?" Gwen protested a bit too vehemently.

Inez chuckled. "Honey, he did mouth time with you on national TV. We all saw your eyes go glassy—and his, too. We all saw the steam pour out of your ears. We all saw the set lose focus there for a minute. The chemistry between the two of you was unbelievable."

Gwen pursed her lips, refusing to dignify Inez's exaggerations with a reply.

"And he also has the ability to diagnose everything that's wrong with my wedding set design. Marjorie told me you told her he told you it's a catastrophe just waiting to happen. Thank God he noticed before it was too late."

Inez's babbling was reaching the bounds of incoherence. Gwen took another sip of coffee, hoping it would make the world more intelligible. "Don't thank God," she said. "Stephen Chambliss happens to be the best carpenter in San Francisco. He did some work for George Maynard, and he did a repair on my co-op. He knows what he's doing."

"I'll bet he does," Inez purred.

Gwen resisted the urge to fling her coffee at Inez. It had cooled down some so it wouldn't do anywhere near the damage Gwen would have liked to inflict. Besides, she needed it in her bloodstream far more than she needed it dripping off Inez's nose. "In any case, you don't have to go overboard with the thank-you's. Marjorie's paying him good money to fix your set."

"Whatever it takes. I defer to his expertise."

"Don't defer too fast. Let's hear what he has to say, and take it under advisement."

"Oh, come on. If he said he wanted to fly me to the moon, I'd defer to him."

"If you want to fly to the moon, you ought to throw your lot in with the astronaut."

"There's more than one way to fly, Gwen." Inez thought for a minute. "You know what we ought to do? We should have a little 'last night out' before the wedding—you, me and a few other friends—but instead of going to one of those male strip joints, we could invite Steve to my apartment."

"And ask him to strip?"

"Why not? If he'll take Marjorie's money, maybe he'll take ours."

Gwen recalled the morning Marjorie and Diane had gotten Steve to strip off his shirt—for free. Maybe he was an exhibitionist. Maybe he'd get a kick out of shimmying around Inez's living room in a jockstrap.

And maybe Gwen was certifiably insane to consider such an idea.

Before she could tell Inez to put a lid on it, the door opened and Marjorie ushered Steve into the office. Inez looked up, her eyes growing wider and rounder the longer they remained on him. When she glanced back at Gwen, she was grinning like a smitten schoolgirl.

Gwen wondered where she'd seen a smile like that before. Then she remembered seeing two such smiles, a matching set, one Marjorie's and one Diane's, that fateful morning in Gwen's apartment when they'd cranked up the thermostat.

"Good morning, ladies," Marjorie singsonged, annoyingly chipper for such a dreary day. Behind her, Steve looked awake and alert, if less cheerful than Marjorie.

His hair glittered with tiny raindrops, and he wore a flannel shirt and carried a battered denim jacket over his shoulder.

Damn the man for looking so virile.

Gwen gave him a fleeting, feeble smile and then became deeply engrossed in her coffee while Marjorie introduced him to Inez. "Dig into those doughnuts, Steve."

"Thanks," he said, sounding mildly embarrassed. He selected a plain doughnut from the platter and took a hearty bite.

"Why don't you tell Gwen and Inez about your brush with fame?" she suggested as she prepared a cup of coffee for him.

"It isn't fame," he admitted sheepishly. "Someone hung a bed sheet from the window of the building across the street from mine. It says Show Us Your Tools, Steve, in big red letters. I know a few people on the block, so I'm figuring it's one of them. Who else would know my address?"

"You're listed in the telephone book, aren't you?" Gwen asked.

"I'm not the only Chambliss in San Francisco."

Inez laughed. "There's probably a bed sheet hanging across the street from all the other Chamblisses, too."

Gwen glanced at Steve the instant he glanced at her. Their eyes locked, and she saw both laughter and wariness in his eyes, and something more, something she couldn't interpret.

Heaven only knew what Steve saw in her eyes. She averted them, once again deciding that memorizing the surface of her coffee was safer than looking at him.

While she watched the steam patterns rising from her cup, Marjorie and Inez described the concept of the wedding set to Steve: landmarks of San Francisco portrayed in a stylized way, arranged around the bridge, which was to function as an altar of sorts. The minister performing the marriage was to stand at the top of the ramp, with Inez and Tom scaling the bridge to him. The wedding party would be surrounded by flowers, high and low, and the audience would serve as the ceremony's witnesses.

Afterward, Gwen would wander through the audience with her microphone, just as she did during all her shows, and audience members could ask questions of the bride and groom. Some surprise guests were expected—the mayor, the evening news anchors, Inez's entire family from Albuquerque. "We're having a private party at the St. Francis Hotel Saturday night," Inez told Steve. "But the actual wedding will be on the air."

From the corner of her eye, Gwen noticed him jotting notes on the diagram Marjorie had spread before him.

"The whole concept probably seems silly to you," Inez added, "given that you're not the marrying type."

Steve shifted in his chair. His foot bumped Gwen's under the table, and she had to exercise extreme control to keep from flinching. "I suppose if you *are* the marrying type," Steve said, "you may as well have the kind of wedding you want—even if it's on a mock-up of the Golden Gate Bridge on TV. A marriage is a public statement, isn't it?"

"Well, this marriage is as public as you can get," Marjorie interjected. "And the logistics are mind-boggling. We want to be sure we've got a feasible set to work on."

Steve studied the blueprint for a minute longer, then drained his coffee cup and stood. "What I really need to do is have a look at the actual set, see what's workable and what has to be redone. If you can point me in the right direction—"

"Gwen, why don't you take him downstairs to the studio?" Marjorie requested. "The stagehands won't be there today, so Steve can have the run of the place, and he doesn't have to worry about stepping on any union toes."

There was no way Gwen could refuse to escort him to the studio. Disguising her reluctance behind a phony smile, she rose from her seat and stalked to the door, avoiding eye contact with Marjorie and Inez. Steve lifted his jacket from the back of his chair and followed her out.

Except for them, the hall was empty. As they walked in silence to the elevator, she was surprised to feel her tension wane. Steve made her uneasy, but at least she didn't have to put on a show of nonchalance for Inez and Marjorie. She could be just as openly nervous around him as she wanted.

He seemed, if not equally nervous, then far from relaxed. He held on to his jacket with one hand and shoved the other into his pocket. His gaze was fixed on a distant point straight ahead of him, and his shoulders were hunched.

His apparent discomfort made her tension wane even more. Whatever existed between them, it obviously bugged him almost as much as it bugged her, and she found that gratifying.

"So they hung up a sheet?" she said to break the ice.

He cast her a diffident smile, which broke a little more ice. "With red letters." He shook his head. "As a famous television personality, you must have to put up with a lot more than that."

She shrugged. "People occasionally come up to me in the supermarket or a restaurant, but it's no big deal. I like it, most of the time. At least—" she grinned "—I like it when they have something nice to say about my show."

"You mean, people actually bother you while you're eating or shopping just to say something *not* nice about your show?"

"It's the price of fame, Steve. I'm a public personality. If I couldn't take it, I would have chosen a different career."

The elevator door slid open and they stepped into the vacant car. The relative tranquillity of the building soothed her bristling nerves another notch. Steve, too, seemed to unwind a bit. He removed his hand from his pocket and stopped staring obsessively at the button panel. When his gaze collided with Gwen's this time, his smile seemed genuine.

His smile, his gaze, his confidence shadowed by a hint of doubt...it all combined with his vexatious good looks to reawaken her memory of how she'd felt in his arms yesterday, how his mouth had felt on hers, how his body had moved against hers. She chased the memory into a dark corner of her mind, knowing it would reemerge whenever she looked at Steve, whenever she caught him smiling at her the way he was smiling at her now. Memories like that couldn't be extinguished. They could only be managed—if she was careful not to let her guard down.

The elevator stopped with a slight lurch that made her gasp. Hoping Steve hadn't noticed her jumpiness, she waited with strained patience until the door slid open and she could escape into the second-floor corridor.

"You're kind of tense, aren't you," Steve observed.

Damn. He *had* noticed. He'd probably noticed the way she'd been jolted when his foot had nudged hers under the table, too. And the way she couldn't look directly at anyone, and the way her voice was edged in breathlessness, and her cheeks were aglow with heat. After her valiant attempts to keep things pleasantly shallow with him, he had unilaterally decided to plunge into the deep end—and drag her down with him.

"The studio is this way," she snapped, then started down the hall.

Two steps were all it took for her to realize that he hadn't budged. Sighing, she planted her hands on her hips and pivoted to face him. He looked as irritated as she felt. "The thing is," he said, his voice low and gravelly, "I don't get involved with ladies I'm working for."

He made it sound so simple. Yet despite the logic of his statement, she couldn't shake the feeling that she and Steve *were* involved, that they didn't need to be kissing to be involved. That merely standing alone together in the echoing corridor, they were involved.

She stared at his tread-soled work boots, the tan leather, the thick laces. Then, mustering her courage, she lifted her gaze to his. She saw the truth in his eyes—and the truth was that he wanted her, wanted her with a hunger he did nothing to conceal.

"What would you have done if I hadn't broken from you yesterday?" she asked, not sure she wanted to hear his answer.

"*I* would have ended the kiss."

His eyes told her he wouldn't have. "Why?" she challenged him.

"Because you're not my type."

She felt as if she'd been slapped. Furious, she spun away. He reached out, clamped his hand around her and pulled her back to him. His fingers molded to the slender curve of her upper arm, and his other hand took her other arm, and he hauled her close and planted a hard, angry kiss on her lips. His mouth moved ruthlessly, his tongue demanded entry, and she wondered what he would have done if she'd resisted.

She didn't, though. She couldn't. Her anger matched his—and so did her desire for him. As his fingers dug into her arms, hers dug into his shoulders. As his tongue pushed past her teeth she parried him, hating him for making her want him so much.

This time it was impossible to say which one of them ended the kiss. She was still incensed when she pulled back. "Not your type, huh," she muttered once she could breathe normally.

"Not even close," he whispered, then drew her back to himself, gently this time, his fingers relenting and sliding up to her shoulders. He brushed his lips lightly over hers, then closed his arms around her, pressing her head against his shoulder so he couldn't kiss her again. She felt a faint shudder ripple through him as he regained control of himself. "I don't know what it is, Gwen. I really don't go for high-powered career women. I don't know what it is about you."

She really didn't go for blue-collar laborers, but she knew damned well what it was about Steve that made her nestle against his tall, powerful body, and tuck her head into the hollow below his chin, and savor the possessive strength of his embrace. The man exuded more sex appeal than any single human being was entitled to have. When she held him, when she inhaled his clean, musky aroma, when she felt the solidity of his arms around her, the taut masculinity of his body against her... she knew exactly what it was about Steve.

Her only defense was to deny it. "I've always gone for eggheads, myself," she informed him.

He stroked one hand up and down her spine, consoling and arousing her at the same time. His large hands covered so much of her back. She wished she could feel them directly on her skin, his thick, hard calluses, his work-roughened palms caressing her, smoothing her like the sandpaper he'd described on the show yesterday.

His voice filtered down to her from above her head. "Eggheads?"

"Intellectual heavyweights," she confessed. "College professors. Researchers. Men who wallpaper their offices with their advanced degrees."

"Really?" He sounded astonished.

She drew back so she could see him. Evidently he found the idea of Gwen paired up with an intellectual heavyweight hilarious. His eyes, truthful as ever, glinted with suppressed amusement.

Indignation flared inside her. "You're laughing at me."

"No," he swore—but he *was* laughing at her, his low chuckle roiling the air.

"What's so funny? Do you think I'm too stupid to find intelligence a turn-on?"

"No, I just..." He convulsed in fresh laughter. "Eggheads? You and an egghead?"

Typical lowbrow, she thought bitterly. He was mocking that which he could never understand—that cerebral intercourse was as fulfilling as the other kind.

Then again, maybe how fulfilling the other kind was depended on the man. Somehow, she suspected that with a lover like Steve, the other kind would be incomprehensibly fulfilling.

It was a perilous thought, and she steeled herself against it. Easing out of his arms, she turned from him. "Let me show you the studio, okay?"

"Sure." He slung his arm around her shoulders, as if he considered her nothing more nor less than a pal, and strolled with her down the hall. She could have asked him to remove his arm, and told him he was an insufferable jerk, and resolved then and there that no part of his body would ever again come within ten yards of her.

But his arm felt too good around her, too confoundedly natural, and his pace matched hers too well. And the sensation of his last fleeting kiss lingered on her lips, sweet and tender, making her wonder, against her will, exactly how fulfilling Steve could be.

Chapter Seven

Steve leaned against one of the vertical braces and studied his notes. The bridge would have to be dismantled and rebuilt, but the foliage problems could be overcome without too much hassle, if Inez would abandon the flower box concept and go with cut flowers. The cable car would have to be enlarged a bit so the wedding party could slide onto the benches without climbing over one another's laps. And Steve would recommend nothing thicker than half-inch plywood for the TransAmerica Tower.

Some things were easier to make sense of than others.

He'd been alone in the studio for an hour, poking around, pacing the stage, examining the underpinnings of what had been constructed so far...and thinking about Gwen, trying to figure out why in God's name he couldn't seem to keep his hands off her. Sure, she was pretty. Even in a baggy T-shirt and frayed jeans, with her hair a mop of tangled waves and her face devoid of makeup, she was pretty. But so what? Lots of other women were pretty, too.

And lots of other women weren't searching for an egghead to hook up with. An egghead! Geez.

Sighing, he closed his eyes and filled his lungs with the tangy scent of fresh pine boards. It was a smell he could understand, the way he understood nails and rulers, aching muscles and sweat. There wasn't a single egghead aspect to carpentry.

He had covered several sheets of paper with ideas about the set. If Marjorie wanted him to come back to the studio so he could explain them to Mr. Trivelli, he would. Given what Steve was charging for his services, he could make a return trip—as long as it wouldn't entail spending any time alone with Gwen Talbot.

He folded his notes, leapt down from the stage and made his way past the dimly lit rows of seats and up the hall to the elevator. Exiting onto the seventh floor, he glanced in the direction of Gwen's office and was relieved to see the door shut. He didn't allow himself to contemplate whether she was inside. It was safer not to think about her at all.

Eggheads, he muttered under his breath as he rapped his knuckles against Marjorie's open door before entering her office.

She thanked him profusely for his recommendations, and he thanked her somewhat less profusely for the check she handed him. She was seated in a high-back leather chair behind a desk at least as large as Gwen's, and looking quite the VIP. Grinning up at him, she tapped her fingertips together and said, "So tell me, Steve, what do you think of fame?"

He used to think of it in the abstract, something far removed from his own experience. True, one of his closest friends—Ki—was an author, his name immortalized on the spines of books, and another—Deke—owned a multimillion-dollar corporation, which entitled him to a certain degree of celebrity. But Ki and Deke were just plain guys in spite of their fame. They drank beer, they used foul language with the best of them, and they caught no more fish on their weekends at the cabin than Steve ever did.

He had the feeling that Marjorie was talking about a different breed of fame: the kind that entailed having your name painted on a bed sheet and hung from apartment building windows.

"There are worse things in life, I guess," he said, folding Marjorie's check and sliding it into his wallet.

"I've been going through my phone mail this morning," she told him, "and nearly all of it is about you." Her smile was gleeful. "You were a hit yesterday."

He shrugged noncommittally. He'd watched the tape he'd made of the show on his VCR and hadn't considered himself a hit. The stuntman had looked better on the small screen. The cowboy and the astronaut had worn more eye-catching costumes. The detective had had an interesting tough-guy manner. All Steve had done was to be himself—exactly the same person he'd been for the past thirty-three years without attracting the least bit of attention.

Now, apparently, he was doomed to endure his proverbial fifteen minutes of fame. No doubt it would last only until Monday afternoon, when "The Gwen Talbot Show" turned somebody else into the star of the day.

"I'm glad the show went well," he said modestly. "But I don't think it's going to make me famous."

"It already has made you famous," Marjorie declared. "I hope you've got the moxie to make the most of it."

"Meaning what? Should I sell my life story to the tabloids?"

Marjorie laughed. "If they offer you enough money. All I'm saying is, judging by my messages, you're a hot property at the moment."

Steve laughed, too. The notion was too ludicrous not to laugh at. "Well, thanks for the warning. I'll be leaving now; I've got a project to finish up across town." Not to mention the twenty-seven people who had called his office yesterday for estimates. "Have Trivelli get in touch with me if he's got any questions."

Back in the corridor, Steve hurried past Gwen's closed door, suppressing the urge to whistle his way past, as if her office was a graveyard. If she was inside, she stayed inside. He made it into the elevator without seeing her.

Talk about notions being too ludicrous. Why should he be so spooked by Gwen he wanted to whistle away the bad karma? If he *had* seen her stepping out of her office, surely he would have been able to resist touching her again. Wouldn't he?

Fortunately, his resolve wasn't tested. He made it down to the first floor and out of the building without running into her.

A cluster of women loitered on the sidewalk near the door. When he stepped outside into the late-morning drizzle, they raced toward him. "Steve!" one of them shouted, as if she were his long-lost cousin. "Hey, Steve! Can I have your autograph?"

So this was the fame Marjorie had predicted. He recalled her advice that he should make the most of it. And why not? His allotted fifteen minutes might extend to thirty minutes or even an hour, but it wasn't going to last. He might as well enjoy it for what it was worth.

"Sure, you can have my autograph," he said grandly, plucking a pen from the chest pocket of his shirt. "Have you got something for me to write on?"

The woman, who appeared to be not much beyond adolescence, extended her hand palm down. "Sign it on *me*," she requested.

Stifling a laugh, he propped her wrist in his left hand and did his best to sign his name on the rain-dampened skin below her knuckles. When he released her, she flexed her hand, studied the signature and let out a delighted shriek. "I'll never wash again!"

Whatever turns you on, he thought, relieved that the other women asked him to sign pieces of paper rather than their body parts. He let them coo and fuss over him for a few minutes, and decided he *did* enjoy it. Who wouldn't want to be fussed over by a bunch of devoted women?

"Listen, ladies, I've got to run," he finally said, when he began to grow tired of their gushing over how clever he'd been on "The Gwen Talbot Show," and how cute his smile was, and how he should never cut his hair. "Thanks for massaging my ego."

"Any time you want to get massaged someplace else, just let me know," teased the young woman with the inscribed hand.

Chuckling, he waved goodbye and strode down the block to the parking lot where he'd left his van. If enough perky women flocked around him during what was left of his time in the limelight, maybe he would find among them someone who could put Gwen out of his mind. Someone down-to-earth, the very opposite of an egghead. Someone who didn't have eyes like blue-tinted crystal, and hair like spun gold, and lips that lured, and a body that fit much too well against his.

By the lot's entry gate, he hesitated. A woman was lurking near his van. When she saw him, she grinned and sauntered over. Tuning out his exasperation over Gwen, he smiled politely and reached for his pen.

"Hi," the woman said in such a husky voice he wondered if she was sick. She appeared to be around his age, with thick dark hair and the sort of bosom he generally associated with *Playboy* centerfolds. "You're Steve Chambliss."

"That's right," he said laconically. He had pretty much used up his supply of charm on the other women; he could be pleasant with this one only so long before his irritation about Gwen rose back to the surface.

"We've got a lot in common," she purred, gazing up at him with heavily made-up eyes.

"Do we?"

"You're not the marrying type. Neither am I. Who wants to be tied down? All I want is fun. And I'll bet that's what you want, too."

"Fun is okay," he mumbled, not really into trading come-on lines with a strange woman, no matter how well endowed she might be.

"I've got something to show you," the woman murmured, inching closer to him. Her flowing white blouse was unbuttoned all the way to her cleavage, then tucked into the waistband of her skin-tight slacks.

He gave her a chilly smile. "Look, I've got to—"

"Come here, Steve," she beckoned, leaning forward and spreading the edges of her blouse wide, offering him a close-up view of two voluminous mounds of white flesh unfettered by a bra. Startled, he sprang back a step.

"Don't run away," she scolded, her lower lip shaping a perfectly round pout and her eyes shining with purpose as she advanced on him. "You're a man, right? *All man.* I saw you on TV. Now, don't you want to see me?"

"I've seen enough, thanks." He sounded husky, too. His throat was parched. The only part of his body that responded to the woman's endowments was his brain—and his reaction wasn't positive.

She wasn't about to give up, however. "They're 38Ds, and they aren't surgically enhanced. They're one-hundred-percent genuine. You're looking at the real thing, honey."

"Good for you." Although he'd been around the block a few times—in the company of an aggressive woman on more than one of those circuits—he felt like a prepubescent kid with this sharkette. If he'd been given to blushing, he would have been the color of a fire engine by now.

"Why don't you touch them, Steve?" she cajoled. "I think you'd like that. I know I would."

"I'll pass, thanks."

"But they *want* you to touch them," she insisted, as if her breasts had minds of their own.

"Look—I—uh..." He searched the street, desperate for an excuse to get away from the woman. A silver Acura was cruising slowly down the block. Behind the wheel sat a woman with eyes like blue-tinted crystal and hair like spun gold.

He might have wanted to elude Gwen inside the building, but now he couldn't imagine a more welcome sight. "You see," he said, addressing the woman and her breasts, "the thing is, I'm not available. I'm already involved with someone. Gwen!" He waved frantically at Gwen, praying for her to slow down. "Gwen, darling!"

The voluptuous woman grabbed his arm before he could escape to the Acura, which had pulled to the curb near the gate and was idling. "That's not your darling. That's Gwen Talbot, the TV talk-show lady."

"And the love of my life. Why do you think I appeared on her show? She and I are together. Gwen!" He tugged his arm free of the woman's grip and sprinted to the Acura. "Gwen, love! Let's get something to eat, babe." He leapt into the passenger seat and slammed the door.

Gwen stared at him. Her silence was decidedly hostile. *"Babe?"* she finally said.

"I'm sorry," he whispered. "Drive this thing, would you? That lady is a fruitcake. I've got to get away from her."

"Babe? I hate that word."

"All right, you hate it. Shoot me. I'd prefer that to spending another second with that nut." He cast a nervous glance over his shoulder at the buxom dark-haired woman.

"Babe? And you told her I was the love of your life? Do you have any idea who she is?"

Steve suffered a twinge of dread. What if the woman were someone important—a diva in the San Francisco Opera Company, a local philanthropist, or—God forbid—the wife of one of the TV station's executives? Steve sank into the upholstery and muttered, "I give up. Who is she?"

"How should I know? She could be anybody."

"Just drive around the block, would you?"

Grudgingly, Gwen shifted into gear and coasted to the corner. "You don't even know who she is, but you out-and-out lied to her and said I was the love of your life."

"I'll issue a retraction, okay? Just keep driving."

Looking none too pleased, Gwen steered around the corner and pulled to a halt in front of the delicatessen Steve had noticed yesterday when he'd come downtown to tape the show. He remembered thinking he could take

Gwen there for coffee after the taping. He remembered thinking it might be fun to explore a few possibilities with her.

Maybe he was as insane as the lady with the mammaries.

Beside him Gwen simmered, her hands tight on the wheel. He took in the elegance of her car, the leather bucket seats, the wood-paneled dashboard, the built-in CD player, the carpeted floors. Gwen's car was definitely the deluxe model—like Gwen herself. Even in her old jeans and sweatshirt, she belonged in a vehicle like this.

Steve belonged in his van, with its dented front bumper and its rear loaded with tools and plywood. No matter how turned on he was by her, she was never going to be the love of his life. And she'd made it extremely clear she would never be his, or anybody's, *babe*.

"All right," he said quietly. "I'm sorry, Gwen. I wasn't thinking of the consequences when I opened my mouth."

"Figures," she grumbled, although her anger seemed to ebb. "What did that woman do to you? You looked positively terrified."

"She showed me her breasts and invited me to touch them."

"Her breasts?"

"They were huge. She wasn't wearing a bra, either."

"Spare me the details," Gwen snapped. Then she sighed and shook her head. "You must have made quite an impression on her yesterday."

He groaned. "Marjorie told me that, judging by her phone mail, I'm going to be famous."

"Judging by mine, you already are."

"Great." He felt like cursing, but a laugh came out instead. The windshield grew misty, blurring the neon signs and placards cluttering the deli's front window. "Does this mean I'm going to get the best tables at the best restaurants?" he asked.

Gwen grinned mischievously. "I doubt it. Those tables are usually reserved for bigger fish."

The mist coating the windows became denser, beading and streaking. Her engine was still humming in neutral, but she didn't turn on the wipers. Enclosed with Gwen in the snug confines of her car, Steve could almost believe they were completely isolated, cut off from the reality on the other side of the wet glass, just the two of them and all the electricity they seemed to generate simply by being in close proximity.

The current made him warm, made him want to reach across the console and haul her onto his lap. "Gwen, look..."

"Don't say it," she cut him off.

How could she know what he'd been about to say when he himself hadn't a clue? Maybe he would have told her that, regardless of everything that was wrong between them, he desired her. Maybe he would have suggested that they have themselves a sweet little no-strings-attached affair and get it out of their systems. Maybe he would have informed her that while he wasn't a certified egghead, he did happen to have attended a decent college on a scholarship, and graduated with a degree in business, and had landed a job that required the wearing of a suit and tie.

But he was under no obligation to prove himself to her. If she didn't like him the way he was, then she was no better than Janet, who had insisted she loved him but would have loved him even more if only he still had one of those suit-and-tie jobs.

"It isn't you, Steve," she said apologetically. "It's me."

"What's you? You mean, your taste in eggheads?"

She glanced away, staring first down the block and then at the soft-drink sign in the deli window. "I'm new in town. I don't know anybody. When I left Dallas, I broke up with the man I'd been dating there. It wasn't exactly an easy break-up, and . . ."

Here he'd been resentful about feeling pressured to explain himself to her, and instead she was explaining herself to him. She was no more obligated than he was. "It's all right, Gwen—"

"No. It's not all right. You need to know this."

"Know what?"

She sighed. "I *am* the marrying type."

He studied her in the car. The windows seemed to be fogging from the inside now, from the heat building between him and Gwen. She looked so vulnerable in her limp sweatshirt, with her hair scraggling down her back, that when he thought about hauling her into his lap now, it was because he wanted to comfort her, not to kiss her.

What the hell—he wanted to comfort *and* kiss her. Not necessarily in that order, either.

"The man back in Dallas would have married me. I'm thirty years old, Steve. I want to start a family. I want to settle down, and build a life with someone, and make a commitment, for better or worse, till death do us part. But this offer to move the show to San Francisco came along, and he flat out refused even to consider moving with me."

If anyone other than Gwen had been telling him this, Steve would have felt as uncomfortable as he had when the loony-tune in the parking lot had exposed her twin peaks to him. The baring of souls embarrassed him. When a woman started spilling her guts, it was usually because she wanted to create an intimacy where Steve was trying to avoid one.

But Gwen was spilling her guts for exactly the opposite reason: to prevent an intimacy from developing between Steve and herself. And ironically, it only made him want to be closer to her.

"The guy must have been an ass," he said bluntly.

Gwen flashed him a wide-eyed look, and then a hesitant smile. "He had his own career to think about."

"What was he, a professional egghead?"

Her smile grew poignant. "More or less. He directed geological research for one of the petroleum companies."

Steve was underwhelmed. "There isn't much call for petroleum research in these parts. The guy would have had a hard time finding a job here."

"I don't blame him for refusing to move to California with me. And I hope he doesn't blame me for refusing to stay in Dallas with him. But the point is, even though it didn't work out, I still hope something will work out for me with someone. I wanted to stage Inez's wedding on my show because weddings are important. I dream of having one of my own someday soon. I'm a romantic, Steve. And I'm looking for Mr. Right."

To his amazement, Steve suffered a sudden, sharp pang of emotion deep inside him, a tender regret that he couldn't be her Mr. Right, her romantic ideal, the man with whom she would build a life. He'd never felt anything like it before, an almost visceral longing to make a real commitment to a woman.

But then he came to his senses. Making a commitment to Gwen would mean spending the better part of his life with a woman who drove a fancy car and lived in a posh apartment and earned a bundle. And hell, he didn't even know her well enough to know whether she'd make him drink his beer out of a glass. He didn't *want* to know her that well.

All he wanted was to get her into bed. Right?

But he didn't want to hurt her. Ever. She'd been honest with him, and he would do whatever was necessary to avoid causing her pain. "I'd better go," he decided.

"Sure thing, *babe,*" she said. She must have intended it as a joke, but it came out sounding pensive.

If she'd asked him not to leave, if she'd expressed the slightest concern about his safety in a world of voluptuous groupies, if she'd told him she trusted him, or wanted his friendship, or simply wished to figure out why, no matter what she said or how he felt, something drew her to him...he would have found any excuse not to leave her car.

But she had enough self-preservation not to beg him to stay. So he went.

INSTINCT TOLD HIM not to drive to his office. If people could look up his home address, they could certainly look up his business address, and even if he'd successfully evaded the flasher when he sneaked back to the parking lot and into his van, some other weirdo could be waiting to ambush him at his office on the southern end of the city.

He decided to check in with Karen on his cellular phone. Sounding half harried and half amused, she informed him that twenty more people had called his shop and asked to speak to him. "Seventeen were women," Karen reported. "Two of the men asked if you were gay. The last one asked if you install kitchen cabinets. I think he was legit, but you never know."

"I'm going to the Presidio," Steve resolved. "If the kitchen guy is legit, he'll call back."

"You could be raking in some big bucks on these calls, Steve. Plus, all the calls you got yesterday—"

He visualized the flasher's plump appendages and shuddered. "We'll work it out later, Karen. Most of these people aren't interested in hiring me. They just want to talk to a celebrity. According to the producer of 'The Gwen Talbot Show,' I'm famous." According to the star, too. The star who'd been brave enough to come clean with him, to fend off his passion with the truth. The star who had a hell of a lot more courage than he did.

The star who had breasts in just the right proportion to the rest of her, breasts he wanted to caress, and kiss, and...

The star who was searching for a husband.

He spent the afternoon finishing up the attic bedrooms in the Victorian, then went home, happy not to have a date even though it was a Saturday night. He spent Sunday watching a football game on the tube, thumbing through the newspaper and talking with his sister Marilyn, who said two women who'd come into her beauty shop on Saturday for perms offered her ten dollars cash for information about him. When he'd asked what information anyone would be willing to pay ten dollars for, she'd giggled and said, "The size of your tools."

If that was what fame was all about, Steve really hoped his fifteen minutes would be up soon.

GWEN WONDERED HOW MANY days a person could go without sleep before she collapsed and required medical attention.

Ever since Steve had departed from her car at midday on Saturday, she'd thought about nothing but him. Oh, there were brief lapses—ten minutes Sunday morning when a newspaper headline caught her eye, a pleasant stretch of playing solitaire on her computer until her mind went numb, a perusal of the takeout Chinese menu someone had slipped under her door. But mostly she'd thought about Steve, about the way he'd filled her car not just physically but spiritually, transforming the atmosphere, making it vibrate with energy. About the way he'd kissed her and held her and fought his own yearnings, and won the battle, and lost it. About the way he'd managed to get her to open up to him, without inviting, without demanding, but simply by being there.

About the way he'd called her *babe,* which she hated— and *love of my life*... which she liked much more than was healthy.

Nighttime was the worst, though. Nighttime, when she ought to have been asleep, Steve seemed more with her than ever. Simply curving her hand around the bedroom doorknob, she thought about him repairing her door, making it match, making it right. She pictured him shirtless, working, fixing things, so her bedroom would be enclosed, private, safe for her dreams. She imagined his strong fingers, his broad shoulders ...

And she didn't sleep.

By Monday morning, she was becoming rather annoyed. He was just a man, for crying out loud. A mere mortal. A guy with a screwdriver and a long screw. Why in the world was she so obsessed with him?

She staggered out of bed, fatigued and bleary-eyed, at a quarter to seven. She'd set the timer on the coffee maker for six-thirty; a full pot of coffee was waiting for her, hot and therapeutic. She filled a ceramic mug and carried it with her to the foyer. Swinging open the front door, she found the morning newspaper on the mat in the hall.

She lifted it, shoved the door shut with her hip and shuffled back into the kitchen. She blew on the surface of the coffee and took a sip, all the while scanning the front page for items that would distract her from Steve. The president's latest budget initiative. Unrest in Eastern Europe. A new strain of the flu invading from Asia. The score of yesterday's 49er's game.

She sipped some more coffee, flipped a few pages and decided to read the "Around Town" column. Light gossip about people she'd never heard of was all she could handle when she was running on too little sleep and two mouthfuls of caffeine.

Good morning, San Francisco!

If you haven't heard of Stephen Chambliss by now, you're either dead or dreadfully out of the loop. The local carpenter who appeared on the recently transplanted "Gwen Talbot Show" has made a major impression not only on all the impressionable women in our fair city by the bay, but on "La Gwen" herself. Ms. Talbot, one of San Fran's most enchanting newcomers and a powerhouse in the world of TV talk shows, has been romantically linked to the stud with the stud-finder, the naughty equipment and the come-hither smile. Several witnesses claim to have heard Chambliss crooning endearments to her on a busy downtown street this weekend. After he'd bellowed a few steamy words of love for all to hear, the hot, hot couple tore off in a snazzy silver car.

As they say in TV-land, stay tuned.

Across the bay in Oakland, people probably thought an earthquake had struck. But it was only Gwen screaming.

Chapter Eight

"What the hell...?" Steve gasped, sprinting his way past a cameraman and a crazed woman with a microphone who chased him from his van to the door of his office, shouting questions about his sex life.

Inside the office, Karen sat on the corner of her desk, her arms crossed and her lips twisted in a smirk. "Hey, there, superstar," she taunted. "Why don't you talk to the nice reporter?"

"Nice?" He locked the door and leaned against it, glowering through the glass at the woman who continued to aim her microphone at him as if it were a loaded semiautomatic. *"Nice* people don't ask whether you prefer the missionary position or something more acrobatic. At least," he added, "they don't ask unless you're both naked and ready to get acrobatic together." Scowling, he attempted to communicate to the reporter, with hand signals through the window, that she should go away. It took all his self-restraint not to flip her the bird.

Karen waved at the reporter; unlike Steve's, her hand signals were decidedly friendly. "Don't be such a stick-in-the-mud, Steve. Go have a word with her. She's from 'Behind the Headlines.'"

"That sleazy tabloid TV show?"

"It's not sleazy. I watch it all the time."

Steve's frown increased to encompass the woman who managed his office while he was at job sites. Karen wasn't much older than him, but she was married and had two schoolage children. She was probably the perfect representative of "The Gwen Talbot Show's" audience demographics. If she also watched "Behind the Headlines," so, no doubt, did most of the other millions of women who had seen Steve on Gwen's show last Friday. No wonder the reporter was wagging her microphone at him.

"I don't get it," he muttered, engaged in a staring contest with the reporter through the pane of glass. "Why does she want to talk about my sleeping arrangements on TV?"

"You're news," Karen explained simply as she crossed to the counter where a pot of coffee stood brewed and ready. She filled two plastic mugs and carried them back to the door. "Didn't you read the 'Around Town' column in this morning's newspaper?"

"What 'Around Town' column?" Steve asked, reaching out to take one of the cups.

Karen deliberately bypassed him, angling her head toward her desk. "Page eight. See for yourself." She opened the door, smiled warmly at the reporter and extended the two mugs to her. "Give him a couple of minutes, and then maybe he'll talk to you. Meanwhile, here's some coffee for you and your camera operator."

"Thanks," the reporter said, taking the cups and returning Karen's smile.

Steve watched his assistant with exasperation. "Why are you encouraging her to stick around? I want her gone."

"She's been out there since six-thirty, waiting for you. She could use some java. Page eight, Steve. Stay focused."

"If you gave *me* coffee, I'd be focused," he grumbled under his breath. Karen returned to the counter to fill another mug as he leafed through the newspaper on her desk. There, on page eight, was the column she'd mentioned. Apparently, "Around Town" was a regular feature of the newspaper, although Steve had never noticed it before. He read the paper for the news, the scores, the movie reviews and the business stories on housing starts and interest rates. He couldn't care less who was seen holding hands with whom at the ballet.

He started caring real fast. "'Naughty equipment'?" he blurted out after his first read-through of the column.

"How long *are* your screws, Steve?" Karen asked, smiling benignly.

"Long enough to screw you to the wall." He bent over the newspaper and reread the column more slowly, unsure whether to laugh or curse. "'Steamy words of love... hot, hot couple...' Gwen is going to be royally ticked off."

"She made you, Steve—"

"She did not! We kissed, is all. That little kiss on her show," he emphasized, not wishing to admit to anyone that he and Gwen had kissed off her show, kisses so steamy that "hot, hot" seemed a gross understatement. If Gwen didn't want to be a hot, hot couple with him, he would protect her reputation, even if doing so meant lying to Karen and the rest of the universe.

Karen laughed. "What I meant was, she made you the most famous carpenter in San Francisco, if not the entire United States. Speaking of which, when are you going to start going through that stack of messages?'' She gestured toward the "in" basket on his desk, across the room from hers.

Steve gazed in the direction she'd pointed. A thick pile of pink phone-message slips was spilling over the top of the basket. He groaned. "Are any of them for real?"

"All of them are for real."

"I mean, work-related."

"Oh, maybe a couple. I starred the ones I thought might be income-producing. Although I've got to tell you, Steve, some of those women might be willing to pay to have you work on them. Especially if you take your time and make it smooth."

He shook his head. If only he hadn't made all those suggestive remarks on the air, if only he hadn't felt compelled to prove that bravery in the face of danger wasn't the only valid measure of masculinity.... If only Gwen Talbot's beautiful eyes and delicate smile hadn't inspired him to flights of sensuality. "I thought it would be a gas, going on the show."

"And it was, wasn't it? Talk to the reporter outside, and you'll be on TV again. It'll be another gas."

It would *give* him gas, more likely. But as he sipped his coffee, it occurred to him that if he talked to the reporter from "Behind the Headlines," he could clear up the matter of his relationship, or lack thereof, with Gwen. It was his fault the newspaper had written that they were an item. He'd been the one to call her *babe* in public. He owed it to her to correct the misunderstanding so she could find Mr. Right and get married.

Sighing, he put down his mug, folded the newspaper shut and stalked to the door, determined to cope with the reporter as bravely as the detective on Gwen's show coped with criminals and the astronaut coped with weightlessness.

He twisted the bolt and inched the door open. The reporter shoved the microphone into the crack and shouted, "Is it true Gwen Talbot is carrying your baby?"

He held up his hands to silence her and guffawed at the patent absurdity of her question. "Look, lady—I'll talk to you, but first I get to establish some ground rules."

The woman, whose face was a mask of shine-free makeup and whose leather-and-chiffon outfit had obviously jumped off the hanger of some chi-chi boutique, gave him a skeptical smile. "What ground rules?"

"We do the interview outside. You let me finish my answers to your questions. You don't ask me any questions about my anatomy."

"Only your tools, eh? Fair enough. Come on out and let's get you on tape. You know, you're even cuter in real life than you are on the tube."

"Yeah, sure," he muttered, even as he ran a comb through his hair. It didn't do much good; the moment he stepped out into the dewy morning air, a breeze tossed the thick chestnut locks out of place. He had on his usual work clothes—a T-shirt and jeans, boots and his belt— and frankly, he didn't think he looked particularly cute. He certainly didn't *feel* cute.

The reporter waved over her cameraman, who stood Steve in the parking lot where the sun would strike his face. "I'll do the lead-in later," the reporter told the cameraman, then shoved her microphone between her chin and Steve's. "So, is Gwen Talbot carrying your child?"

"No. Gwen Talbot and I aren't romantically involved." The early-morning light caused him to squint, but he refused to look away from the camera. He wanted it evident that he had nothing to hide.

"A lot of people who saw you and her smooching on her show last week won't believe that."

"A lot of people believe the earth is flat. All I'm saying is, Gwen and I have never been lovers."

The reporter turned toward the camera. "This, from the man who claimed on Gwen Talbot's show that carpenters weren't fighters, they were lovers. So, Steve—" she spun back to him "—when you said you were a lover, who were you referring to?"

"At the moment, I'm not involved with anyone."

"Hear that, ladies?" she squawked at the camera. "He's up for grabs! Let me ask you this, Steve—if Gwen Talbot showed any interest, would you make a play for her?"

"I refuse to speculate," he said, sounding uncomfortably like a politician. "In any case, she's much more interested in settling down than I am. If there are any intelligent, mature, stable guys watching this show—" *millions of them, no doubt,* he thought sarcastically "—they ought to give Gwen a call. She's a terrific woman."

"So what are you saying, Steve? You're not intelligent, mature or stable?"

The reporter was sharper than he'd expected. He struggled to come up with an equally sharp response. "Maybe I'll want to settle down someday," he conceded. "But not right now."

"We already know you're intelligent. Our research has indicated that you attended Beckett College back East on a scholarship, and graduated in the top quarter of your class. There's a bit of the bookworm in you, isn't there, Steve?"

"I crack open a book every now and then."

"Wow. Ladies, this man is to die for. He reads, he's gorgeous, and check out his tool belt! Tell us, Steve, do you sleep in that thing?"

The cameraman zoomed in on Steve's belt. He should have ended the interview right then and there...but mischief flared inside him. Knowing his words would come back to haunt him, he tossed caution aside and answered, "No. When I'm in bed I don't wear anything."

"Wow!" The reporter sank slightly, pretending her knees had turned to water. "Okay, ladies—here are the facts about Steve Chambliss: he's smart, he reads, he's got bedroom eyes that ought to be licensed as deadly weapons, and...*he sleeps in the raw.* You can stand in line and take a number, folks. I saw him first!" With that, she grabbed Steve's arm and walked with him around the building, out of the camera's view.

As soon as they'd reached the side alley she released him and her swooning demeanor vanished. "Great job," she said. "Thanks for coming through."

"Thanks for not asking me how long my screws are."

"I saw 'The Gwen Talbot Show.' They didn't look much longer than three, four inches—which is too short to mention, if you know what I mean. Anyway, thanks for your time. We'll be running this piece on tomorrow's show—unless something important happens, you know, like an assassination or something."

"I'm glad to hear you've got your priorities straight," Steve muttered. "Now, if you'll excuse me, I have a business to run." He took the reporter's empty coffee mug and left the alley for the comforting familiarity of his office.

As he stepped inside, the phone started to ring. "Chambliss Carpentry," Karen answered, then grinned slyly at Steve. "Oh, yes, he's here and he's definitely single. And he's got the best tools in the business. Would you like to talk to him?"

Steve slumped in his chair, although he would have preferred to hide under his desk. He stared at his office manager, then at the flashing hold light on his phone, then at Karen once more. She was snickering.

Steve cursed—partly at her, partly at the flashing light, but mostly at himself. Inhaling for fortitude, he punched the button, lifted the receiver and listened to the morning's first romantic proposition.

As Gwen entered Marjorie's office for a pretaping powwow, she almost didn't recognize Diane, who was standing at the coffeemaker with her back toward the door. She had on a black micromini skirt, black fishnet stockings, black sandals, spiky hair—and a baggy white T-shirt.

First that ghastly write-up in the "Around Column," and now Diane was wearing a garment that wasn't black. Clearly the world was coming to an end.

Gwen was still gawking at Diane as Marjorie circled the conference table with the day's script. "Hot, hot!" Marjorie chirped.

"Watch it, or someone around here's going to get iced," Gwen threatened. Diane pivoted with her cup of coffee—and Gwen let out a tiny shriek as the front of the white T-shirt came into view. Silk-screened across it was Steve Chambliss's handsome face and broad shoulders. Large passion-red letters below the picture spelled out: Wanna See My Tools?

"Oh, my God." Gwen stumbled to a chair and sat. "Where did you get that?"

"Do you like it?" Diane struck a modeling pose. "Eighteen dollars, down on Fisherman's Wharf."

"Not to worry," Marjorie assured her. "I spoke to the manufacturer Saturday night. That's a still from our show, but we're getting a cut of the action."

"Is Steve?"

"I would assume he is."

"What do you think?" Diane asked, swiveling and striking another pose. "Is it hot, hot, or what?"

"I'm going to be sick," Gwen groaned, burying her head in her hands.

"Don't be sick," Marjorie ordered her. "We're doing a show on math anxiety today. Can we review the script?"

"Only if she takes that disgusting shirt off," Gwen snapped, then grabbed Diane's arm before Diane could actually remove her shirt. "No, keep it on. But honestly—I don't think Steve would have approved this. Are you sure the manufacturer got the proper permissions from him?"

"If you're worried about it, why don't you give Steve a call? After all, you and he are on a 'steamy words of love' basis, aren't you, *La Gwen?*"

Gwen stuck her tongue out at Marjorie. The infantile gesture brought no relief. She would have preferred to break something, smash something, maybe take scissors to the picture on Diane's shirt. She'd like to slice off Steve's nose, maybe an ear . . . and definitely those bright scarlet letters gloating about his tools.

"Are you going to tell us what the steamy words of love were?" Marjorie asked.

"No. I'm going to talk about math anxiety." She reviewed the show's guest list—a high school math teacher, a young woman working on her Ph.D. in mathematics at

UC-Berkeley, and a group of students from a local middle school. Simply thinking about something—*anything*—that didn't relate to Steve made her feel marginally better.

The meeting went smoothly, once she arranged her chair so she couldn't see Steve's face leering at her from Diane's chest. The show went smoothly, too. In fact, it went so well Gwen was tempted to suggest that from now on, "The Gwen Talbot Show" should stick to tame, intellectual subjects and avoid the more flammable fun stuff, even if moving in a tame direction caused her ratings to plummet.

Back in her office after the taping, Gwen decided to telephone Steve. She honestly didn't believe he would have approved the shirt, not after the way he'd made a spectacle of himself trying to elude his crazed fan in the parking lot down the street. He didn't seem all that enamored of the spotlight; Gwen suspected that he would have abhorred the notion of having his likeness silk-screened across T-shirts and sold—assuming the manufacturer had bothered to consult with him about the shirts before he'd opened up shop on Fisherman's Wharf.

She spun through her Rolodex in search of Steve's office number, and dialed. His line was busy.

Slamming down the phone, she closed her eyes. Diane's shirt flashed across her mind, followed by a vision of Steve himself, his glittering eyes and wicked smile. For all she knew, maybe he *had* approved the shirt. Maybe his act with the buxom woman in the parking lot had merely been a ploy to get close to Gwen. Maybe he'd been looking for a way to kiss her again. Lord knew, things got mighty exciting whenever they kissed.

She tried his number again. Busy.

Strange way of doing business, she thought. If he was in such demand as a carpenter, he ought to have more than one line. Then again, maybe he did. Maybe all his lines were tied up with women begging to have a look at his tools.

She hit the redial buttonr once more. This time she heard a ringing, and then a woman's voice: "Chambliss Carpentry, can you hold?"

Gwen barely said yes before she heard the click relegating her to telephone purgatory. She studied the rest of the week's schedule while waiting for the woman to return to the line. Tomorrow's show was "Jealousy: the Green-Eyed Monster." Wednesday, a chat with a local congressman on national health policy. Thursday, an author promoting a weight-loss book. Friday, a soap-opera actress who had recently launched her own line of costume jewelry. It looked like a gratifyingly calm, civilized week of shows.

"Sorry to keep you waiting," the woman's voice recited through the phone. "Can I help you?"

"I'd like to speak to Steve Chambliss, please," said Gwen.

"You and everyone else," the woman lamented. "I'm sorry, but—"

"This is important," Gwen interrupted. "It's business."

"I'll take a message. What's your name, please?"

Gwen took a deep breath. She didn't want to leave her name. It was bad enough that "Around Town" was trumpeting a bogus relationship between her and Steve; heaven knew to whom Steve's receptionist would leak the news that Gwen was just one of the millions of women badgering him on the phone.

The hell with it. He probably had authorized the T-shirts. And other than that, what did Gwen have to tell him?

"Never mind," she said, then hung up. And called herself a dozen different kinds of coward.

AFTER A WHILE, chronic insomnia became a state of being for Gwen, kind of like white noise, so ubiquitous she no longer paid attention to it. By the end of the week, she'd learned to function on a half hour of REM slumber and a pot of coffee a day.

One advantage of living in a constant daze was that the Steve Chambliss T-shirts no longer bothered her. By Friday they had become the new uniform at work: Marjorie showed up at work wearing one under an Armani silk blazer, and the techies who operated the cameras and lights on her show all had on the shirts with their jeans. Diane left a neatly folded Wanna See My Tools? shirt on Gwen's desk, tied up with a bright pink ribbon.

She could deal with the shirts. She could get through her shows faking zest and energy. She could even—difficult though it was—sit through a broadcast of "Behind the Headlines," a sensationalistic show that usually featured stories on sleazy criminals, mothers who'd lifted cars to rescue trapped children, parrots that testified at murder trials and the like. Fortunately, someone had given Marjorie warning that Steve was going to appear on the show, and Marjorie had warned Gwen.

She'd set her VCR to tape the Tuesday show that featured him, because she wouldn't be home when it was on the air. But in fact, once she'd viewed the tape of the show, she couldn't bring herself to erase it. It became a part of her permanent videotape library, and she watched it again and again, mesmerized by Steve's sexy squint, by his chivalrous effort to undo the damage of Monday's "Around Town" column, by his insistence that he and Gwen were not lovers . . . by his claim that he didn't wear anything in bed.

As long as he was on tape, or on a T-shirt, or somewhere else in the city, she could cope. He was a fantasy, and since she was currently on her own and unattached, she was allowed to fantasize. Once she closed her magnificently functioning bedroom door and heard that perfect little click as the latch slid into place, she could fantasize about anyone and anything she damned well wanted.

In person, though, coping was harder. The morning after Steve's appearance on "Behind the Headlines," she emerged from the ladies' room to find him standing in the hall, chatting with one of the set builders. She ducked back into the bathroom, spent ten minutes she couldn't spare fixing her hair, and then emerged to find him still out in the hall, shooting the breeze with the skinny, young, ponytailed workman.

Gwen wasn't going to spend the rest of the day hiding in the ladies' room. Squaring her shoulders, she moved in dignified strides down the hall toward the elevator, hoping he wouldn't notice that she was holding her breath.

"Hello, Gwen," he murmured.

Her breath left her in a sputtering gasp. "Oh—hi, Steve," she said with absolutely phony casualness. Then she dove into the elevator and pounded all the buttons with her fist, figuring it didn't matter what floor she landed on, as long as it was a different floor than the one where Steve was standing. As the door began to slide shut, she glanced out to see Steve watching her, a bemused smile on his face. She smiled back, grinding her teeth so tightly her jaws ached for an hour afterward.

After that, she resolved to avoid the studio where he was working. But when Inez buzzed her Friday morning and asked how the revamped wedding set was doing, Gwen had to admit she hadn't checked on it all week.

Inez was obviously suffering from premarital jitters. "Trivelli told me it was taking longer to redo the cable car than he'd expected. And the TransAmerica tower—"

"Don't worry," Gwen reassured her. "I'm sure it's going to be fine."

"What if they're having a problem? What if it looks awful?"

"I'll check on it today," Gwen told her.

"Promise?"

"Sure." As long as Steve wasn't there. As long as checking on her friend's wedding set didn't require her to make an ass of herself in front of the sexiest carpenter in San Francisco.

The taping of her show with the soap-opera actress went splendidly. Gwen was actually feeling upbeat when she signed off, thanked her guest and steeled herself for a stroll down to the studio where the wedding set was being constructed.

From the doorway at the rear, she observed the stage-hands hammering, sawing and painting under the watchful eye of Frank Trivelli. Given his age and portly build, Trivelli looked rather comical wearing a Steve T-shirt with the Wanna See My Tools? boast stretched across his round belly. The younger workers all had Steve T-shirts on, too. Only one person in the auditorium wasn't wearing a Steve T-shirt. He was wearing Steve's face, though, Steve's sturdy chin, his thick mane of hair, his broad shoulders and narrow hips and cocky smile and dazzling eyes.

He was huddling with Trivelli near the apron of the stage, a blueprint in his hands. Gwen backed out into the hall, reasonably certain he hadn't noticed her.

For God's sake! She was acting more foolish than she had in high school, when she'd had a massive crush on Billy Hoffman, who had gotten a perfect 1600 on the SATs and considered her nothing more than a fluff-brained cheerleader. Every time she'd seen Billy in the hall she'd gotten warm and breathless—exactly the way she felt right now.

Steve Chambliss was no Billy Hoffman—and Gwen was no high school cheerleader. On the other hand, according to the report on "Behind the Headlines," Steve had gone to college and he occasionally read a book. Which wasn't quite the same as scoring 1600 on the SATs, but the man wasn't exactly a mental midget.

Whoopee for him. He was a stud, a cutie-pie, a sometime bibliophile whose tools had become the major topic of discussion for a ridiculously large portion of the Bay Area population. At this point, he was less fond of her than Billy Hoffman had been back in high school. If Steve had had any personal interest in her, he wouldn't have gone on television and invited every smart, single man within the sound of his voice to ask her out.

Not that anyone had followed Steve's exhortation and asked her out.

Not that she would have gone out with any man, no matter how smart or single, who made a habit of watching "Behind the Headlines."

Feeling like a spy, she flattened herself against the corridor wall, sidled to the door and shifted her head just enough to peek around the edge of the doorway. Trivelli was studying the diagrams; Steve was surveying the stage. His hands were on his hips, making his shoulders look wider and craggier under his shirt.

God. Why did he have to be so damnably good-looking?

Sighing, she shoved away from the wall, marched down the hallway to the elevator and punched the up button. When the car didn't arrive immediately, she forsook it for the stairs. She didn't want to be in the corridor when Steve emerged from his conference with Trivelli.

As far as Inez's wedding set went, she would return to the studio to inspect it later, when Steve wasn't around. And as for herself, as for her embarrassing, lingering infatuation with Steve Chambliss... She would simply have to get out and start meeting some men. Once she found someone more to her taste, someone who could take over the starring role Steve currently held in her dreams, she could forget about him.

IT WAS THE STRANGEST thing: he was sure he'd glimpsed Gwen.

He'd thought he had seen a movement in the doorway at the far end of the studio, and he'd glanced up from the blueprint. The woman in the doorway was cast in shadow by the brightly lit hall behind her, but even if he couldn't make out her features, he would have known Gwen anywhere. The golden sheen of her tousled hair, the slim dimensions of her figure, the easy grace of her posture...

Hell, even if he hadn't seen her he would have known she was near. She only had to be within range and hormones started flooding his system. He knew this, because during the past week, as he'd dropped in to observe the progress on the wedding set, he'd always known when Gwen was near.

He would walk past the studio where her show was taped, and his body would lurch to attention. When her show was on the air, he'd hear her voice through the speakers mounted around the building and his muscles would string tight; his tongue would slide across his lips searching for the taste of her. One morning when she'd strolled past him and tossed him a smile, he'd almost chased her into the elevator, hit the emergency-stop button between floors, and...

He didn't want to contemplate what he would have done to Gwen Talbot if they'd been trapped between floors in a jammed elevator. It was too tempting a fantasy. Too powerful. Too downright adolescent.

Even when he wasn't in the same building with her, she was a part of his life. For the past four nights, he had come home from the deck project down in Pacifica, flopped onto the sofa with a beer and clicked on his VCR to watch that day's "Gwen Talbot Show." As if he had nothing better to do than to listen to some congressman drone on and on about universal health coverage, or to be lectured on the destructive nature of jealousy. He hadn't really cared what her guests were saying, anyway. All he'd cared about was the host of the show.

Was she seeing anyone else? he wondered. Was a manly egghead currently making use of her platform bed? Should Steve have paid closer attention to what the experts on her Tuesday show had been saying about the green-eyed monster?

He tried to convince himself he didn't care who she was sharing her bed with. He tried to tell himself he was watching her show only out of curiosity, to see how he measured up against her other guests. But that was only so much rationalization.

He was watching the show because he wanted to see her.

And now he was sure she'd been in the studio where Trivelli was building the wedding set. If only for a second, Gwen had been there.

He'd spent the past week being swarmed by women, many of them wearing those godawful T-shirts some clown had decided to market. Steve didn't really mind the shirts—he'd negotiated a decent royalty for himself from the manufacturer, and as long as no one thought that the creepy picture on the shirt actually resembled him, he didn't care if the whole world wanted to wear the things. He'd sent one to his sister in Connecticut, one to his parents to give Mrs. Donahue down the street—either to confirm or to disprove that he was a bum—and one apiece to Ki, Tripp and Deke.

Women in Steve Chambliss T-shirts approached him on the street every day, as did women in tank tops, tube tops, semisheer blouses and lace bustiers. Women telephoned his office. Women telephoned his home. And yet, after one fleeting instant when he'd shared the same air with Gwen, he realized how little any of those other women could ever mean to him.

What could Gwen mean to him? She didn't want him in her life. She didn't need him. She would be better off without him. But...

But there was still that spell, that magic, something about her that changed his molecular structure. Something so strong, so irresistible, that he didn't even have to see her to know she was there.

Trivelli seemed to have the set under control, so Steve took his leave and headed back to Pacifica to finish up the deck job he had there. He stopped at his bank's automatic teller machine to deposit the final payment check on his way home, then cruised past the flock of women standing guard near his building, representing a variety of generations but all of them wearing his face on their baggy cotton T-shirts. He gave them an amiable wave before veering onto the driveway to the residents' parking lot behind the building. The small band of women had been gathered outside his building at around 6:00 p.m. for the past few days to welcome him home; then they always dispersed. They seemed harmless enough, so he always favored them with a wave.

That evening, though, he'd been too restless to find the Steve Chambliss welcoming committee amusing. Just five hours ago, he'd seen Gwen—if that fraction of a second he'd glimpsed her actually counted as *seeing* her. Tonight he didn't want to deal with other women. He wanted to think only about Gwen, the woman he'd set free on that tabloid TV show, the woman who had provided him with enough details of her recent love life to persuade him he could never be her Mr. Right. The woman who clung to his memory like the damp gray San Francisco fog rolling in off the ocean tonight, refusing to let the day's heat burn her away.

He stopped in the lobby for his mail, then climbed the stairs to his second-floor apartment. He needed a shower and some food, but not as much as he needed a better, longer look at Gwen. He rewound his videotape to the beginning of her show.

There she was on his TV screen, looking captivating in a lime-green dress and dangly earrings. He remembered the first time he'd met her, when he'd come to her apartment to fix her bedroom door. She hadn't been able to keep her hair from getting tangled in her earrings. Were they the same ones she was wearing on today's show? He stopped the tape, rewound it and started it up again, this time leaning forward and concentrating on the gold jewelry adorning her earlobes.

Cripes! He couldn't believe he was obsessing over her earrings. Whatever she'd done to him, his inability to shake off the aftereffects was beginning to trouble him in a big way.

Her guest was some woman he'd never heard of before, although the audience seemed enthralled by her. Gwen identified her as an actress on a soap opera, but she wasn't on the show to talk about her acting career. Rather, she was there to promote a line of jewelry she had designed.

Steve stopped the tape and studied the frozen image on his screen. He decided Gwen's earrings were much prettier than anything the actress had created.

Well, of course he did. Gwen's earrings belonged to the sorceress herself. He was helpless before their bewitching glitter.

A caustic laugh escaped him. He sucked down some beer and started the tape rolling again.

A buzz on his intercom broke through the chatter coming from the screen. Grumbling a pungent curse, he freeze-framed the tape once more, crossed to the speaker by his door and pressed the button. He hoped whoever had buzzed him wasn't one of the ladies from outside the building. He was feeling a bit too sour to engage in cheerful banter with them.

"Yeah?" he growled into the mouthpiece.

"Steve?"

Damn. It sounded like Gwen. He must be delirious, imagining her everywhere.

His silence prompted her to speak again. "Steve? It's Gwen."

Definitely delirious. He pictured that fleeting moment he'd spotted her hovering in the studio doorway, just a shape, a shadow, yet exerting so potent a pull on him he'd wanted to shove Trivelli aside and fly up the aisle to her. And now some lady was downstairs, claiming to be Gwen.

"Steve?" she said again.

"Yeah."

"Can I see you?"

He felt the last of his self-control, his sanity, his self-protective instincts draining away. Gwen's presence—assuming the woman standing in the lobby at the other end of the intercom was truly Gwen—couldn't make him any crazier than he already was. "Sure," he said. "Come on up."

Chapter Nine

"I brought a peace offering," she announced.

She'd brought herself, which was more than Steve could have hoped for. She stood in his doorway, dressed in a floral-print skirt that flowed loosely down past her knees, and a plain white blouse that, thank God, didn't have his face printed on it. Her hair was pulled back into a ponytail, her earrings were complicated, her feet were shod in sandals, and her hands held a foil-wrapped plate. Her teeth worked on her lower lip and her eyes glistened with uncertainty.

If he revealed how thrilled he was to see her, he would likely scare her off. Besides, he felt more than just thrilled. He felt pretty uncertain, himself.

"Come on in," he said, training his gaze on the plate in her hands because it was safer than looking at her face.

"They're cookies," she said as he closed the door behind her. "I baked them...." Her voice trailed off.

He turned and found her staring at the television, where her image was still frozen on the paused VCR. He smiled sheepishly. "Man, I'm just addicted to that 'Gwen Talbot Show.' Have you ever watched it?"

Still holding the plate, Gwen frowned. "That's today's broadcast. You taped today's broadcast?"

It was too humiliating to admit that he'd been taping her show all week, that he'd needed his Gwen fix at the end of each day. He covered his embarrassment with a joke: "I've been shopping around for some cheap jewelry to match my tool belt. I figured I might learn something about accessorizing from the guest you had on today's show. That was her favorite word, wasn't it? Accessorizing."

Gwen managed a speculative smile. "You taped my show."

"I was curious to see how I stacked up against your other guests."

She eyed him dubiously, but fortunately didn't question him further. Which probably meant she'd figured out the truth: he didn't give a damn about her other guests. He'd taped the show only to see her.

Well, if she'd caught him, so be it. He wasn't going to defend himself, or deny anything. He'd wanted to see her, and TV was the least hazardous way to go about it. If she didn't like it, she could take her peace offering and leave. If she did like it, she could throw herself at him.

She didn't throw herself at him, but she handed him the plate, which was good enough for now. He folded back the silver wrap and helped himself to one of the cookies. Oatmeal chocolate-chip, laden with brown sugar and magnificently chewy. "You made these?" he asked after swallowing his first bite.

"Yes."

"They're great." He extended the plate toward her, and she declined with a shake of her head. After taking a second cookie, he set the plate down on the coffee table. "Really outstanding," he murmured, taking a hearty bite. "You made these for me?"

She nodded. Now it was his turn to be flattered, and her turn to look as embarrassed as he'd felt when she'd discovered herself on his VCR.

"When did you make them?"

"This afternoon. After I saw you with Frank Trivelli at the studio where Inez's wedding is going to be held."

"You could have saved yourself a lot of time and effort by coming in and saying hello," he pointed out, although he was secretly pleased that she'd gone to the trouble of baking for him. The groupies who had been hounding him on the streets of San Francisco over the past few days hadn't given him cookies. One had tried to give him her underpants, but frankly, he'd rather have Gwen's cookies.

She turned so she was no longer facing the television set. "You're right, Steve," she said, her gaze on the window. "I should have come in and said hello. It was stupid of me."

"Hey, I could have said hello to you."

"You saw me?"

"In the doorway." He offered a crooked grin. "On the stupidity scale, I'd say we're pretty evenly matched."

Gwen's tension seemed to ebb. Her shoulders lost their stiffness and her smile no longer looked forced. "Has it been a rough week for you?"

If she was talking about his bout of Gwen-itis, it had been exceedingly rough. But he wasn't prepared to admit that. "You mean, the fans mobbing me?"

"And that horrible tabloid TV program, and the T-shirts, and—"

"I'm getting a cut of the action with the shirts," he told her. "Are you?"

"My show is. Marjorie saw to it."

He nodded his approval. "As for 'Behind the Headlines,' I was glad the reporter gave me the opportunity to set the record straight about you and me. No sense having all those eligible bachelors thinking you're off limits." He dared to touch Gwen's arm, and she lifted her face to his. The connections—gaze to gaze, skin to skin—caused longing to twist tight inside him. He parried it by resorting to humor. "You aren't carrying my baby, are you?"

She laughed. "If I am, we'd better notify the Pope."

"Boy. The tabloid headlines would be wild if we pulled off a miracle like that." He let his hand drop and grimaced inwardly at how empty his palm felt without the warmth of her skin against it, how strangely empty his soul felt at the thought that he and Gwen weren't expecting a baby, immaculately conceived or otherwise.

What was he, insane? He didn't want a baby, not with Gwen, not with anyone. Fatherhood meant sacrificing freedom, losing sleep, giving up everything Steve lived for: the right to make decisions without taking anyone else into account. The right to go where he wanted, when he wanted. The right to be as inexcusably selfish as he wanted to be.

His face must have reflected his thoughts—although at that moment they were such a jumble he had no idea what Gwen saw in his expression. "What are we going to do, Steve?" she asked, her voice soft.

He couldn't handle a heavy conversation with her right now. He couldn't even handle his own perilous mental meandering. He couldn't make promises—to love her, to leave her alone, to laugh off whatever continued to draw him to her, and bind him to her, and make him crazy with anger and desire and affection for her.

For the moment, all he could handle was her friendship, her company, her cookies and the kindness her gift implied. "What we're going to do is go out for dinner," he resolved, refusing himself the temptation of one more cookie along with the far greater temptation of Gwen herself. "Give me ten minutes to shower, and then we'll hit the road."

He took less than ten minutes. Knowing that she was in his living room made shutting himself inside his bathroom difficult. She was so close; he wanted to be with her. Forget about their being wrong for each other. Forget about her fancy career and his habit of guzzling beer straight from the bottle. All that mattered was that he and Gwen were going to spend an evening together—in a public restaurant, where they wouldn't be able to get themselves in trouble.

They would behave like a normal couple on a date. They would discuss politics, their favorite movies and whether or not marijuana ought to be legalized. Then Steve would take Gwen back to her apartment and...not kiss her. Just drop her off, go home and take another shower. A long, cold one.

And in the meantime, he would stop fantasizing about inviting her to strip off her clothing and join him in this quick, hot shower.

The image of her body, damp and steamy as water pounded down on her, was too potent. He yanked the faucets shut, climbed out of the stall and toweled himself dry. He shaved in record time, then raced into the bedroom for clean clothing—khakis and an oxford shirt instead of the work apparel she always saw him in—combed his hair, checked his wallet to make certain he had his full complement of credit cards, and stepped into a pair of moccasin-style loafers.

Back in the living room, he found Gwen by the window, peeking around the drawn curtain. The television and VCR were turned off, the newspaper sections folded neatly on the coffee table and his half-empty bottle of beer planted atop the newspapers, as if Gwen couldn't bear to let one more water ring join the other 452 that stained the table.

What was it about women that they couldn't tolerate a little clutter? he wondered. What was it about them that they couldn't control their compulsion to tidy things? He was sure there must be a few women on the planet who were as sloppy as he was. Why was he doomed to fall for the ones who neatened every room they entered?

Sloppy women probably wouldn't bake cookies, he decided—or if they baked them, they'd mistake the salt for sugar, or accidentally mix a dust ball into the batter. And anyway, an admitted slob like Steve didn't have the right to expect perfection in others.

Gwen came about as close to perfection as he could manage. Any closer and he'd be ready to chuck his bachelorhood out the window for her.

"Anyone out there?" he asked.

She let the curtain drop and turned from the window. If she didn't do a double-take, she came awfully close. "You look very nice."

He grinned. "It's my Halloween costume. Last year I went out trick-or-treating as a grown-up."

She smiled, then motioned toward the window. "Someone's hung a sheet from a window across the way. It says, We Know You're in There, Steve. Come Out With Your Tool Up."

"Oh, God. They're getting worse. Last night, the sheet said, How Long Is Long?"

"You mean, there's a sign out there every day?"

"Since a week ago," he confirmed. "Whoever is hanging them must have cleaned out the entire linens department at I. Magnin."

Gwen peeked around the drape one more time, smiling and shaking her head. "If it's any consolation, your adoring fan club seems to have dispersed for the night."

"They usually take off a few minutes after I get home. I guess they were lucky they stuck around as long as they did today. Getting to eyeball the famous Gwen Talbot herself was probably like a two-fer for them."

"They had no interest in me," Gwen confessed, adjusting the strap of her shoulder bag and stuffing her hands into her skirt's side pockets. "One of them asked me if I was Gwen Talbot, and I said no, and that was that."

He feigned shock. "And here I thought you were so honest."

Gwen shrugged. "I was afraid of what would happen if I told them the truth. One of them might have tried to sneak up to your apartment by hiding inside the foil wrap."

"Let's go," he said with a smile, holding open the door for her. "Do you have any preferences about where to eat?"

"I really don't know much about the local restaurants," she confessed. "I hardly know anything about the city at all. Ever since I got here, I've either been working on the show or fixing up my apartment. I haven't even ridden on a cable car yet."

"You haven't? Then it's high time you had the grand tour," he declared, locking his apartment and ushering her down the hall to the stairs. "Did you drive over here?"

She shook her head. "I took a bus. Two buses, actually. I've always thought a good way to get to know a city is to use public transportation."

"An equally good way," he said as they reached the bottom of the stairs and he steered her toward the rear entrance of the building, "is to use the Chambliss chariot. Do you mind?"

"Mind?" She studied his commercial van, parked in his assigned space in the residents' lot. "Of course not. You don't think it's too conspicuous, do you?"

"If I've learned anything from recent experience, Gwen, it's that anyone who wants to track me down is going to track me down. They don't need a truck with Chambliss Carpentry painted on the sides to find me."

"What you ought to do," she teased, "is paint your face on the van, with big block letters bragging about your tools."

"I've got plenty of tools in back," Steve said as he unlocked the passenger side and helped her up into the seat. He recalled how much Janet had hated traveling anywhere in his van. She'd always insisted on driving, all the while nagging that he ought to consider buying a real car. But how many vehicles did a single guy need? His accountant had supplied him with a formula for calculating how much of the van's use was business and how much personal, and Steve didn't give it another thought.

He climbed in behind the wheel and discovered Gwen peering over her shoulder into the rear of the van. "Those don't look like tools. They look like boards."

"Trust me. The side compartments are crammed with all sorts of equipment. If you'd like, after dinner we can drive somewhere and build a trestle table. I've got everything we need."

"How did you wind up being a carpenter?" she asked as he coasted down the driveway to the street.

He headed west, toward Point Lobos. "I like building things."

She shot him a skeptical look. "Surely there's more to it than that. You were an honors student at Beckett College. With a degree from a top-notch school like that, you could have become just about anything."

"Hey, wait a minute." He laughed modestly. "If you saw how I studied, you'd know how limited my talents were. This is Golden Gate Park, by the way."

She stared through the windshield at the verdant stretch of trees and grass and gardens, but her mind remained on the conversation. "So you're saying, carpentry was the only thing you could have done?"

He felt a twinge of defensiveness. "It was what I wanted to do," he said tersely.

"Then you're very lucky," she said.

He shot her a quick glance. "In what way?"

"That you've been able to support yourself doing what you want to do." She settled back in her seat. "I can just picture you as a little boy, tinkering with one of those kiddy tool chests."

"Never had one of those," he told her. "I used to use my father's tools. He was always fixing something or other. We lived in a sixty-year-old duplex—my grandmother upstairs and us downstairs. Something was always breaking—the stairs, the furnace, the caulking around the windows. My dad and I would fix it. I was his trusty assistant."

"Is your father a carpenter?"

Steve shook his head. As a rule, he didn't discuss his parents much. But he recognized the need to put some distance between himself and the woman sitting next to him. He understood that asking her if she minded being chauffeured around town in his van had been a kind of test. She'd passed it—which meant he had to give her a more difficult test, one that would force her to acknowledge that they made a lousy couple.

"My father drives a truck," he said. To underline the point, he added, "My brother's an auto mechanic. My sister's a hair stylist."

"That's nice," said Gwen, not a trace of condescension in her voice.

"They all expected better of me," he explained, a little less defiant given her easy acceptance of what he'd told her. "I was the Chambliss who got the college scholarship. I was supposed to graduate and land a respectable job. In fact, I *did* land a respectable job. And I hated it, so I quit." Why was he telling her all this? Why wasn't he pointing out the Arboretum, the Japanese Tea Garden and all the other points of interest dotting the park?

He knew why. He wanted to give her every chance to reject him, to withdraw, to cut off the current that circled around them, linking them as surely as if it were an iron chain.

"I said it before, and I'll say it again. You're very lucky," Gwen insisted. "Not many people are able to earn a living doing what makes them happy. To say nothing of being the best at it in all of San Francisco. I wish I could say I was the best talk-show host in the city."

"I bet you are."

"I'm basically the *only* talk show host in the city," she said, then laughed. "Most of the shows are taped in New York, Los Angeles or Chicago."

They had reached Point Lobos, a bluff overlooking the Pacific Ocean. Steve parked the van in the lot of a stucco building that housed a snack bar and a maze of terraces. He climbed out and came around to her side to help her down from the high seat.

She filled her lungs with the salty, misty air. "I love that smell," she said. "I grew up near Denver, and then I lived in Dallas. The only time I ever smelled the ocean was on vacations. It's so bracing, so alive."

"Come on," he said, taking her hand and leading her down a flight of steps to the first terrace. The tiles were slick with moisture, and he told himself he was holding on to her so she wouldn't slip. "Let's go ogle the seals."

Ragged outcroppings of rock, dark and shiny, protruded from the frothing spray of the ocean several hundred feet off the shore. "Are there seals there?" she asked, frowning.

"It's hard to see them, especially when it's foggy out. They blend in with the rocks—look, there's one."

Gwen squinted at the rock where he'd spotted a seal moving. She let out a squeal of pure delight. "I can't believe it! I've never seen a seal anywhere outside a zoo."

"Well, that's what they look like in real life. See, there goes another one," he said, pointing to a seal as it waddled to the edge of a rock and dove into the water.

"Wow! This is so exciting!" She clapped her hands and gave a little jump. To him, the excitement was in viewing the seals with someone who could take such unabashed joy in the sight. "Look, Steve!" She grabbed his arm and tugged. "It's climbing back on. Is that the same one who just jumped off? Maybe it's a different one."

"From this distance they all look alike."

"Excuse me," a deep baritone behind him broke in. "You're Steve Chambliss, aren't you?"

Steve turned warily. The man who'd approached him was beefy and balding, on the far side of middle age.

"I'm sorry for butting in," the man said, acknowledging Gwen with an apologetic nod, "but I recognized you from those shirts, you know? If I don't get your autograph, my daughter'll kill me."

"Well. I don't want to be responsible for an act of murder," Steve said, relieved to be accosted by someone who didn't personally have the hots for him—and someone who apparently didn't recognize Gwen. After Steve had appeared on "Behind the Headlines" to disavow any relationship with Gwen, he would be hard-pressed to convince anyone that his outing with her tonight was strictly about friendship, not romance. As it was, he hadn't quite convinced himself.

He scribbled his name for the man on the back of a picture postcard, then waved him off. Returning his gaze to Gwen, he sighed. Her childlike exuberance had vanished; the mood was broken. "So much for that," he muttered.

"Does all the attention bother you?" she asked as they climbed the stairs back to the parking lot.

He was glad to see no one lying in wait for him by the van. "I never dreamed of being a celebrity," he told her, helping her into the van and then resuming his place behind the wheel. "I never had a burning desire to sign autographs. In my family, being the center of attention meant getting pressured, so it wasn't something I wanted."

"What did they pressure you about?"

"Winning the damned prestige job. The one I hated." He sent her a smile, but he doubted there was much humor in it. "I started out doing carpentry back home in Connecticut, but I had to move away. Being that close to my parents . . . All I ever heard from them was that I was a terrible disappointment, throwing away my education and wasting my opportunities. I could have had a great career, been a hotshot professional, but I'd given it all up to hammer nails. They saw me as a failure. After a while, I just said the hell with it and moved to California."

"Some parents just can't accept us as we are," Gwen commiserated.

Her words startled him—in particular, the word *we,* as if she'd experienced the same friction with her parents. How on earth could they consider her a failure? She was famous, she was affluent, she was smart and beautiful and all the rest.

She answered his unvoiced question. "My parents wanted me to be Miss Popularity. They considered it the greatest thing in the world when I made the varsity cheerleading squad in high school."

"You were a cheerleader, huh." He permitted himself an appreciative glance at her lithe body and her lush blond hair. Of course she'd been a cheerleader. He could picture her in one of those short skirts, waving her pompoms, doing splits in the air.... In fact, he could picture it much too vividly, almost as vividly as he'd pictured her standing in the shower with him.

"But the minute you become a cheerleader," she continued, "all the smart boys avoid you. I was always getting crushes on the National Merit Scholars. They didn't want anything to do with me. They thought that because I was a cheerleader I was by definition an air-head."

"Then they weren't so smart."

"They made assumptions. I can't say I blamed them." She reminisced, a wistful smile tracing her lips. "I always wished I was smarter. I envied the geniuses, the ones who actually understood what we were supposed to be doing in the physics lab. I had a framed lithograph of Albert Einstein hanging in my bedroom. But all my parents wanted was for me to be the prom queen, and to find Prince Charming and settle down.''

"They aren't proud of your accomplishments?''

"They've come around—maybe more than your parents have. I think they're pleased by my success. Which isn't to say they wouldn't be even more pleased if I got married.''

"So, they're the reason you're looking for Mr. Right.''

"No. If I were doing it for them, I would have found him long ago. I wouldn't have left Dallas—I would have stayed there and married my boyfriend. I do things on my own terms, Steve. I don't let my parents determine my life for me. I'm thirty years old. I take responsibility for my own decisions.''

How very mature, he thought dryly, wondering whether she was trying to convey some sort of message to him—that he *wasn't* mature, that he *wasn't* responsible. But he was. Responsible, anyway. And just about as mature as he could manage with a schoolboy crush.

Besides, what was so mature about jumping up and down and clapping for the seals on the rocks? Steve would bet his wedding-set consulting fee Gwen was going to squeal over the cable cars, too.

He considered driving to Fisherman's Wharf, then realized he'd never find a parking space there on a Friday night. Instead, he drove to her apartment. Before she could question him, he explained: "We'll walk over to the Wharf and catch a cable car from there.'' He slowed near her building, searching the crowded block for a parking space.

"Why don't you pull into my building's garage?'' she suggested. "There's usually an extra space or two there. I think it would be better than leaving your van visible so close to my house.''

Steve appreciated her caution—and he appreciated even more not having to knock himself out finding a place to park along the sloping streets of the Marina district. Gwen passed him her garage key, which he inserted into the lock by the door. It groaned open and he pulled in.

Within a few minutes, they were strolling through the balmy evening toward the Wharf. Fog curled lazily above the bay, swirling like diaphanous banners in the warm dusk. As accustomed as he was to San Francisco's striking vistas, the zigzagging hills, the incredible blue of the water and the endless fog, the city's exotic features struck him as more romantic tonight than they usually did. He'd walked this route dozens of times before, but Gwen made everything different, somehow.

She gazed around her in wide-eyed wonder as they passed Fort Mason and entered the razzle-dazzle of Fisherman's Wharf: the tacky museums, the souvenir shops, the arcades and the open seafood sheds where crabs could be bought fresh-boiled. Steve hurried her past two T-shirt shops that displayed Wanna See My Tools? shirts prominently in their windows. He slowed with her to watch a street performer juggle a knife, a flaming baton and a fluorescent light bulb, and tossed a dollar into the guy's can. Another dollar went to the blues guitarist across the street, and then they reached the cable car turnaround.

"It's wonderful," she murmured as they joined the line of passengers waiting for the next cable car.

"It's kinda touristy, don't you think?"

"I'm too new in town to care." Her eyes narrowed slightly and she whispered, "Don't turn around. The woman behind you is wearing a Steve shirt."

He laughed. "Ah, the price of fame."

"Are you sure it doesn't bother you? If she gets on the cable car with us, she's going to see you."

"If she grabs my shoulder and spins me around, she's going to see me, too." He gave the woman a brief, furtive glance. "Those shirts are really ugly. I can't believe people are paying eighteen bucks for them."

"If that shirt had Calvin Klein or Ralph Lauren on it, she'd have paid a lot more."

"Thanks for putting me in my place," he muttered, trying hard not to succumb to fresh laughter. Gwen looked as if she were also struggling against a laugh. Her nose twitched, her eyes grew filmy, and she lost the battle, convulsing in giggles just as the cable car clanged to announce its arrival at the turnaround.

A crowd of people descended from the vehicle, chattering, pointing out the sights, aiming their cameras and checking their watches. Steve pulled enough money for two fares from his wallet and they inched along the line. When they were no more than a couple of feet from the door, one of the disembarking passengers dashed over to him, bellowing, "Steve Chambliss! Millie, look! It's Steve Chambliss!"

He braced himself for the onslaught. The woman who had been standing behind him and Gwen in blissful ignorance suddenly comprehended whose back she'd been staring at and hurled herself at him. Several women who had been admiring the juggler at the corner raced over. The passengers waiting to board—at least twenty people, some with cameras—closed in on him so swiftly, pawing and pinching and chanting his name, that he had less than a second to grab Gwen's hand before he lost her in the mob.

He couldn't see her, but he could feel her slender fingers squeezing tight around his hand. Their cool, silky strength helped him regain his equanimity. "I'm sorry," he said politely to his swarming fans. "I'm sorry, I've got to—"

The crowd surged forward, shoving him toward the cable car. Someone poked a pen at him; someone else jabbed him with a piece of paper bearing a phone number. Someone shouted, "Show us your tools!" and several other members of the mob picked up the demand. "Show us your tools! Show us your tools!"

He clung to Gwen, hauled her to the steps and nudged her ahead of him into the car. The conductor wriggled around him and planted himself at the top of the steps, barring entry to the teeming hordes below. "Stand back, stand back!" he barked. "No more room! You'll have to wait till the next car." To Steve he whispered, "Go on back, forget the fare. Just go find a seat and we're outta here."

Steve guided Gwen down the aisle to a bench and they dropped wearily upon it. The other passengers stared openly at him, but given the conductor's stern protectiveness, no one dared to make a fuss over him.

An elderly woman with a large shopping bag and a small cane leaned toward him. "Excuse me—are you a rock-and-roll star?" she asked.

He smiled. "I'm afraid not." His smile grew less tense as the conductor clanged the bell and steered around the U-turn, leaving the crowd at the terminus and beginning the tracked ascent up the steep street.

Next to Steve, Gwen wilted. "That was scary."

"They were harmless."

"They would have gladly torn my arm from its socket if it would have brought them closer to you."

He looped his arm around her, wanting to reassure her. She rested her head on his shoulder, and he could feel a slight shiver ripple down her back. He would have liked to believe it was a shiver of desire, but he suspected it was simply a reaction to the near-riot he'd caused.

"These cable-car rides aren't usually so frantic," he told her. "And they're usually a lot more crowded. You're not getting an authentic experience."

"It'll do for now." Abruptly she sat straighter. "Look at that!" she gasped as a cable car passed them going down the hill.

At first Steve wasn't sure what had prompted her shock. Then he saw it: on the tail end of the cable car, the advertising placard bore a flagrantly sexy model wearing a Steve T-shirt, along with the words: "If you'd been watching 'The Gwen Talbot Show' on San Francisco's Channel 9, you would have seen his tools!" Below it was the logo for the station that carried Gwen's show.

Steve watched the billboard vanish down the hill. "This is getting a little weird," he said.

Gwen looked guilt-stricken. "It's all my fault, isn't it."

He leaned back slightly so he could view her. Her eyes were round, shimmering, and she looked as uncertain as she had when she'd shown up at his door an hour ago. "Do you hear me complaining?" he reassured her. "I'm planning to retire to Tahiti on the royalties from that T-shirt. And it would never have happened without you."

"It would never have happened if you'd kept your shirt on in the first place," she said, then blushed a luscious pink and averted her eyes.

It took him a minute to grasp what she was talking about: the time he'd stripped off his shirt in her apartment when he'd been working on her bedroom door. But it had been so stultifyingly hot in the flat that morning, and he'd thought no one would see him, and . . .

"Really?" he asked, intrigued. "My naked chest was what got me on your show?"

"Of course not." She studied the delicate crisscrossed leather of her sandals, as if unable to look at him. "If that was all it was, I would have asked you to take off your shirt on the air."

"But if I'd left my shirt on in your apartment, you wouldn't have had me on your show," he pressed her.

"I don't know." She seemed extremely uncomfortable, shifting away from him on the bench. "You were good-looking. We wanted a good-looking carpenter."

"Seems like half of San Francisco wants a good-looking carpenter."

"Well, I hope you like being viewed as a sex object."

"It has its pluses." One of which was watching Gwen squirm whenever the discussion flirted with the topic of sex. "I don't suppose *you* view me as a sex object, do you?"

"No," she said too quickly.

He didn't believe her. He doubted she believed herself. Just to be sure they were united in their disbelief, he arched his arm around her once more, pulled her back to him and settled his mouth over hers for a deep, hot, unmistakably sex-object-like kiss.

Chapter Ten

She heard bells. The world shimmied and shook. If she
hadn't been so totally caught up in Steve's kiss, she would
have remembered she was scaling the steep incline of
Mason Street in a cable car, while the conductor of which
clanged a warning chime at every intersection.

But she *was* totally caught up in Steve's kiss, in the heat
of his mouth, the aggression of his tongue, the envelop-
ing pleasure of his embrace. He wasn't a sex object, no.
A sex *subject,* perhaps. A sexual, sensual man.

She could do nothing but kiss him back, meeting the
pressure of his lips and matching the thrusts of his
tongue. She nestled within his arms and felt the warmth
of her own desire blossoming inside her. That other people shared the cable car with her was irrelevant. That
anyone standing along the sidewalks could view the torrid moment through the windows and the open sides of
the car, that gossip columnists and tabloid TV reporters
could blare headlines about Gwen's sex life, that Steve
had several times proclaimed himself to be the wrong
man for her...

When he kissed her, none of that seemed to matter.

As if from a great distance, she heard the voice of the
elderly woman seated across the aisle, muttering, "He *is*

a rock-and-roll star, isn't he. Only a rock-and-roll star would behave like that in public."

Steve's laughter caused his lips to vibrate against Gwen's. Laughing as well, she hid her face against his shoulder. "Better cool it, Elvis," she whispered.

His arms relented around her, becoming less possessive, more comforting. He raveled his fingers into her ponytail, separating the strands of hair. "You ought to be grateful I kept my shirt on, at least," he taunted gently.

In truth, she wasn't grateful. She wanted his shirt off. She wanted *her* shirt off. She wanted things she shouldn't want, things that were only going to bring her heartbreak down the road.

"I could..." She broke off nervously.

He inched back and gazed into her eyes. "You could what?"

She swallowed, then found the guts to say, "I could fix us something to eat at my place."

He continued to study her face, reading the subtext of her statement, understanding what she was offering. "After tasting those home-baked cookies of yours, I'll eat anything you can serve up," he murmured, his grin indicating that his words also carried more than one meaning.

As the cable car slowed to a stop at a corner, Steve stood, took her hand and hoisted her to her feet. He belatedly paid the conductor their fares and thanked him for rescuing them from the rampaging masses at Fisherman's Wharf. Then he propelled Gwen down the steps to the street.

Her feet had scarcely touched the pavement when a flock of women emerged from a health-food café across the street and darted into the traffic, causing cars and buses to slam on their brakes and honk their horns. "It's Steve Chambliss, the sexy carpenter!" one shouted, while another bellowed, "I love you, Steve! I love men who aren't the marrying type!"

Steve broke into a gallop, pulling Gwen along behind him. He ducked around the corner, spotted a taxi and dove for it, easily beating out a slow-moving gentleman who had lifted his hand to signal the driver. Steve pushed Gwen ahead of him onto the seat, jumped in and slammed the door. "Just drive," he said.

The cabbie glanced at Steve and Gwen in his rearview mirror. He saw a man and a woman, flushed and sputtering with laughter—and perhaps a dozen frenzied fans chasing the cab down the center of Sacramento Street, half of them wearing Steve T-shirts.

"Are you famous?" the driver asked.

"No," Steve lied, then gathered Gwen back into his arms. His lips brushed over hers, lazily, languidly.

"You'd better give him my address," she whispered before his kisses lulled her into blissful incoherence. "He's got the meter running."

Steve impatiently recited the address to the driver, then lowered his mouth to hers again. He half lifted her onto his lap, cradling her in his arms, running his hand up along her side, caressing. Rubbing and rubbing until it felt right—that was what he'd said on her show. He'd been talking about sandpaper and more, about sex and passion, about tools and skills. She felt her soul growing smooth beneath his practiced fingers, as smooth and soft as velvet. When his thumb skimmed the outer curve of her breast, she moaned softly.

Perhaps the cabbie was used to having couples necking in the back of his car, because he didn't say a word until they'd reached her street. In a way, Gwen wished he had been one of the loquacious hacks she usually got stuck with. If she'd had to listen to him expound on the ghastly state of the universe and the ghastlier state of his tips, she might not have found herself so gloriously lost in the sensations Steve was awakening within her. She might have cleared her mind enough to remember that he had no interest in settling down and getting married, that despite his college background he was about as far from an egghead as it was possible to be, that he was no more and no less than an incredibly virile carpenter looking for a good time.

But as long as she kept kissing him, as long as she remained wrapped in the dreamy passion of Steve's kisses, Gwen wanted nothing more than what he was—and what he was doing to her. She wanted a mindless, meaningless, irresistible night with a man who was all wrong for her. She would have plenty of time for regret when it was over. But if she didn't do this, if she didn't give in to it, she would spend the rest of her life wondering what she'd missed.

Steve sighed and slid his hand down to her waist. It took her a minute to realize the cab had stopped in front of her building. She extricated herself from his arms, hating to break from him but consoling herself with the knowledge that soon they would be inside, and he would be once again kissing away her ability to reason and act logically. Soon enough she would be returning to the passionate dream.

He paid the driver and assisted her out of the cab. Her legs felt shaky, her head light. Her hands trembled as she rummaged through her purse for her keys. Unable to find them, she panicked—not so much because she was upset about being locked out as because the longer it took to get inside, the greater the likelihood that she would come to her senses before she and Steve could finish what they'd begun.

He pulled her hand away from her purse, dug into his pocket and produced her keys. "You gave them to me so I could get into your garage earlier," he reminded her.

She smiled meekly, embarrassed that she'd been so swept away she hadn't even remembered what she'd done less than an hour ago. She wanted him to open the damned door as quickly as he could, so she could be swept up again.

Her wish came true, literally. The instant they were inside the building, he swooped her into his arms and carried her up the stairs. "You're going to break your back," she said, linking her hands at the nape of his neck and savoring the thick, dense hair that fell in soft waves below his collar.

"You seem to forget," he shot back, showing absolutely no strain, "that I'm a big, tough hombre. The sexiest carpenter in San Francisco. Carrying a hundred-pound *babe* is no sweat."

"I'm not a babe," she scolded. "And I weigh more than a hundred pounds."

"I must be even stronger than I thought." He lowered her to her feet outside her apartment door, unlocked it and handed her the keys. She preceded him into the foyer, then closed the door.

They stood facing each other in the amber light. The air was scented by the dense bouquet of white lilacs on the table, and by the salty sea aroma wafting in through her open windows. Steve's eyes reminded her of the sea, green and gray and full of life.

"Are you hungry?" she asked.

"Starving," he whispered, lifting her back into his arms and kissing her, feasting on her, devouring her. She sank against his chest as her entire body responded to the onslaught of his kiss. No other man's kisses had ever turned her on so thoroughly. No other man had ever made her so eager to abandon herself to him.

He carried her down the hall he'd painted to the door he'd repaired and across the threshold he'd rebuilt. Gwen reached around his shoulder to nudge the door shut. She smiled at the satisfying click of the latch sliding into place. "Doesn't that sound good?"

"Music to my ears," he murmured, skimming her jawline with his lips and then grazing the underside of her chin. He lowered her to her feet on the thick area rug beside her bed. His hands spanned her waist and tugged her blouse free from the waistband of her skirt.

He was going fast, and she was glad. She wanted his hands on her, her hands on him. She wanted their bodies to join as their mouths had—and *then* she wanted him to go slow, because carpenters didn't rush things. They took their time. They were lovers, not fighters.

Cool air whispered across her skin as he unfastened the buttons of her blouse and drew back the fabric. A deft flick of his thumb and her bra came undone. And then she felt his hands, his warm, leathery palms, his callused fingertips stroking, skimming, floating up her back and forward, under her arms and down to circle her breasts, cup them, knead them until her entire body was burning with the same hunger Steve had confessed to in the foyer.

She clawed at his shirt, desperate to touch him as he was touching her. She struggled with the buttons, and although her efforts seemed to amuse him he didn't help her. It took forever to get the shirt open, forever to reach inside and feel the sleek, hot skin of his chest, the flexing muscles along his rib cage, the taut surface of his abdomen. When her fingers teased along the edge of his trousers he gasped and pulled her closer, bringing his hands around to her back and down to her hips. He pressed her against himself, making her feel him, making her wild with desire.

"Ste-e-e-eve!" It came through the window, shrill and rude. "Steve Chambliss! We want your tools, Steve!"

"Oh, God." It was half a groan, half a laugh. His breath was shallow, rasping, and his hands continued to knead her bottom, guiding her against his aroused flesh.

Gwen rested her forehead against his chin and labored to breathe normally. "How did they find us here?"

"Who the hell knows? Maybe the cabbie cruised through the neighborhood, announcing our arrival."

"You told him you weren't famous."

"Maybe he recognized me, anyway. Maybe telling my fans I was here was his way of getting me back for lying to him."

"*St-e-e-e-e-eve!*" the voice from outside pierced the bedroom. "I want to be your sex slave!"

"Just what I've always dreamed of. My own personal sex slave."

Gwen wondered how close she'd come to fulfilling the job requirements for that particular position. But her ardor was cooling down enough that she probably wouldn't qualify. "I had you fix my bedroom door because I treasure my privacy," she complained. "Apparently, a door that closes isn't enough. This is ridiculous."

"You could close your windows."

"I like fresh air. And even if the windows are closed, I can hear noise from the street. Which usually doesn't bother me." She let out a weary breath, straightened up and glared at the window. "Maybe I should call the police."

"And tell them what? A woman is screeching like a cat in heat outside your apartment?"

"I like to have my windows open. I *don't* like to have cats in heat screeching at my guests."

Steve brushed his hands lightly over her breasts, but he couldn't seem to get back into the mood, either. Releasing her, he crossed to the window and peeked out. "Cripes. There are five of them out there."

"Isn't it ironic," Gwen muttered. "Here you are, the sexiest carpenter in San Francisco, and your fans are destroying your sex life."

He turned, and the smile he gave her was so enchanting her breath grew erratic again. "I'm not about to let them destroy it. Are you up for a ride?"

"They know where you live, too, Steve. If we leave, they'll just follow us there."

"I was thinking of a longer ride than that." He methodically buttoned his shirt, then crossed back to her and dropped a light kiss on her brow. "Go get your toothbrush. We're cutting out."

"Where are we going?" she asked, wary but curious. "A cheap motel?"

"A cabin in the mountains. You might want to bring a change of clothes, while you're at it. We could spend the whole weekend there if you want."

"A cabin in the mountains?" A fresh flicker of desire sparked to life inside her. It was almost too romantic—a cabin in the mountains, a whole weekend, Steve.

She'd gone unkissed and untouched by him long enough that a shred of sanity had taken hold inside her, demanding a hearing. "Where is this cabin? Whose is it? How will we get there?" *What if I fall in love with you? What if you walk away from me because I'm looking to settle down and you're not? What if I end up in a mil-*

lion pieces after this weekend at a cabin in the mountains with you?

"Go get your toothbrush," he said. His grin was so beautiful, so full of promise, she decided to worry about ending up in a million pieces some other time.

In five minutes she'd filled a tote with her toothbrush, her hairbrush, a pair of jeans and some fresh underwear. Steve looked depressingly dressed when she found him in the living room, spying on his loudmouth admirers from the corner of the window. But when he turned to Gwen, she saw the glint in his eyes, a flash of carnal pleasure that made her hope the cabin wasn't too far away.

"Would you mind if we took your car?" he asked. "I'm afraid if we drive off in the van those lunatics will follow us."

"We'll definitely take my car, then. But maybe you should drive. I don't know where we're going."

"Sure." He studied her for a moment, his longing practically tangible. "They're going to recognize us through the windshield."

"I could paint a mustache on you," she joked, and then decided it was actually a pretty good idea. "Come on. I'll use an eyebrow pencil—it'll wash off. And I've got an adjustable baseball cap somewhere—the Texas Rangers. I hope you don't mind..."

A few minutes later, they were in as complete a disguise as she could muster on short notice. Steve's hair was wet and slicked back under the cap, and she'd drawn a rather attractive shaggy mustache on him. She had removed her earrings, tied a scarf into a dramatic turban around her head and donned a pair of sunglasses with light-sensitive lenses. In the evening gloom, their lenses were almost clear enough to look like regular glasses.

"Gee," Steve said, inspecting his reflection in the mirror above Gwen's sink. "Maybe next year for Halloween, I'll trick-or-treat as a grown-up with a mustache."

"And I'll go as Isadora Duncan." Scribbling on his upper lip had been odd. Every time her fingers had touched his face, he'd sucked in his breath, fighting his response to her touch. Just seeing the tension in him, sensing it in his rigid posture and feeling an answering tension inside herself, had made her want to keep touching his lip, brushing it, rising on tiptoe and kissing him....

Wait till you get to the cabin, she'd told herself at the time. Either Steve's cabin would provide the perfect place for a tryst, or else the drive to the cabin would provide the perfect opportunity for her to rethink the entire idea of letting this tryst take place.

Incognito, they hurried down the stairs to the silver Acura parked in the garage. Gwen released the trunk and tossed in her tote, then handed her keys to Steve. There was something unnervingly domestic about granting him such frequent access to her keys. She remembered the first time he'd been to her apartment, when she'd left her front door unlocked for him. The man had an uncanny way of making her want to open up to him—her home, her car, herself.

He revved the engine and smiled at the powerful drone echoing off the concrete walls. "Nice wheels," he said as he backed out of the parking space. He pushed the button to open the garage door, and she pretended to be engrossed in her manicure as he drove past his fans. They were a motley assortment—young, old, varying heights and weights—but they looked uniformly silly in their Steve T-shirts. They glanced at the car, then turned back to the second-floor windows, hooting and whistling and calling for Steve.

"If I ever get sick of carpentry," Steve decided, shifting gears and leaving the noisy women behind, "I guess I can get a job in espionage. How can those ladies claim to love me when they don't even recognize me?"

"Do you actually expect a group of ninnies like that to exhibit any consciousness of the world around them?"

"Don't call my fans ninnies," Steve reproached, feigning indignation. "They obviously have great taste in men."

"Unless the men are sporting fake facial hair."

"All right, so they're ninnies," he conceded with a laugh.

They were heading toward the Bay Bridge. "Don't you need to pick up your own toothbrush?" she asked.

He shook his head. "I've got stuff at the cabin."

"Where is this cabin, anyway?"

"Tahoe."

"Lake Tahoe?" She sat up straighter. "I've never been there. I hear it's gorgeous."

"It is. I'll give you another grand tour tomorrow."

Not tonight, she thought. It would be too dark to tour the lake, the surrounding mountains.

Not tonight, because tonight Steve was going to make love to her.

The thought sent a frisson of sensation through her, part anticipation, part anxiety. She knew becoming intimate with Steve was a bad idea. He didn't love her, she couldn't let herself love him, and as delightful as a simple physical fling could be, she wasn't cut out for flings. This was definitely a bad idea.

Yet there was a certain inevitability to it. From the first time he'd shown up at her apartment and announced he was there for her bedroom, she had somehow known, in some secret, womanly part of herself, that one way or another she was going to wind up in bed with him.

Tonight's encounter reminded her of the tornadoes that used to rip through central Texas every now and then. They were bad, too, but they couldn't be avoided. When they came, they came. And when they were gone, you dusted yourself off, assessed the damage, gathered whatever was left and got on with your life.

She hoped the damage after this encounter wouldn't be too horrible. She hoped she would be able to get on with her life once the storm blew away.

"We've got a little more than a three-hour drive," he warned her as the twilight darkened around them. "We ought to stop somewhere to eat along the way."

Apparently he was hungry for more than just her. She herself was too keyed up to think about eating. "Whatever you want."

"We can stop around Sacramento. There are plenty of fast-food places near the highway." He glanced at her, then reached across the console and patted her knee. "Not exactly what I'd planned on when I asked you out for dinner, but in retrospect, I think we'd have had a hard time trying to dine out in any restaurant in San Francisco. We would have been mobbed."

"Your groupies would have crawled under the table to catch your crumbs," Gwen agreed. "I don't care about an elegant dinner. Fast food is fine." Actually, it wasn't what she'd planned on, either. But none of this evening was what she'd planned on. When she had shown up at Steve's door with the plate of cookies, what she'd planned on was to apologize for having avoided him all week, when it was her fault that his likeness had been turned into a public icon. Her show had stolen his privacy from him, and instead of taking responsibility for that, she'd been hiding from him.

And from herself. She'd been hiding from exactly what was happening right now: the sexual undertow that dragged her away from solid ground, that pulled her toward him no matter how hard she fought it or tried to rationalize it away. She'd been hiding from the fact that, no matter who Steve was or how ill-matched she and he were, she couldn't stop wanting him.

The rush hour traffic was thinning out. The dusk sky was painted with streaks of mauve and rose; palm and oak trees cast long shadows in the waning light. Gwen reran the entire evening through her mind: her arrival, Steve's apartment, his obvious pleasure at seeing her, his willingness to show her the city he called home. The scraps of information he'd told her about his family back East.

There was a great deal more she wanted to know about him, and she had a three-hour drive in which to learn it. Shifting in her seat, she studied him in the dim light. His makeup mustache was smeared, but the baseball cap suited him, even if it didn't match his spiffy clothing. He had opened his window a couple of inches, and the warm, dry air of the East Bay tugged at the fringe of hair protruding from the cap.

"Tell me about her," Gwen said.

He flicked a glance her way. "Who?"

"The woman who made you drink your beer from a glass."

He unbuttoned the cuffs of his shirt and rolled the sleeves up, one at a time, one hand always on the wheel. He opened his window the rest of the way, and rested his elbow on the sill. All the while, he contemplated her question, as if it were a multiple-choice quiz and he was reciting eeny-meeny-miny-moe to come up with an answer.

At last he ventured a reply. "Her name was Janet, and we broke up a year ago."

"Were you married?"

"Nope. It never got that far."

"Because you wouldn't drink beer from a glass?"

His smile was bittersweet. "I suppose, if everything else had worked out, I could have learned how to chug suds in a civilized manner. We talked about marriage a few times. For a while, it seemed that was the direction we were headed in."

"But . . . ?"

"But she wanted to change too many things about me."

Gwen couldn't think of anything she would want to change about Steve, other than his attitude toward marriage. But then, Janet must have known Steve a lot better than Gwen did.

"What did she want to change?"

Steve smiled wryly. "Welcome to 'The Gwen Talbot Show,'" he intoned. "Is this an interview?"

"No," she retorted. "It's a question." A question she was entitled to ask as someone who might well end the evening in bed with him, making love.

Evidently he heard the sharp edge in her tone, because he stopped needling her and provided a straight answer. "She wanted me to be more of an executive type. She wanted me to dress like this—" he gestured toward his tailored trousers "—and drive a car like this." He waved around him at Gwen's Acura. "She used to introduce me to her friends either as a construction engineer or the president of Chambliss Carpentry, as if I were a corporate officer or something. That's not my style." He fell silent for a while. "She was smart, and funny, and we were great in bed together. I thought we had a shot, but . . . I don't like being introduced to people as the president of a carpentry company. I'm a carpenter."

Gwen couldn't care less whether he thought of himself as an executive or a tradesman. What she cared about was his pride, his fierce determination to buck all the pressures placed on him by the people he was closest to, and to be true to himself. It took her full supply of willpower not to cover his hand with hers, not to lean across the gear stick and press a kiss to his lips, even at the risk of getting eyebrow pencil smeared across her mouth. It took her entire reserve of self-preservation not to declare that she was in love with him.

But she kept her mouth shut, neither speaking nor kissing. Steve wasn't in love with her. He probably thought she was smart and funny and . . . well, as far as great in bed, he'd have to judge for himself. In any case, he wasn't going to change his opinion about marriage for her. And she couldn't hope to change his opinion without losing whatever she had with him. He'd been candid about not wanting a woman to change him.

Which left her in limbo, halfway between the seduction that hadn't happened in her San Francisco co-op and the seduction that might happen in his cabin near Lake Tahoe. She had no commitment from him, could never ask for a commitment from him, and wanted him, anyway. She was caught in the eerie stillness that settled over the earth just before a tornado struck, aware that the storm might leave devastation in its wake yet wishing she could feel the fear and exhilaration and sheer aliveness the tornado would bring.

She knew it would happen. She had no choice but to settle back in her seat and wait for it to come.

Chapter Eleven

Somewhere east of Sacramento they stopped for burgers and fries. At a convenience store just down the road from the fast-food place on the frontage road, Steve purchased a quart of milk, a loaf of whole-wheat bread and a few oranges, so they would be all set for breakfast. He filled the tank with gasoline. And then they headed into the night.

The silence in the car gave Gwen too much time to think. She turned on the radio, but the deejay's chatter grated on her, and she turned it off. She hadn't had the foresight to stash any CDs in her tote when she'd left San Francisco.

She fidgeted with her purse, shifted in her seat, eyed the illuminated dashboard. "You're nervous," Steve guessed.

"A little."

He didn't appear the least bit nervous. He had scrubbed off his mustache in the rest room at the hamburger joint, and he'd tossed the baseball cap into the back seat of the car. His hair had dried in the balmy breeze that gusted through his open window; the thick, tawny locks flew back from his face, throwing his profile into relief in the reflected glow of the headlights.

"Second thoughts?"

She smiled. "I'm up to about fifteenth thoughts. I keep trying not to think, but I can't seem to help it."

"Gwen." He took her hand, drew it to his knee and tucked it protectively beneath his own hand. She felt the hard contours of his thigh against her knuckles. "There's something pretty incredible going on between us. You know that as well as I do. I'd be lying if I said I knew exactly what it was or where it's taking us, but it's there."

"Yes." Her voice emerged as barely a whisper.

"It's been there all along. And I don't think it's going to go away on its own."

"I don't know about that. Maybe if we just ignore it..."

"We just ignored it all week. And look at us now."

She looked at him. She desired him. She desired him even more than before, because in addition to being the sexiest carpenter in San Francisco, he was amazingly honest. As far as Gwen was concerned, honesty in a man was an aphrodisiac.

"This cabin I'm taking you to," he said, "has four bedrooms."

"Four?"

"So if you want your own room—not that I'd vote for that, but if you're really uncomfortable about the whole thing, we can work something out."

"Four?" She'd thought he was bringing her to a rustic one-room dwelling, a place where people stashed their skis when they were ready to head down to the casinos on the Nevada side of the lake. "Four bedrooms? What is it, a mansion?"

He laughed. "It's big, but it's hardly fancy."

The house she'd grown up in, in an affluent suburb of Denver, had been charmingly middle class—and it had only had three bedrooms. "It must have cost you a bundle."

"Actually, no, it didn't."

She frowned. "It isn't yours, is it."

"It's twenty-five percent mine. Three friends and I own it together."

"Oh." She figured it was one of those time-share vacation homes—although even at that, the size boggled her mind. "Are your friends going to be there tonight?"

"Not a chance. Tripp lives outside Chicago, Deke lives down in Atlanta, and Ki is all over the place. They use the cabin when they can, and we try to get together there for some down-and-dirty poker once a year or so, but they don't tend to drop in on the spur of the moment. I'm the lucky one who lives within driving distance. Then again, I'm the unlucky one who gets to fix everything in it that needs repairing."

"So you use it more than the others do?"

He shrugged. "We all use it. Deke is a millionaire, so he can jet anywhere he wants. Ki travels a lot in his work—he's a writer, always doing research on the road—so I imagine he squeezes in visits whenever he can work in a detour through the Sierra. As for Tripp, the cabin was originally in his family. They used to be rich, so they built it big. And when Tripp couldn't scrape together the money for taxes on the place, we all chipped in."

"You bought a share of the cabin for one quarter of the property tax? What a deal!"

"We're really good friends," Steve explained. "It was more than just that we didn't want Tripp to have to sell the place. We're like brothers. We wanted to do it for him, he wanted to do it for us—" a faint smile traced Steve's mouth "—and maybe we'd all had one too many beers when we drew up the contract. But it's worked out well, so far.''

"How do you know these men? How did you happen to become friends with a millionaire from Atlanta?"

"We went to college together. All four of us." His smile grew playful. "And I'll tell you right now, Gwen, there's not an egghead among us."

"That I can believe," she muttered, although she was also smiling.

At around ten o'clock, they arrived at the cabin, a sprawling two-story A-frame on a private road that cut a winding path through the mountains. Even though the crescent of moon shed little light, Gwen could see the fir forest looming on either side of the road. She could smell the clean pine scent. The cabin was nestled in a small clearing, massive and inviting and—she couldn't deny it—terribly romantic.

No other cars were parked near the house. Apparently, as Steve had promised, they would have the entire place to themselves.

She climbed out of the car and inhaled the crisp mountain air. A few stars stabbed the night sky, glinting high above the spires of the fir trees surrounding the cabin. Circling it was a broad deck with a hot tub built into it; a second deck overlooked the evergreen forest from upstairs. As far as cabins went, this one was rather elaborate.

Steve carried the groceries, Gwen, her tote, as they crunched up the unpaved walk to the front door. Steve unlocked it, reached around the doorframe for a light switch, and then beckoned Gwen inside.

The interior lacked the closed, stuffy atmosphere of a building that hadn't been used in some time. The furniture might have been in need of dusting, but no more so than the furniture in Steve's apartment in San Francisco. The main room was dominated by a massive fieldstone fireplace; on the floor in front of it lay a white bearskin rug.

"Oh, Lord!" She erupted in laughter. "A bearskin rug. You and your buddies must have spent your college years reading girlie magazines."

"We put that there as a joke," Steve confessed as he headed through a doorway into the kitchen, turning on lights as he went. "We felt it made a statement."

"A very trite statement about the male libido." Turning her back on the awful rug, Gwen gazed around the room. The furniture was old but sturdy, the tables scuffed and the upholstery faded. It had a comfortable, lived-in look, making another statement about the four bachelor owners of the cabin.

Steve continued on into the kitchen with the groceries, and Gwen followed. The kitchen was also unglamorous but functional, with the requisite appliances and a few telltale coffee stains on the counter by the sink. Steve opened the refrigerator to assess the food supply, and Gwen offered her assistance in emptying out the bag: the milk, the bread, the oranges...

And a box of condoms.

Steve glanced over his shoulder and saw what she was holding. "Those don't need to be refrigerated," he said, reaching around her to take the box, then pulling her into a hug. He rested his chin on the crown of her head and closed his arms around her. "You're angry with me," he half asked.

"No." She wasn't, really. Just...uneasy. His having bought contraceptives seemed so premeditated. There was nothing wrong with that, of course; this entire trip had a certain premeditated aspect to it. Steve's assurances about the abundance of bedrooms didn't nullify the fact that they both knew why they had driven all this way. "No," she repeated, wishing she could convince herself. "I'm not angry."

"But you'd be happier if I hadn't tossed those into the bag at the store."

She tried to laugh off her nervousness. "Actually, I would have thought that four randy bachelors in a cabin like this would have plenty of protection lying around, without having to buy more."

"Sure. We go through millions of those things every week. I figured I'd better stock up, just in case. Better safe than sorry."

She hated herself for taking everything so seriously. She wished she could simply accept that, as he'd said, something incredible existed between them, and ignoring it wasn't going to make it go away. She might as well enjoy it for what it was. A weekend of fun or a tornado of cruelly destructive force—either way, she ought to face it head on.

She would start by facing Steve head on. Turning in his arms, she peered up into his strong, luminous eyes. "Steve, I'm sorry I'm acting like such a drip."

"A drip? Is that what you were acting like?"

"What do you think I'm acting like?"

He rested his hands on her shoulders and scrutinized her face, mulling over his reply. "I think you're acting like a woman who doesn't take sex lightly."

"You do take it lightly, don't you." It sounded mo[re] like an accusation than a question.

He considered her charge, then shook his head[and] grinned sheepishly. "It's going to destroy my [reputa]tion, but no. I don't."

"But you do wish I'd stop getting so uptigh[t"]

He slid his hands toward her neck, extending his thumbs along her chin and tilting her face higher. "I wish you would trust me. And yourself," he murmured, then lowered his mouth to hers.

His kiss wasn't fierce or demanding, but instead was so lush and sweet and seductive that it had the effect of making up her mind for her. She would love Steve this weekend, and let him love her, and pay the price when the bill came due.

His room was upstairs, under a sloping ceiling, with a window that captured what little moonlight there was and layered the room with silver. His bed was broad and old, with a maple headboard and a sagging mattress. Before he drew her down onto the bed, he opened the window to fill the air with the fresh fragrance of the mountains.

He returned to her, his hands purposeful, his lips warm and lingering. He kissed her mouth, her eyelids, the tip of her nose. He released the barrette that held her hair and kissed the nape of her neck. He opened her blouse and kissed her bare shoulders, opened her bra and kissed her naked breasts.

They didn't speak. Speaking was too close to thinking, and Gwen was beyond that, now, beyond anything but the moment, the passion building between them. She tore at his shirt, reached for the buckle of his belt and ___ienced a keen twinge of arousal as he grabbed her ___essed it lower, against his fly, so she could ___ her. His mouth came down hard on ___ by a need that was just as sweet ___ enous way.

___ e way, dropped to the floor, ___ Steve and Gwen tumbled down ___ ir legs entangled, their bodies ___ hands across the strong width of his shoulders, the smoothly muscled planes of his back. He ran his fingers over her breasts, squeezing, teasing, stimulating her nipples until they hurt and then soothing them with gentle flicks of his tongue. His hand rode the swell of her hip and slid down the outer surface of her thigh to her knee, bending it, easing her legs apart so he could slide back up along the inside.

A shaky sigh escaped her as he brushed his fingertips against her, and another as he pressed deeper, discovering her heat and dampness. He entered her with his finger, and she cried out, her hips arching, her soul already on fire as he nudged her knees farther apart and rose above her. She filled her hands with him, stroked him, tightened her fingers around him and reveled in his shuddering groan. And then he pulled her hands away, braced himself above her and thrust, deep and hard.

They were a perfect match, their bodies latching, sealing each other and locking out the rest of the universe. He moved and she moaned. She rose to him and he gasped. They rocked each other, clung to each other, kissed each other, abandoned themselves to each other until nothing was left but sensation, explosion, the wild, wondrous rapture of two lovers meeting and merging and melting into ecstasy.

For a long time afterward Gwen didn't move. She lay still, her eyes closed, her arms closed around Steve's strong body, and savored the weakening ripples of bliss that washed through her, undulating from her scalp to her toes and then back to the very center of her consciousness. She was aware of Steve's weight, his breath floating across her temple, his fingers languorously twining through her hair.

"Hey," he finally whispered. "Are you alive?"

"More or less." She smiled and opened her eyes. "I think that qualifies as my very first California earthquake."

In the faint light she could just barely make out his grin, the glint of his straight white teeth, the crinkling skin at the outer corners of his eyes. With obvious reluctance, he lifted himself off her and eased onto his side. "Now, down to business. Would you like me to set up one of the other bedrooms for you?"

She pretended to punch him. He caught her fist and kissed her knuckles, then laughed. "You can go sleep on that stupid bearskin rug," she grumbled.

He brushed a lock of hair back from her cheek, then leaned forward and kissed her. "I've got news for you, *babe.* Neither of us is leaving this bed tonight."

"Is that so?"

"Yes. That's so." He ran his hand through her hair again, weaving his fingers into the disheveled strands.

"Not even if we hear a group of Lake Tahoe women shrieking through the window that they want to be your sex slaves?"

He chuckled and rolled his eyes. "God forbid."

"I'll tell you, Steve—after what just happened here, I think I've got the right to put up some new billboards in San Francisco saying, It's True—He *Is* the Sexiest Carpenter."

"It ain't the carpenter, it's the tools," he joked, then kissed her again. His smile faded a bit when he said, "It wasn't the tools, either. It was *us,* Gwen. The two of us together. You know that, don't you?"

What she knew was that she'd never felt anything near as intense with any other man. She would have liked to believe she'd contributed something to the overwhelming pleasure of their lovemaking, but she knew herself.

She knew what her past encounters had been like—and they'd been nothing like this.

"It was you, Steve. I'm not . . . I'm not all that experienced. All I did was lie there, and—"

"Transmutation. Isn't that one of those egghead words?"

"Transmutation?"

"Or regeneration . . . *Catalysis*. Maybe that's the right term."

"Catalysis?"

"Two organisms acting upon each other, coming together and transforming each other. It's a mutual process, a two-way street."

"Well." His seriousness took her aback. She decided to inject a little humor, before her thoughts veered off in a dangerous direction and she acknowledged how deeply in love she'd fallen. "I don't know if we're organisms, but we certainly did come together."

He smiled at her joke and kissed her knuckles again. "The point being, this is one of those times when the sum is greater than the parts." He let his free hand drift down through her hair to her back, along her spine to her bottom, where he molded his palm to the rounded flesh. "You turn me on like a switch," he murmured. "It's like electricity. You just press the button and I'm on."

"Like a power tool."

"A zillion volts," he whispered, rolling onto his back and lifting her onto him, arranging her legs around his hips. He moved his hands from her thighs to her belly, then higher to her breasts, cupping and warming them, and then gliding up to her shoulders and pulling her down for a steamy kiss. "I'd take you to the hot tub," he said, moving his hands to her back and down again, to her hips. "But power tools in water are too hazardous. We'd probably kill ourselves."

"The bed is fine," she said in a surprisingly thick tone. Less than a minute ago, it seemed, she was laughing and sparring with him. Now, all of a sudden, she was seething with reawakened yearning. She felt him between her thighs, as aroused as she was. His hands tightened on her hips, moving her slowly, sensuously against him, rubbing her in a rhythm she couldn't resist. She writhed, throbbed, ached, with an emptiness only he could fill.

And then he filled her, surged inside her, ignited her. Her last coherent thought, before her body surrendered to the storm, was *catalysis*.

IT WAS BETTER than he could fathom, better than he'd ever known sex could be.

Sure, the cabin had its stud trappings—the bearskin rug, the hot tub, the breathtaking views—anything a man might believe he needed to put a woman in the mood. But Steve was in the sexiest place in the entire house, and everything he needed, everything he believed, was right there with him. He was in his bed, in Gwen's arms, in her body, and he couldn't imagine wanting to be anywhere else, ever again.

She had collapsed on top of him, her body a graceful tangle of silken skin, soft flesh and angular bones. She was hot where he was still inside her, wet, pulsing around him in receding tremors. He knew some women were able to have multiple orgasms, but Gwen seemed to be aiming for a record.

As for men, he thought they were supposed to peak in a single, splendid shot. But it was different with her. He seemed to go on and on and on.

She was obviously exhausted. So was he. Yet remaining inside her, feeling her muscles flexing around him, made him hard again. "Hang on," he whispered, rotating with her until she was under him.

She looked utterly, gloriously wanton in the pale moonlight. "I can't," she moaned, shaking her head and closing her eyes.

Disregarding her weary protest, he began to move again, slowly because he lacked the energy to go fast. Each time he plunged into her he got harder; each time, she rose a little higher, absorbed a little more of him. Her eyes fluttered open and she shook her head again.

"Just stay with me," he pleaded, feeling his strength return bit by bit.

She opened her mouth to object, but he silenced her with a kiss. Her tongue chased his into his mouth, and he felt even stronger. Her fingernails scraped the skin of his back, her body bucked off the mattress and her breasts crushed against his chest. "Steve—"

"Shh." He lifted her legs around his waist and thrust deeper, quicker, until she was sighing and digging her fingers into his shoulders. Still he wanted more of her, all of her. He wanted her with a greed he hadn't known he was capable of.

He reached under her and rose onto his knees. She settled in his lap, her head pressed to his shoulder and her arms tight around him. His body surged upward, straining, striving to break free.

She cried out, her release liberating him. He soared through the fires of hell and into heaven, clinging to her as she quivered around him. He felt dampness on his skin—sweat or maybe her tears as she buried her face in the hollow of his neck. His legs were incredibly sore, his muscles fatigued, but he would never let her go, never.

"No," she murmured, her voice muffled and breathless.

"No?" He sounded just as breathless.

"In answer to your earlier question, no, I'm not alive. I died happy, though."

He wanted to share in her humor, but somehow he couldn't bring himself to. Something about making love with her frightened him. He had never gotten into drugs, but he imagined that the most dangerous must be something like this, making a person feel so unspeakably wonderful, he became instantly, incurably addicted.

Steve was addicted to Gwen. He didn't love her; he *couldn't* love her. She was looking for a husband—an intellectual one at that. Steve couldn't think of anything further from what he was than intellectual husband material.

And yet . . .

And yet he simply couldn't imagine ever letting her go.

Chapter Twelve

They made breakfast side by side, Gwen slicing the oranges while Steve toasted the bread and located an unopened jar of strawberry jam in one of the cabinets. The blended aromas of citrus and fresh-brewed coffee filled the air.

It was all alarmingly homey—not just the appetizing breakfast smells, not just the easy efficiency with which Gwen and Steve moved around the kitchen and each other, but the way they'd awakened in each other's arms, drowsy and warm and smiling, as if to wake up together was the most natural thing in the world. Gwen wouldn't mind waking up to Steve every morning.

But that happily-ever-after scenario wasn't possible. Not with him.

He piled their breakfast onto a tray and carried it outside to the deck. Passing through the living room, which was bathed in morning light, Gwen got a better look at the fireplace, the worn, well-used furniture and that ridiculous bearskin rug. Once she'd joined Steve outside on the deck, she got an eyeful not just of the thick, verdant forest surrounding the cabin but of the hot tub.

She wanted to think of Steve only the way he'd been last night: demanding yet generous. Macho yet tender.

Caught up in his own pleasure yet never for an instant losing sight of hers.

In the sharp, glaring sunlight, however, she could no longer believe in the magic that had overcome her last night. She knew that the man seated beside her on the deck, clad in a pair of jeans torn at the knee, and an old Beckett College T-shirt and beat-up canvas sneakers, was the very same man who had appeared on her television show and announced to everyone within the sound of his voice that he had no interest whatsoever in getting married, because marriage meant allowing a woman to change him. If Gwen wanted to convince him he was wrong about that, she would have to change his mind—and in changing his mind, she would only prove that he'd been right.

She stared at the hot tub, which was covered with a tarp, and imagined it bubbling and steamy, occupied by a harem of scantily clad bimbos, there for the entertainment of the four bachelors who owned the cabin. She could divine no place for herself in the scene she visualized, no safe haven for a woman who wanted to settle down, to create a home with someone, a family, a lifelong, committed relationship.

"Four bachelors," she murmured, unable to erase the bawdy vision from her mind.

"Hmm?"

She turned to him, shifting her chair so she wouldn't have to view the tub anymore. "I'm just contemplating the idea of you and your three bachelor buddies sharing this place."

"And?"

"And the picture I see has an overabundance of testosterone in it."

Chuckling, he popped a corner of toast into his mouth and licked the jam from his fingers. Then, propping his feet up on the deck railing, he leaned back in his chair and cradled his mug of coffee in his strong hands. "We try to keep the testosterone at a manageable level."

"No orgies?"

"Not within recent memory." She must have looked vexed, because he emphasized, this time solemnly, "No. No orgies."

"So it's just four guys and a case of beer?"

"Throw in a deck of cards and some fishing poles, and you've pretty much got it."

"In other words, you don't bring all your lady friends here to seduce them." She'd intended to sound flippant. But to her chagrin, she heard a catch in her voice. She wondered if Steve had heard it, too.

If he did, he was polite enough not to comment on it. "Are you asking me for an itemized history of my sex life?"

"No." She honestly didn't want to know about his past.

"Not an egghead among them," he remarked, smiling genially.

She knew he was trying to lighten her mood. She also knew that his attempt was doomed. This wasn't about the women he used to date, or the men she used to date. It was about Steve and Gwen and her unshakable conviction that, no matter how gorgeous a hunk he was, how amiable a companion, how tender a lover, when all was said and done he was an overgrown boy who liked to hang out with his unmarried chums, surrounded by bearskin rugs and hot tubs and all the other accoutrements of playboy living.

"It's none of my business," she mumbled, regretting that she'd started this conversation even though she knew it was necessary if she was ever going to straighten out her head about Steve.

"The truth is," he said, "Tripp, Ki, Deke and I were never into bringing women here. We all saw this cabin as a place for hanging out, doing guy things, just being ourselves and not having to worry about making a good impression on anyone of the female persuasion. It was almost like a club in a tree house, with a sign on the door that said No Girls Allowed." He smiled at a private memory. "The four of us even swore a solemn oath never to get married."

"A solemn oath?" Perhaps she shouldn't have been surprised that Steve's closest friends would be men as marriage-phobic as he was.

"We were maybe nineteen or twenty at the time. One of us had gotten trashed by a girl—I don't even remember which of us it was. Anyway, we stocked up on beer, and when we were really swimming in the suds, we made a pact that none of us would ever get married because women were more trouble than they were worth."

"How lovely," she said dryly.

"We were kids. What did we know?"

Not much less than you know now, she thought with a sudden, searing bitterness. For God's sake! She didn't want to sit in the bracing sunshine of a Sierra morning with an allegedly grown man who had reached the conclusion over a dozen years ago that women were more trouble than they were worth. She had just spent the past night sharing the most profound intimacies with Steve, exposed and vulnerable and helpless to do anything but love him—and here he was, just hours later, bantering with her about how he and his pals had sworn not to take women seriously.

She knew he was joking...yet a seriousness underlined his humor. He had sworn an oath. Women weren't worth it.

"Take me home," she said abruptly.

Steve bolted upright, his feet hitting the deck with a resounding thump, his smile disappearing and a shadow falling across his face. Beneath his furrowed brow his eyes burned, green and silver, churning with astonishment and anger and confusion. Gwen recalled her ruminations about tornadoes and braced herself for the one that seemed about to touch down between her and Steve.

"You didn't just say what I thought you said, did you?" His voice was low and taut.

"What I said was, take me home. I want to go back to San Francisco."

"Why?"

Because I'm in love with you, and you're never going to be what I need you to be. Because I gave you my heart last night, and you're too foolish to know what to do with it. Because sooner or later you're going to run away from me, and I see no reason to delay the inevitable.

"Gwen—"

"Please." She pushed herself to her feet and stared at her half-full mug of coffee. She didn't want to discuss anything; she didn't want to argue with him. She didn't want to consider the possibility that she was overreacting. Her intuition had warned her all along that Steve was the wrong man for her. It was already too late to protect herself from the anguish of loving and losing him, but she could still take steps to protect her sanity. "Let's just go."

Before he could say another word, she fled into the house.

A BREEZE RUSTLED through the forest, causing the fir needles to tremble. Cotton-ball clouds drifted across the sky. Far in the distance a hawk glided in graceful loops above the treetops.

The magnificence of the scenery made no impression on Steve. The tranquillity of the Sierra morning escaped him. He was in shock.

What the hell was that all about?

What had he done wrong?

What was he going to do now?

One thing he knew: it was easier to fix a warped doorframe than it was to make sense of a woman. Especially when he couldn't find the cracks in his relationship with Gwen, the damaged joints, the splintering seams.

Sighing, he rose and went inside, determined to figure out what had gone so drastically awry between him and Gwen. Their lovemaking had been spectacular. That morning, everything had been smooth between them, warm, affectionate. Peaceful, but with an underlying comprehension that last night had been magnificent, that the desire that bound them together was big and powerful and immeasurably exciting. Steve had planned to drive her down to the lake after breakfast, maybe take her out in a boat, buy her lunch at one of the hotels, show her a casino, and then return to the cabin, to bed, to each other. He had assumed things were just fine between them.

Obviously he'd assumed wrong. He reviewed everything they'd been talking about, and tried to pinpoint precisely what had triggered her unexpected snit. That nonsense about the pact he, Ki, Tripp and Deke had made so many years ago? That had been a laugh, a goof, nothing to take seriously. If she'd wanted to take anything seriously, why not last night? Why not take seriously what happened when he kissed her, when he touched her, when his body found hers and fused with it? If anything was serious, it was the awesome passion that held them in its thrall.

Her coffee mug was in the kitchen, but she wasn't. He left the tray on the counter by the sink and headed up the stairs, where he found her in his bedroom, gathering her few things into her tote.

He wanted to cross the room and pull her into his arms, to kiss her until she succumbed to reason, or yearning, or whatever would vanquish her sudden animosity. But if he closed in on her she might feel threatened, and if he touched her she might scream. So he lounged in the doorway, effectively blocking her escape even though he left her plenty of space to move around the room.

"What's going on?" he asked when she didn't acknowledge his presence after several minutes.

She folded her skirt, decided she'd done a bad job of it, shook it out and folded it again. "Don't make me say it."

"Say what?"

After all that meticulous folding, she jammed the skirt into her bag and lifted her face defiantly to him. "You're a terrific guy, Steve. You're amazing. I think..." She faltered for a moment, averted her eyes and blinked a few times. "It doesn't matter what I think," she continued, sounding less defiant. "What matters is that we both know this isn't going to work out in the long run. So I think—" she swallowed to still the tremor in her voice "—we should just quit while we're ahead. Okay?"

No, he wanted to object. Maybe she was ready to quit. He wasn't.

But if she was, what was the point in fighting her? If she was convinced that whatever was going on between them wasn't going to work out, who was he to try to persuade her otherwise?

She gripped the tote in one fisted hand, slid the strap of her purse onto her other shoulder and glowered at him. He felt like an hourglass, all the sand draining out of him, leaving him hollow and spent.

His gut told him she had everything all mixed up, but his brain told him she could, in fact, have it perfectly straight. If the long run meant marriage and accommodation, compromise and diminishing freedom, he didn't want the long run any more than she did. Just because they were phenomenal in bed together didn't mean he wanted to turn his life inside out for her. He liked things the way they were. He didn't want anything to change.

Maybe he ought to thank her for saying what needed to be said, and doing what needed to be done.

Still, a heavy sense of loss weighed on him as he collected his wallet and keys from the dresser, as he grabbed the trousers and shirt he'd worn last night and stalked out of the room. In the kitchen, he rinsed the mugs and turned off the coffeemaker. He emerged to find Gwen waiting for him by the front door.

It was going to be a long, horrible drive back to San Francisco. And no matter how grateful he should be, how relieved that Gwen had committed euthanasia on their affair so it wouldn't die a lingering, painful death, how pleased that nothing in his life was going to have to change, he couldn't shake off the icy desolation that filled him when he thought about never having Gwen in his arms again.

THE LIGHT ON HIS answering machine was flashing like a strobe when he let himself into his San Francisco apartment, carrying a thick stack of mail and nursing his wounded pride. He tossed the mail onto the coffee table and punched the message button on his machine.

Beep: "Hello, this is Candy Rasmussen from *Bay Area Magazine,* calling for your comments on the gossip that you and TV talk queen Gwen Talbot are an item. Please call me at..."

Beep: "Alexandra Hoover from "Society Profiles" here. My spies have spotted you and the host of "The Gwen Talbot Show" carousing around town. Any truth to the rumor? My number is..."

Beep: "Hi, my name is Lynnette, and I want to make you happy. Call me at..."

He rewound the tape without listening to the rest of the messages. He remembered the first time he'd gone to Gwen's apartment. Her phone hadn't stopped ringing. At the time, he'd thought the constant phone calls were due to her having just moved into a new place, but maybe they had also been a measure of her fame. Maybe any blip on the celebrity radar screen resulted in a life sentence of incessant telephone calls.

He resolved to contact the phone company and have his number changed.

Trudging to the kitchen, he noticed the plate of cookies Gwen had baked for him. His first impulse was to throw them away. His second was to savor them, one at a time, pretending each cookie was a piece of her, each chocolate chip a kiss from her. But then, once he'd eaten the last cookie, he would feel even more bereft than he already did.

Saying goodbye to her in the garage of her apartment had been bad enough. Parking her Acura and crossing the cold concrete floor to his van, watching her hover by the garage door switch so she could close it behind him... That was the worst. Seeing her face in his rearview mirror as he exited onto the short driveway, and then watching the motorized door slide down, cutting her off from him...

A few pungent curses filled his mouth. He vented them, and then another couple for good measure. The hell with the long run. Why couldn't he and Gwen have enjoyed the short run while it lasted?

He grabbed a beer, popped off the bottle cap and took a long swig. If he drank enough, maybe he would rediscover that brainless bliss he'd enjoyed so many years ago, when he and his buddies had sworn themselves to eternal bachelorhood. It would take a lot of beer to numb his mind that thoroughly, but Steve had no plans, no place to go, nothing to do but hang around the apartment and mope. He might as well mope drunkenly.

He returned to the living room, rummaged through his mail and discovered most of the envelopes contained fan letters, which he wasn't in the mood to read. Flopping onto the sofa, he clicked on the television. When he lifted the remote control, he accidentally hit the VCR button, and Gwen materialized on the TV screen.

The last thing he'd been watching before she had appeared on his doorstep with that plate of homemade cookies was the tape of her Friday show, the one with the actress hawking her costume jewelry designs. In a fit of masochism, Steve let the tape keep running, although he muted the sound. He didn't want to hear the actress's boring lecture on accessorizing. All he wanted was to see Gwen.

He saw her...and felt her hands on him, felt her body surrounding him. He saw her hair and felt it brushing against his shoulders, snagging on his overnight growth of beard. He saw her body, modestly clothed on the show but naked in his mind, all satin skin and womanly curves. If he turned the sound back on he would hear her voice and remember the way she'd sighed, the way she'd moaned, the way she'd cried out in joyful surrender when she came.

His phone rang. He ignored it. After the fourth ring the answering machine clicked on. He heard his own taped voice inviting the caller to leave a message, and then the beep.

"Steve? It's Marjorie Bunting. I'm sorry to bother you on a weekend, but I'm desperate. I'll be at the studio until around four. After that, you can reach me at home—I think you've got my number there. Please call me as soon as you can. I've got a real crisis on my hands."

What a coincidence, he thought sourly. *I've got a real crisis in my life.*

Still, Marjorie wasn't a gossip columnist or a pea-brained nymphet. Before she could hang up, he lifted the phone from the cradle. "I'm here, Marjorie," he said, keeping all traces of emotion out of his voice. "What's your crisis?"

"Oh, Steve—thank God I've reached you. It's Frank Trivelli. He's had a heart attack."

Steve assumed that by heart attack, she meant a physical ailment, not the gnawing pain he was feeling in the metaphorical region of his heart. He sat up straighter, aware that he ought to be saddened by Marjorie's news, even though it took him several minutes to remember that Frank Trivelli was the foreman of the construction crew building the set for the wedding show.

"A heart attack," he murmured. "That's too bad. How is he?"

"He's going to be fine. The doctors expect him to make a full recovery. But in the meantime, he's going to miss a few weeks of work."

"Uh-huh."

"The thing is, Steve, Inez's wedding is next week, and the set isn't finished yet. We need that set completed by Friday morning."

Steve thought he had exhausted his supply of curses, but he discovered a few more inside him. Marjorie didn't have to elaborate; he knew what she was asking of him. He also knew that he couldn't go to the studio and oversee the last few days of set construction without running the risk of crossing Gwen's path. He might be masochistic enough to want to watch her on television, but he wasn't sure he was willing to take a chance on bumping into her.

"That could be a problem for me," he hedged. "My schedule is jam-packed."

"Whatever anyone's paying you, I'll pay double. We'll work around your schedule. I can have the crew here nights if need be. Steve, we've got to have that set ready to roll by 10:00 a.m. Friday."

"Can't Inez get married on Gwen's usual set?"

"No, she can't. For one thing, we need the larger audience space. For another, we need the larger stage—she's got attendants, ushers, the minister. And this is her dream wedding. You've met her, Steve. Are you prepared to tell her she can't have her dream wedding?"

"Well, I—"

"And finally, we've got ratings to think of. Gwen's been hyping the wedding show for weeks. The station's been talking it up on the evening news because Inez is their meteorologist. Every evening at 6:20, before she broadcasts her weather report, the anchorman does a countdown. On Monday evening's news he's going to say, 'Four more days till Inez ties the knot.' It's big, Steve, and we need to have *that* set in *that* studio.''

"I've already vetted the blueprint," he reminded her. "Someone else can oversee the final construction."

"No one knows the set the way you do, Steve. Come on," Marjorie wheedled. "It's Frank Trivelli's deathbed wish—"

"You just told me he was going to be fine."

"Well, just in case he takes a turn for the worse. Would you want it on your head that you refused to fulfill someone's dying wish?"

Steve understood that the wish was Marjorie's, not Trivelli's—and the temptation to land Marjorie on her deathbed brought a mirthless smile to his lips.

But he knew he would have to say yes. Not for Trivelli, not for Inez, not for Marjorie, and certainly not for Gwen. He would have to say yes because as a professional he was responsible for the project, obligated to see it through to its completion.

"All right," he yielded, feeling that gnawing pain settle deeper into him, spreading from his heart to his soul, leaden and icy. "You want me to make sure the thing gets done? I'll help you out."

"I love you, Steve," Marjorie gushed. "If you ever grow tired of all your fans, let me know. I'll dump my husband and run off to Acapulco with you."

Steve did her the favor of laughing, then promised to stop by the studio Monday morning to gauge exactly what needed to be done. After accepting her copious thanks, he said goodbye and hung up.

Monday morning. That would give him the rest of Saturday and all day Sunday to drink himself into oblivion. Or to go out and amuse himself with Lynnette and all the other groupies who wanted to make him happy, no strings attached.

Or to figure out what in God's name had transformed Gwen from the most eager, responsive, satisfying woman he'd ever slept with, the most electrifying, the most *catalyzing,* most beautiful, tantalizing, resplendent lover in the solar system . . . what had turned her from all of that into a cold fish.

But first, he was going to finish his beer, turn the VCR back on and eat some cookies. And then maybe have another beer.

THE LILACS IN HER FOYER had shriveled overnight; instead of fragile white drops, the petals were grayish brown, the branches shedding them across the table like dirty snow.

It must be a sign, Gwen thought glumly. A sign of death, dryness, discontent.

The messages on her answering machine droned on: Reporters seeking confirmation that she and Steve Chambliss, the studliest carpenter in San Francisco, were a couple. Inez, hoping Gwen had marked Thursday evening for their final "girls' night out" before the wedding. Marjorie, calling from the office with the shocking news that Frank Trivelli had been stricken with a heart attack. "But don't worry," Marjorie had said. "The doctors say he's going to pull through. And as far as getting the wedding set finished, I'll take care of everything."

It wasn't like Marjorie to reassure Gwen. Marjorie was always the one to panic, and Gwen considered it part of her job to reassure her producer. Perhaps Marjorie had a sixth sense about these things, though—perhaps she knew Gwen's lilacs had died and she was in no condition to cheer anyone up.

She trudged down the hall to her bedroom, trying to ignore the subtle twinges and mysterious aches in her muscles and joints, souvenirs of the previous night's physical activity. Her stiff neck was more likely a result of how rigidly she'd sat during the long, quiet drive back from Lake Tahoe. Her headache was no doubt a symptom of stress, and her heartache...

She reached for her bedside phone and dialed Marjorie's number. "It's Gwen," she identified herself. "What hospital was Frank Trivelli admitted to? I'd like to send him flowers." She pictured the desiccated lilacs in her foyer and grimaced.

"I already sent some from all of us. And he's going to be fine."

"What about the set?"

"Not to worry. Your favorite carpenter is going to make sure the work gets done."

He's no favorite of mine, Gwen wanted to retort. He was just a little boy in a gorgeous man's body, a funny, sexy, devil-may-care devil. Mr. Wrong.

"By the way, Gwen, what's going on with you two? I've been fielding calls from the media all morning. Tell me everything."

"There's nothing to tell," Gwen muttered. "He heard I'd never taken a cable car ride, so he took me on a cable car. A couple of people saw us and made a fuss." *They saw us kissing. They saw Steve enter my building with me, and never leave. And we drove far, far away and made love all night, and now there's nothing to tell.*

A drop of moisture hit the night table, and she realized it was a tear. How absolutely humiliating, to let a big, brawny hunk like Steve break her heart. She was used to weeping over National Merit Scholars, not working-class heroes with long screws.

"Well, sorry if it causes you any grief," Marjorie said, sounding not the least bit contrite, "but my answers to all the press people were deliberately ambiguous. These rumors are going to do wonders for your ratings."

"My ratings!" Gwen grabbed a tissue, mopped her damp eyes and replaced self-pity with healthy indignation. "How could you lie to them? There's nothing going on between me and Steve Chambliss."

"But you went on a cable car together, didn't you?"

"There was a sweet gray-haired grandmother on the cable car, too. Why don't you drop some ambiguous hints about my relationship with her?"

"Gwen, I'm only thinking of giving your ratings a goose."

"Who gives a damn about my ratings?"

"I do," Marjorie snapped. "And so should you."

Ordinarily, Gwen gave a damn. But at that moment, all she gave a damn about was that Steve couldn't be a little more responsible, a little more ready to make a commitment. All she gave a damn about was that if only he loved her enough, he would be willing to change for her.

And the one thing he never wanted to do was change for a woman.

"Listen, Marjorie, I've got to go. Do me a favor, please, and don't give any more ambiguous answers when it comes to my personal life, okay? If anyone asks, just tell them it's none of their business. And thanks for sending the flowers to Frank."

Marjorie must have sensed defeat in Gwen's tone, because she retreated, as well. "No problem. I'm sure we'll have an update on his progress Monday morning."

"Okay. I'll see you Monday," Gwen said, then hung up the phone. She was no longer crying, no longer angry. What she was, she decided, was miserable.

She hoisted herself off her bed and glanced out the window. No one was camped near her building, neither groupies nor press people. Maybe everyone would leave her alone. Maybe they'd all gather across town at Steve's place, where they could harass him with Gwen's blessings.

He didn't want to change? Fine. Let him be his own free self, surrounded by gossipmongers and shrieking fans, his moves monitored and his face plastered across every cable car in town. Let him be hassled, badgered, madly adored by the entire city of San Francisco.

Gwen, meanwhile, would buy some new flowers for her foyer, and get on with her life.

Chapter Thirteen

She arrived at the studio at seven-fifteen Monday morning, hoping to avoid Steve. She knew he would be in the building at some point during the day to touch base with the crew constructing the wedding set, but she wanted to get upstairs without seeing him.

Thus, she was exasperated to find herself emerging from the elevator at the second floor, where the studio for Inez's wedding was located. Gwen had no reason to be there; even if people happened to be working on the set so early in the morning, they certainly didn't need her input. Yet she couldn't seem to stop herself from wandering down the hall, smiling and nodding at a few of the technicians from the overnight staff who were heading in the opposite direction, anxious to get home after eight hours of broadcasting colorized old movies and infomercials.

When she saw the door to the studio up ahead, her heart raced. She felt like a dieter compelled to stroll past a bakery for the thrill of inhaling the fresh-baked smells of forbidden cakes and pies. She assured herself that this was merely a test of her willpower—she could walk right past the studio without looking inside. And even if she couldn't, Steve wouldn't be there yet. It was much too early.

Nearing the studio, she heard a rapping noise through the open door, a hard, steady, echoing rhythm. Someone was hammering nails inside. She hesitated.

The real test of the dieter, she reminded herself, was not to flee from the bakery but to saunter past it as if it didn't matter. And anyway, the hammer wielder was probably just one of the crew members on loan from the theater on Geary Street. They came and went at odd hours, working their TV studio jobs around their theater jobs. No chance Steve would be the one working on the set.

At that hour, he would just be waking up. He would be stumbling through his cluttered living room to his kitchen in search of coffee. Or maybe he'd be stumbling over the shoes of an adoring fan who'd spent the night in his bed. He had so many fans, and they were universally willing, and none of them seemed inclined to make demands on him. None of them wanted to change a thing about him. They thought the sexiest carpenter in San Francisco was perfect just the way he was.

This was not a productive line of thought. Gwen fought off the one-two punch of jealousy and bitterness, squared her shoulders and marched toward the open door. Why be frightened of whoever was hammering nails on the set? If Steve had a groupie in his bed, surely he'd still be under the covers with her, not here slapping a set together.

Her gait slowed slightly as she neared the doorway. She sucked in her breath, then took another step. And another, smaller one that placed her in the open doorway—where her vision was filled with the sight of the sexiest carpenter himself.

He was kneeling on the mock-up of the Golden Gate Bridge, dressed in his standard T-shirt, jeans and tool belt, his right hand gripping a hammer, his left hand setting up a nail. Two more nails protruded from his clenched mouth.

Her first impulse was to shout at him that storing nails in his mouth was an unsafe practice. Her second was to race down the aisle, wrap her arms around his waist, press her cheek to the strong arch of his back and tell him that like his air-head groupies, she was available to him on his terms, no questions asked, no demands made.

Her third impulse was to run for her life.

She stifled them all. To make herself less conspicuous, she stepped back into the hall and angled her head so she could spy on him as he worked. Alone on the stage, his work space illuminated by a single overhead spotlight, he was utterly focused on his task, almost possessed. He propped a nail and whacked it into place, then plucked a nail from his mouth, propped it and whacked it. His right arm moved in a fierce arc, his biceps bulging and flexing. He looked nowhere but at the bridge he was building.

Given the force of his swing, he should have been able to drive each nail into the wood with a single blow. Yet he pounded the nails three, four, five times, smashing them flush with far too much vigor. No one should have that much energy so early in the morning.

Having used up his mouth's supply of nails, he stood and strode to the edge of the stage, where he scooped a handful of nails from a box. Then back to the bridge, where he whammed and slammed them into the boards as if they were his enemies and he was battling them to the death.

Was he as frustrated as Gwen? As upset? Had he spent last night, as she had, hating the wretched emptiness of his bed and hugging a pillow to ward off loneliness? Or had he spent it raining curses upon her soul?

Or—the idea refused to leave her—had he spent it in the lustful company of a fan?

If he had, she reminded herself once more, he wouldn't be smashing the nails into the wood the way he was. He'd be too tired.

His strength awed her. His single-mindedness unnerved her. The powerful breadth of his shoulders made her loathe her self-protectiveness, her faith in forever-after and her inability to set aside her dreams and goals and live for the moment.

He ran through his resupply of nails, working at a relentless pace, as if he intended to complete the entire set that morning before any of his crew showed up. Because he was too intent on his work to notice her, she drifted back into the doorway and watched him, mesmerized by the smooth athleticism of his movements, the sinewy power in his arms, the flexibility of his legs and spine as he bent and twisted and aimed his hammer.

After he'd pounded the last nail into place, he stood and stretched, rolling his shoulders in circles, rocking his head from side to side. For the first time, she got a clear view of his face in the light.

He looked dreadful.

He looked handsome, of course. But fatigued, his eyes framed in gray, his forehead scored with frown lines, his chin darkened with a stubble of beard. His hair was luxuriant with honey-colored highlights in the bright overhead lamp, but it was mussed, the part crooked and the long, thick locks tossed haphazardly back from his brow.

He yawned, stretched again, and froze as his gaze came to rest on her.

She wasn't going to turn and run the way she had the last time she'd glimpsed him working in the studio. Her heart began to beat too fast, pounding with as much force as his hammer had pounded on the nails. Biting her lip and struggling to maintain her composure, she entered the studio.

Without taking his eyes from her, Steve lowered his hammer onto a nearby piece of scaffolding, leapt down from the stage and started up the center aisle as she started down it. They met halfway, surrounded by theater seats and swarming shadows, both instinctively halting when there was still a buffer of a few feet between them. She noticed the vein in his neck move as he swallowed. His eyes were bloodshot, his lips turned down at the corners. He seemed uncomfortable, and she realized he wasn't happy to see her.

"I didn't expect anyone to be here so early," she said when she couldn't stand the silence any longer.

"I had to come early," he explained. "I had to sneak out of my house before the sun came up."

"Why?"

"It's been crazy." He glanced away from her and scrubbed a hand through his hair, messing it even more. "I had to unplug my phone while I was home. I had to disconnect my lobby intercom. Yesterday, when I went out to pick up the paper and some bagels, I was mobbed."

"The Steve Chambliss fan club?"

"They've been multiplying like rabbits, Gwen. There must have been a hundred of them outside my building yesterday. It was awful."

She envisioned him, big, strong and indomitable, being chased down the street by a riotous gang of giddy women. The picture made her laugh.

"It's not funny," he snapped. "I've asked the phone company to change my number. If that doesn't work, I'm going to have to move."

"Give it some time, Steve. This too shall pass. Your fans will get tired of you and find someone else to bother."

"I can't wait. You should have seen them, Gwen—all those T-shirts, all those women screaming, 'We want your tools!' And asking..." He drifted off.

"Asking what?"

He turned his gaze back to her. She was nearly staggered by the emotion in his eyes—longing, disappointment, sorrow. "Asking about us."

"You mean, you and me?" It hurt too much to think of her and Steve as *us*.

He nodded. "Are you okay?" he asked, his tone oddly husky.

"Okay?" No, she was devastated. She was disconsolate. She wanted him—only on her terms, not his. She was a woman in love with the wrong man. How in God's name could she possibly be okay? "I'm fine," she lied.

He cupped his hand around her cheek, and for an insane moment she hoped he would kiss her. He only stroked his fingertips against the hair at her temple, and let his thumb trace the edge of her chin. "I've been going over it again and again, and I still don't know what happened Saturday morning."

An arrow of rage pierced her. How could he not know? It was so obvious. "You're smart, Chambliss. Use your brain."

"My brain tells me..." His voice remained as muted as hers was sharp. "We were perfect together."

"For now," she retorted, despising him for making her spell it out. "For today. But not for tomorrow."

A sad smile twisted his lips. "This is California, Gwen. Tomorrow we could all be killed by an earthquake."

"If that's the way you want to live, fine. I certainly don't want to change your philosophy of life. I don't want to change anything about you."

He sighed and let his hand drop. "The way I want to live my life is..." Another crooked smile. "I want to go back to the way things were before."

Before he'd gotten famous and had a hundred fans lying in ambush outside his apartment. Before he'd met Gwen.

Or before Saturday morning, when she'd decided to listen to her head instead of her heart.

He lifted his arm as if he wanted to touch her again, then thought better of it and shoved his hands into his pockets. "I just—" he struggled to find the words "—I'm trying to use my brain, Gwen. I guess I'm just not as smart as those eggheads you love, because I can't figure out what I did to make you so angry with me. It's been driving me nuts. I tried drinking. I tried taking a walk—and I almost got stampeded by the boob troop. I lay in bed all night Saturday, and all night Sunday, and went over everything we did together, everything we said. And I guess I'm stupid, because I just can't figure out what it was that set you off. It isn't about earthquakes, Gwen. It's about us. Tell me."

She realized that he wasn't used to speaking his heart so openly, or conceding failure so readily. His candor moved her. His eyes beseeched her. His smile twisted her spirit, wringing it as if it were a wet cloth, and the wetness filled her eyes.

She blinked furiously, batting the dampness away. "I can't tell you, Steve," she whispered. "If I tell you, you'll hate me."

"If you *don't* tell me, you won't exactly be number one on my list."

She sighed, blinked again, and stared into the light on the stage behind Steve. If she told him the truth, she would lose him. But if she didn't tell him the truth, he was already lost to her. Because she loved him, she owed it to him to tell. The outcome would be the same either way.

"I know how you feel about women who try to change you," she said, her voice steady despite the lump in her throat and the frantic thrumming of her heart. "I don't want to be just one more woman who tries to change you. But what I want from you would mean you'd have to change."

He stood motionless, absorbing her words. She had dared to hope he would laugh, swing her in his arms and insist that he would be willing to change anything and everything for her—his name, his party affiliation, his hair color, anything. Not that she wanted to change much. Just one tiny little thing: his attitude toward marriage.

But he didn't grab her, didn't smile, didn't shake his head at how silly her worries had been. Which meant they weren't silly.

"You want me to wear neckties and drive a sedan," he muttered.

"No! Of course not."

His gaze grew harder, his expression sterner. The tendons in his wrists stood out as his hands fisted in his pockets. "You want me to be a respectable pencil-pusher. You want me to call myself a company president—"

"Not only do I not give a damn what you call yourself or what you do with your pencils, but I wouldn't even care if you drank beer up your nose with a straw. I'm not your last girlfriend, Steve. I'm not a snob."

"Then what do you want to change about me?"

Tears welled up once more, overflowed and streaked down her cheeks. "I want to get married. I want children, a family. I want to be more important to you than your bachelor buddies." Her voice broke, but she'd gone too far to stop. "You don't fit the bill, Steve. You appeared on my show and announced to the world that you're not that type. And there's a slew of women in San Francisco who are looking for exactly your type. So why waste your time with me?"

It was a rhetorical question, yet she knew the answer. What he wanted with her was what they'd had Friday night, that passion, that soul-deep union, that seamless connection. She wanted that, too. But she wanted more, much more. More than he could give.

It was torture putting her pain into words. She couldn't bear the added grief of listening to him tell her he would never be able to place his love for her ahead of his comfortable bachelor life, never be able to build a relationship with a woman as solid as the bridge he'd just finished constructing on the stage, never be able to make her dreams come true.

Before she would have to hear him match her truth for truth, she spun around and bolted from the studio.

HE CONSIDERED CHASING HER. He considered accusing her of being the lousiest interviewer he'd ever seen, hurling words at her subject and then refusing to let him speak for himself. Weren't proper talk-show hosts supposed to pose a few questions and then get out of the way so their guests could sound off?

But if he chased her, if he sounded off, what would he say? That she was wrong, that he was ready to give up his life of footloose, carefree independence for her?

He had only just met her, for God's sake. And she was right—the city was apparently overrun with women willing to satisfy his every fantasy while asking for nothing in return.

But how many of those women would ever speak to him as honestly as Gwen did? How many of them would challenge him the way she did?

Hell, he had enough challenges in his life, keeping his business profitable, performing his work not just to the customer's satisfaction but to his own exacting standards, finding the time to unwind, to escape to Tahoe for a weekend. He didn't need the challenge Gwen was offering—especially since meeting that challenge would entail changing his perspective on a few things.

Like women, and commitment, and why a life without Gwen Talbot in it seemed like a life without purpose or direction or joy.

He returned to the stage, disturbed by his thoughts and the mournful silence left in the wake of Gwen's departure. Slamming nails into wood wasn't the cathartic exercise he'd hoped it would be. Building things felt like a feeble substitution for building a relationship.

If only he could give her everything she asked for without having to change for her.

He worked until the set builders showed up, then outlined for them everything that had to be completed that day if they were to remain on schedule. By tomorrow the last board and nail had to be in place and the painting begun. He would stop at the studio on Wednesday to check up on the set's progress. Thursday, the flowers would be delivered and the electrical cables taped down, and Friday the wedding would take place.

He designated one of the guys to manage the construction, then packed up his tools and left. He hadn't even haggled a contract with Marjorie for the extra few days of work. Money wasn't the issue here. This was about giving Gwen's friend the wedding of her dreams—something he couldn't give Gwen.

Distracted by his thoughts, he didn't notice the swarm of women outside the studio building's main entrance. The receptionist mumbled something that sounded like, "Good luck!" as he stormed through the security door into the vestibule, and then he swung open the outer door.

They descended upon him like the birds in the Hitchcock horror film, shrieking, pinching, pecking at him. Legions of females, old, young, skinny, fat and everything in between. Hands reached for him, tugged at him, caught in his hair. "Steve! Steve Chambliss!" they screamed. "We love your tools!"

He staggered under the assault. He knew they didn't mean to hurt him—they loved him, after all. Or at least they loved his tools.

Flattening himself against the concrete wall of the building, he tried to ward them off, but although he was bigger than most of them there were a hell of a lot more of them than there was of him. One aggressive middle-aged woman flung her arms around his neck and gave him a noisy buss on the cheek. An equally aggressive young woman lifted her Steve T-shirt and displayed her breasts for him. "I showed you my tools!" she flirted. "Now let's see yours!"

He reflexively grabbed his belt. These ladies were deranged. He wouldn't put it past them to try to pull off his jeans.

Prying their clinging, clutching hands from his body, stumbling over their clambering feet, he fought his way back to the door and inside. The receptionist must have been watching, because she was holding the inner door open for him. As soon as he was inside, she and he leaned against it together, and she twisted the lock into place.

"I'll call security," she said.

Sinking against the wall, Steve nodded. He lacked the breath to speak.

The receptionist spoke into her phone, then filled a paper cup with water from the cooler and carried the drink to him. "They're maniacs, aren't they."

"Yeah."

"Did they hurt you?"

"Nah." He had a few surface scratches on his arm, his shirt was completely untucked and his cheek was wet where that woman had kissed him, but other than that he was essentially intact.

"Lipstick," the receptionist said, plucking a tissue from the box on her desk and handing it to him.

He wiped the stickiness from his cheek and groaned. He could think of only one woman in the world he wanted kissing him, and it wasn't that crazed stranger on the sidewalk outside.

A security guard arrived, glanced through the window and shook his head. "How did you get here? Bus?" he asked.

Steve shook his head. "I drove my van over. It's parked at the public lot on the corner."

"I'll drive you down there. Follow me."

Steve gratefully accompanied the guard to the elevator and down to the basement. The man's crisp blue uniform comforted Steve, as did the walkie-talkie hooked onto his belt. It wasn't a gun, but it was where a gun would be if the guard were armed. Steve figured that if they got waylaid on the way to the parking lot, they could call for help even if they couldn't shoot their way through the crowd.

In the basement garage, the guard led Steve to a nondescript white sedan. "Why don't you lie down in back?" the guard suggested. "I'll drive you around the corner."

"I really appreciate this," Steve mumbled, climbing into the back seat and ducking below the window level.

"It's the least the station can do," the guard said. "They've been using your mug in all their billboard ads. You're bringing them revenues, you know? Ratings and revenues."

Steve cursed, something he'd been doing with great frequency lately. "When I agreed to appear on that show—"

"'The Gwen Talbot Show,'" the guard said reverently as he adjusted the rearview mirror and then started the engine. "That Ms. Talbot sure is something, isn't she? I wouldn't mind having a hundred broads like her chasing me down the street."

Steve peered over the seat. The guard was old enough to be Gwen's father. It didn't sit right with Steve that an older man should be speaking about Gwen that way. "Gwen wouldn't chase anybody down the street," he argued. "And she isn't a broad."

"You're right about that. She's as slim as a cover girl. A bit short, but man, what a body on her."

It took all Steve's willpower not to vault across the seat and bloody the guard's nose. He reminded himself that his life was in the guard's hands as they cruised slowly out of the garage. For his own safety, Steve had to keep his temper under control. But really, the nerve of the guy, talking about Gwen like that!

Of course, she *did* have a body on her, a body that could do incredible things to a man. Change him, for instance. Change the way he saw things, the way he felt, the way he thought about love.

Through the windows he heard a muffled babble of female voices as the guard drove past the throng. The noise abated slightly, then swelled again as the car reached the corner. "They're all over the parking lot, too," the guard reported to Steve.

He didn't bother to sit up. "My van says Chambliss Carpentry. Can you see it in there?"

"Nope. I'll bet it's over there, where all those women are jumping up and down.

"They're probably stripping it for parts," Steve grumbled.

"Like locusts," the guard confirmed. "You want me to keep driving?"

"You'd better. If I get out here, they'll strip me, too." He gave the driver the address of his office, then pulled himself into a slouching position so he could glimpse the mob scene as they drove past.

The situation at the Daly City line was no better. Nearing his office, he saw a crowd of women, two police cars with their blue lights flashing, and Karen standing on the flatbed of a pickup truck, holding what appeared to be a press conference. After using the Lord's name in vain and apologizing for it, Steve asked the guard to drive him home.

Evidently, the fan club had assumed he wouldn't be home during work hours on a weekday morning. Other than the daily message hanging on a sheet across the street from his building—today it said Let Me Recharge Your Power Drill—he saw no indications that he would be risking life and limb by getting out of the guard's car and sneaking into his building. He thanked the guard, dashed upstairs to his apartment and locked himself inside.

The world had obviously gone mad. He could have his choice of hundreds, maybe thousands, of women. Babes, wenches, hussies, or the unwed daughters of those dimple-faced mamas who made a habit of stuffing telephone numbers into his pockets. He could have any of them, all of them—and he didn't want them.

All he wanted was Gwen.

His answering machine was blinking, but he ignored it. The phone started ringing, but he ignored it, too. He headed straight for the kitchen, pulled a bottle of beer from the refrigerator and removed a glass from the cabinet above the sink.

It was too early to be drinking beer, but he didn't open the bottle because he was thirsty or looking for a buzz. This was an experiment.

Gwen had never asked him to drink beer from a glass. As she'd said, she wasn't Janet. She had never asked him to make the superficial, hypocritical changes Janet had demanded.

No, the change Gwen wanted him to make was real, fundamental, life-threatening. But before Steve could contemplate that, he had to see if he could handle the most trivial change.

He poured the beer into the glass, let the head settle and took a sip. It wasn't quite the same as drinking straight from the bottle. But it wasn't lethal, either. He could survive. He could do this.

Leaving the glass on the counter, he returned to the living room, where his phone had stopped ringing. He wondered when the phone company was going to change his number. As long as his phone was still working, though, he ought to call Karen—assuming she wasn't still holding forth in front of that rabid audience down at Chambliss Carpentry's headquarters—and let her know where he was.

But first, he had to grow up.

He telephoned Marjorie Bunting at the studio. "I need five minutes on Gwen's show," he told her. "Can you give me that?"

MARJORIE HERSELF PICKED Steve up the next morning. He'd put on his one nice blazer, a tailored shirt and a colorful necktie. His hair was neatly brushed, his cheeks clean-shaven and his stomach tied in more knots than were listed in the *Boy Scout Handbook*. He felt like a street punk who'd been washed up and groomed so he'd look respectable in criminal court.

"Are you sure you want to do this?" Marjorie asked.

He donned a pair of dark sunglasses and shoved his hair straight back from his forehead. "I have to do it. I can't live this way anymore."

As Marjorie steered along his building's driveway, he gazed down the street. Three young women had camped out on the sidewalk outside his building overnight. In front of their sleeping bags stood a metal bucket, with a sign above it reading Help Us Buy Steve Chambliss Some Screws. He wondered how much money they'd collected.

"We can't have you on the set," Marjorie informed him, cruising past the girls and turning the corner. "Gwen's guests are acrobats from a visiting Russian circus, and we've got mats and a trapeze set up in the studio. So what we're going to do is put you in another studio and do a remote."

"Whatever." He adjusted the shoulders of his blazer and fussed with his tie. He could have gone on the air dressed in his usual work clothes, but the idea behind this was that he didn't want his fans to view him as Steve Chambliss, the sexy carpenter. He wanted them to view him as Steve Chambliss, the mature private citizen.

It was probably just as well he wouldn't be in the studio with Gwen. If he saw her, up close and personal, he would touch her the way he'd touched her yesterday, a quiet, tender caress, because he would be unable to keep his hands to himself. And because he wouldn't be able to control himself, he would move from quiet, tender caresses to sexy, erotic caresses. He would embarrass himself with confessions about how he would do anything, change anything, be anything she needed him to be, if it would bring her to his bed once more.

He'd be much safer in a separate studio, addressing his comments to a camera.

"Have you prepared a speech?" Marjorie asked.

"A few words."

"We can give you three minutes. Will you need longer?"

"Probably less. I don't have much to say."

"I hope you can be polite about this, Steve," Marjorie cautioned him. "I don't want to put you on the air and have you say you want your fans to drop dead. They're our audience."

"I know. I'll be polite." He stared out the window.

"Give me a preview. How are you going to approach this?"

He sighed. "I'm going to say that I want to be left alone. Celebrity was fun, but I'm not looking for orgy partners. I want to be able to drive my van to job sites, and do my work and live my life without interference."

Marjorie assessed his speech and nodded. "That sounds about right. I hope it helps."

"Maybe once they stop chasing me all over town, the idiots will have more time to watch TV."

"Anything that improves our ratings is fine with me," Marjorie declared.

Driving down the block where the studio was located, they passed a small gathering of women near the front door—a much smaller group than yesterday's army. Apparently word hadn't gotten out that Steve was going to be at the building today. In his natty business attire and sunglasses, he was practically unrecognizable to the hangers-on, who no doubt expected him to look like the ludicrous picture of him that was printed on their T-shirts.

Once Marjorie had parked inside the employee garage, Steve felt one or two of the knots in his abdomen unravel. He was still tense, though. He was still aware, as he'd been through a long day of thought and a long night of restless meditation, that the existence he'd known before he'd met Gwen was no longer available to him. No matter what happened, no matter whether his on-the-air speech brought him the desired result, he would never be able to go back to the way things used to be.

"This way." Marjorie led him from the elevator down a hall to a small room furnished as luxuriously as a holding cell. A folding metal chair stood near one of the pale gray walls. A fluorescent ceiling light glared. A camera man in a Steve T-shirt and jeans, a headset arching from ear to ear, was setting up an elaborate videocam on a wheeled tripod. A small monitor sat on a shelf in one corner.

"Okay," Marjorie said, nudging Steve into the chair. She checked her watch. "We're going to start taping Gwen's show in about fifteen minutes. We'll have the opening titles, some introductory chitchat, and then she'll introduce you. When the light goes on on this camera, you're on the air. Try not to look at the monitor while you're on or you'll get self-conscious. Do you want me to have a makeup person come in and powder your nose?"

"No." There was a limit to how much change he could take. Cosmetics were way over the line.

She asked the cameraman for a peek, and he stepped aside and let her inspect Steve's image in the camera viewfinder. Nodding, she straightened up and smiled. "I'm really sorry you've had such a rough time of it," she said. "Yesterday the parking lot owner at the corner had to call the police because as long as your van was there, the women refused to leave. I understand it got pretty loony."

"I heard." He'd had to take a cab across town at midnight to fetch his van from the lot—and he'd had to pay a small fortune before the owner would release the vehicle.

"This was all supposed to be fun," Marjorie said.

"It *was* fun," he admitted. "But after a while...things got serious." Lots of things had gotten serious, he reflected. Including himself.

"Well, we'll always be in your debt. Here we were thinking Inez's wedding was going to be our coming-out party in San Francisco, but it turned out your show did the trick instead."

Steve nodded vaguely. He was no longer listening to Marjorie. The single black eye of the camera stared at him, and he stared back, wondering what words were going to emerge once he had his chance to speak.

The cameraman murmured to Marjorie that he was being signaled to get everything ready. "All right, then. I'd better go to the studio," she said. "Give it your best shot, Steve. I hope it works."

So do I, he thought, managing a tenuous smile for Marjorie and then turning his focus back to the camera. On the other side of that lens, on the other end of the cables and cords, was Gwen. The woman who loved him so much she wouldn't ask him to change.

The cameraman beamed at him, one of those big, brawny smiles designed to put people at ease. It didn't help Steve. He adjusted the knot of his tie again, raked his hand through his hair and watched the camera.

The theme music for Gwen's show spilled through the monitor, and then Gwen appeared on the small screen, cheerful and animated, her hair a beautiful jumble of curls yet her eyes curiously sad. "Hi!" she chirped as the audience applause died down. "Boy, this show is jumping—literally! Today we've got a few acrobats from the Moscow circus, which is visiting San Francisco this week. Let me tell you, I've seen these folks rehearse and they're not only fearless, they're *bone*less. When you see what they can do, you'll agree they must have rubber bands where you and I have skeletons. We've got some very special entertainment coming up. And later this week . . . well, you've all heard me mention it plenty enough, but I'm going to tell you again: we'll be hosting the wedding of meteorologist Inez LaPorta and restaurant mogul Tom Blanchard. That's Friday's show. Please join us!"

The audience burst into fresh applause.

"And now," Gwen said, subduing them with a wave of her hand, "before we meet these marvelous aerial artists from Russia, I'd like to turn things over to a former guest of mine. I'm sure you all remember him. His name is Stephen Chambliss, and he appeared on a show we did a while back about sexy professions for men."

The audience whistled and clapped. Steve watched the monitor, ignoring their outburst and concentrating only on Gwen. Yes, her eyes were definitely sad. They reminded him of a blue sky with dark clouds drifting in, threatening rain.

Gwen, he whispered. *Gwen, I wish I could be the guy you're looking for.*

"Steve's had quite a time of it since he was on our show. He's become a magnet for women all over the city. He gets mobbed wherever he goes. And he's asked our producer for a few minutes to address his fans on the air. So let's give him a chance to share his thoughts."

The light on the camera in front of Steve flashed on and the cameraman cued Steve with his index finger. Steve belatedly remembered the index cards in his pocket, on which he'd jotted a few notes. He didn't need them, though. He was going to speak from his heart.

"Hi," he said into the camera. "I'm Steve Chambliss, and I'm a carpenter. That's what I am, that's what I do. I'm not a sex symbol. I'm not a star. I'm a carpenter."

Good start. He took a deep breath and continued. "When I appeared on Gwen's show a couple of weeks ago, I never expected that everything in my life would change. I went on the show, talked about my work, told a few jokes, and said I didn't want to get married because marriage meant a woman would try to change me.

Well, I don't know why, but apparently a lot of women in San Francisco saw that as a dare. They've been trying to lasso me ever since.

"It's gotten so I can't walk down a street without being mobbed. I can't get to my job. I can't ride the cable car. I've got women sleeping on the street outside my apartment, women tying up my phone lines, women sending me photographs of them in the buff. It's been strange. I guess most guys would think this is great, but I don't.

"The thing is..." He stared at the camera. "Women are wonderful, but I'm not about to fall in love with any of you women who are chasing me all over town. Love isn't just about sex. It's about being friends, and changing for each other, and trying to please each other. And it's a one-on-one thing.

"I'd like to announce, publicly, that I want to be left alone. I'm not looking for love. I've already found it."

The cameraman tapped his watch. Steve nodded. "I'm running out of time," he said more quickly, "so let me make this fast, and let me make it clear. Gwen, I love you. I miss you. I want you to be my best friend. Will you marry me?"

Silence filled the tiny cell in which Steve sat. The cameraman's eyebrows shot up. Steve's gaze drifted to the monitor, which was now filled with Gwen. She looked stunned.

"Steve?" she said, her voice cracking.

He spoke to the monitor. "Am I blowing it? Are the tabloids going to make our lives hell because of this?"

Her eyes shimmered with tears, but she smiled through them. "If you really love me, our lives are going to be heaven."

"Well, I really love you." Saying it exhilarated him. He felt freer than he'd ever felt when he was free of commitments, free of responsibilities. He realized he was grinning. All the remaining knots in his stomach melted away.

"I love you, too," Gwen murmured.

"Then say you'll marry me."

"I will, Steve. I will."

The audience broke into cheers.

"But I don't want to get married on your show, okay?" he cut through the cacophony. "I've already proposed on your show, and I don't want to have to build another wedding set. I'd rather get married at this nice, secluded cabin I know. It's got a hot tub."

"And a bearskin rug?" She was laughing and crying simultaneously, and she looked ravishing.

"The complete stud setup, *babe*."

"Call me babe again, and the whole thing's off." Still laughing, still weeping, she said, "I think we have to cut to a commercial. Steve Chambliss fans, I'm going to have to ask you to give him back his privacy and let him live in peace. He's about to become a married man." Gazing directly into the camera, into Steve's soul, she smiled and said, "I love you, Steve."

The light on the camera switched off, and Steve bolted from the room, racing off to the main studio so he could kiss Gwen. On the air, if necessary. He didn't care.

He was a changed man, he realized—changed not by Gwen but by *love*, by being in love, accepting love, embracing it. He was changed by the epiphany that nothing was as important, as essential, as necessary to a man, than finding the right woman and being the right man for her.

As he reached the door to her studio, he saw her standing in the wings, watching for him. Her face lit up when he bounded over the wires, past the assistants and into her arms. And then he had the kiss he needed, the kiss he wanted, the kiss he would probably have died if he hadn't gotten.

The audience was still clapping, still hooting and cheering. And Steve felt the earth move, transforming, evolving, realigning itself, making everything that mattered in his life fall perfectly into place.

You asked for it...you've got it. More MEN!

We're thrilled to bring you another special edition of the popular MORE THAN MEN series.

Like those who have come before him, Chase Quinn is more than tall, dark and handsome. All of these men have extraordinary powers that make them "more than men." But whether they are able to grant you three wishes or live forever, make no mistake—their greatest, most extraordinary power is of seduction.

So make a date in October with Chase Quinn in

#554 THE INVISIBLE GROOM
by Barbara Bretton

SUPH6

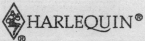

HARLEQUIN®

Don't miss these Harlequin favorites by some of our most distinguished authors!
And now you can receive a discount by ordering two or more titles!

HT#25483	BABYCAKES by Glenda Sanders	$2.99	☐
HT#25559	JUST ANOTHER PRETTY FACE by Candace Schuler	$2.99	☐
HP#11608	SUMMER STORMS by Emma Goldrick	$2.99	☐
HP#11632	THE SHINING OF LOVE by Emma Darcy	$2.99	☐
HR#03265	HERO ON THE LOOSE by Rebecca Winters	$2.89	☐
HR#03268	THE BAD PENNY by Susan Fox	$2.99	☐
HS#70532	TOUCH THE DAWN by Karen Young	$3.39	☐
HS#70576	ANGELS IN THE LIGHT by Margot Dalton	$3.50	☐
HI#22249	MUSIC OF THE MIST by Laura Pender	$2.99	☐
HI#22267	CUTTING EDGE by Caroline Burnes	$2.99	☐
HAR#16489	DADDY'S LITTLE DIVIDEND by Elda Minger	$3.50	☐
HAR#16525	CINDERMAN by Anne Stuart	$3.50	☐
HH#28801	PROVIDENCE by Miranda Jarrett	$3.99	☐
HH#28775	A WARRIOR'S QUEST by Margaret Moore	$3.99	☐

(limited quantities available on certain titles)

TOTAL AMOUNT	$	
DEDUCT: 10% DISCOUNT FOR 2+ BOOKS	$	
POSTAGE & HANDLING	$	
($1.00 for one book, 50¢ for each additional)		
APPLICABLE TAXES*	$	
TOTAL PAYABLE	$	

(check or money order—please do not send cash)

To order, complete this form and send it, along with a check or money order for the total above, payable to Harlequin Books, to: **In the U.S.:** 3010 Walden Avenue, P.O. Box 9047, Buffalo, NY 14269-9047; **In Canada:** P.O. Box 613, Fort Erie, Ontario, L2A 5X3.

Name: _____

Address:_____City: _____

State/Prov.: _____ Zip/Postal Code: _____

*New York residents remit applicable sales taxes.
 Canadian residents remit applicable GST and provincial taxes.

HBACK-OD

Once in a while, there's a man so special, a story so
different, that your pulse races, your blood rushes.
We call this

David Quinn is one such man. And QUINN'S WAY is one such book.

Teacher and single mother Houston Malloy lived your basic middle-class life in Middle
America, until one day a special man—a perfect man—literally fell into her lap. No
doubt Quinn was a hero for her time…but what time was he from?

QUINN'S WAY
by
REBECCA FLANDERS

Don't miss this exceptional, sexy hero. He'll make your HEARTBEAT!

Available in November wherever Harlequin books are sold.
Watch for more Heartbeat stories, coming your way soon!

COMING NEXT MONTH

#557 ONCE UPON A HONEYMOON by Julie Kistler

Self-proclaimed bachelor Tripp Ashby was in a no-win situation…and only Bridget Emerick could help him. His old pal had bailed him out since college—but this time, the sexy bachelor needed the unthinkable…a wife! *Don't miss the second book in the STUDS miniseries!*

#558 QUINN'S WAY by Rebecca Flanders
Heartbeat

When David Quinn appeared out of nowhere and entered Houston Malloy's ordered life—mouthwatering smile, bedroom eyes and all—she thought the man was out of this world. Little did she know how right she was!

#559 SECRET AGENT DAD by Leandra Logan

As a secret agent, Michael Hawkes had stared down danger with nerves of steel. But then he found himself protecting his old flame Valerie Warner—and her twins—in the jungles of suburbia. Twins who looked an awful lot like him…. Michael never saw danger like he did now!

#560 FROM DRIFTER TO DADDY by Mollie Molay
Rising Star

For a couple of hundred bucks Sara Martin bought the wrongfully imprisoned drifter Quinn Tucker for thirty days. But it didn't take long for Quinn to know he was safer in jail, doing his time, than he was out on a ranch with a gorgeous woman and her ready-made family….

AVAILABLE THIS MONTH:

#553 THE MARRYING TYPE
Judith Arnold

#554 THE INVISIBLE GROOM
Barbara Bretton

#555 FINDING DADDY
Judy Christenberry

#556 LOVE POTION #5
Cathy Gillen Thacker

A NEW STAR COMES OUT TO SHINE....

American Romance continues to search
the heavens for the best new talent...
the best new stories.

Join us next month when a new star
appears in the American Romance
constellation:

Mollie Molay
#560 FROM DRIFTER TO DADDY
November 1994

*For sexy bad-boy Quinn Tucker, getting in
trouble with the law wasn't unusual. But
getting "bought" by a gorgeous woman
rancher for a thirty-day parole certainly
was! Could Sara and her twins charm this
drifter into a daddy?*

Be sure to Catch a "Rising Star"!

RISING
STAR

"HOORAY FOR HOLLYWOOD" SWEEPSTAKES

HERE'S HOW THE SWEEPSTAKES WORKS

OFFICIAL RULES — NO PURCHASE NECESSARY

To enter, complete an Official Entry Form or hand print on a 3" x 5" card the words "HOORAY FOR HOLLYWOOD", your name and address and mail your entry in the pre-addressed envelope (if provided) or to: "Hooray for Hollywood" Sweepstakes, P.O. Box 9076, Buffalo, NY 14269-9076 or "Hooray for Hollywood" Sweepstakes, P.O. Box 637, Fort Erie, Ontario L2A 5X3. Entries must be sent via First Class Mail and be received no later than 12/31/94. No liability is assumed for lost, late or misdirected mail.

Winners will be selected in random drawings to be conducted no later than January 31, 1995 from all eligible entries received.

Grand Prize: A 7-day/6-night trip for 2 to Los Angeles, CA including round trip air transportation from commercial airport nearest winner's residence, accommodations at the Regent Beverly Wilshire Hotel, free rental car, and $1,000 spending money. (Approximate prize value which will vary dependent upon winner's residence: $5,400.00 U.S.); 500 Second Prizes: A pair of "Hollywood Star" sunglasses (prize value: $9.95 U.S. each). Winner selection is under the supervision of D.L. Blair, Inc., an independent judging organization, whose decisions are final. Grand Prize travelers must sign and return a release of liability prior to traveling. Trip must be taken by 2/1/96 and is subject to airline schedules and accommodations availability.

Sweepstakes offer is open to residents of the U.S. (except Puerto Rico) and Canada who are 18 years of age or older, except employees and immediate family members of Harlequin Enterprises, Ltd., its affiliates, subsidiaries, and all agencies, entities or persons connected with the use, marketing or conduct of this sweepstakes. All federal, state, provincial, municipal and local laws apply. Offer void wherever prohibited by law. Taxes and/or duties are the sole responsibility of the winners. Any litigation within the province of Quebec respecting the conduct and awarding of prizes may be submitted to the Regie des loteries et courses du Quebec. All prizes will be awarded; winners will be notified by mail. No substitution of prizes are permitted. Odds of winning are dependent upon the number of eligible entries received.

Potential grand prize winner must sign and return an Affidavit of Eligibility within 30 days of notification. In the event of non-compliance within this time period, prize may be awarded to an alternate winner. Prize notification returned as undeliverable may result in the awarding of prize to an alternate winner. By acceptance of their prize, winners consent to use of their names, photographs, or likenesses for purpose of advertising, trade and promotion on behalf of Harlequin Enterprises, Ltd., without further compensation unless prohibited by law. A Canadian winner must correctly answer an arithmetical skill-testing question in order to be awarded the prize.

For a list of winners (available after 2/28/95), send a separate stamped, self-addressed envelope to: Hooray for Hollywood Sweepstakes 3252 Winners, P.O. Box 4200, Blair, NE 68009.

CBSRLS

OFFICIAL ENTRY COUPON

"Hooray for Hollywood"
SWEEPSTAKES!

Yes, I'd love to win the Grand Prize — a vacation in Hollywood — or one of 500 pairs of "sunglasses of the stars"! Please enter me in the sweepstakes!

This entry must be received by December 31, 1994.
Winners will be notified by January 31, 1995.

Name _____

Address _____ Apt. _____

City _____

State/Prov. _____ Zip/Postal Code _____

Daytime phone number _____
(area code)

Account # _____

Return entries with invoice in envelope provided. Each book in this shipment has two entry coupons — and the more coupons you enter, the better your chances of winning!

DIRCBS

OFFICIAL ENTRY COUPON

"Hooray for Hollywood"
SWEEPSTAKES!

Yes, I'd love to win the Grand Prize — a vacation in Hollywood — or one of 500 pairs of "sunglasses of the stars"! Please enter me in the sweepstakes!

This entry must be received by December 31, 1994.
Winners will be notified by January 31, 1995.

Name _____

Address _____ Apt. _____

City _____

State/Prov. _____ Zip/Postal Code _____

Daytime phone number _____
(area code)

Account # _____

Return entries with invoice in envelope provided. Each book in this shipment has two entry coupons — and the more coupons you enter, the better your chances of winning!

DIRCBS